You ar

Yo

You function.

His town is perfect. A shining example of morality. The kind of place you'd raise children in. The kind of place that breeds happy, productive citizens.

He is an exemplary member of the community—goes to Church every Sunday, always punctual and organized, never misses a day of work.

But to achieve perfection, sacrifices have to be made.
This is a world of mandatory mind control.

When one man is forced to confront the holes in his world-view head on, what starts with skipping Church becomes a full-fledged battle for sanity.

Now they're coming for him, to put him back in his place, restore his status as a sedated slave.

In this gripping and suspenseful psychological thrill-ride, you'll follow the narrator's remarkable journey of awareness and self-discovery as the world he once knew is torn apart around him.

If ignorance is bliss, then knowledge is torture.

The Perception Experiment is a poetic and imaginative work of literature, a modern allegory of epic proportions that will leave you emotionally shaken.

THE PERCEPTION EXPERIMENT

JASON GLOVER

THIRDEYE | PUBLICATIONS
THIRDEYEPUBLICATIONS.COM

THE PERCEPTION EXPERIMENT

All Rights Reserved.

Copyright © 2007 by Jason Glover.

Book Design by Jason Glover.

No part of this book may be reproduced or transmitted in any form or by any means, electronic or mechanical, including photocopying, recording, or by any information storage and retrieval system, without permission in writing from the publisher, except for the inclusion of brief quotations in a review.

Library of Congress Control Number: 2006910292

ISBN 978-0-9790981-2-3

Printed in the United States of America on recycled paper.

First Edition, April 2007

Thirdeye Publications

www.thirdeyepublications.com

To all who hear the prophetic words in this book:

You are presented with a choice, and for those who have already found contentment in the arms of slavery, to read further will put that contentment at great risk. However, for those who have grown dissatisfied in their faith and have begun to ask questions, for those who seek awareness whatever the cost, to read further is to commit yourself to the cause of enlightenment, even if the results are unpleasant.

Choose wisely, because afterwards there is no turning back.

The Perception Experiment

Patient number 234214 567875 456799
Override successful
Transmission intercepted

Are we important?
Do our lives mean anything?
So much attention paid to the petty dramatics of one species.
We have to be important.
The question is, to whom, to what?
What makes us so necessary?

Damn, my head hurts. It's Sunday, and I feel like crap. Until recently, I've never just lain here in my bed thinking. The questions keep multiplying, intermingling, evolving. It's too much to handle at 9 a.m.

I should really sit up, wake up, and get moving. And the subject will start functioning: now. And the subject will commence feeling: now. I should really be getting ready to go to Church at ten. But I'm not.

I'm lying here thinking. My mind travels in waves, in currents, along the crests and pond ripples of my blue bed sheets. Strewn about, tossed about, my head put through a blender. A purée of slimy, gray tissue. Nothing quite like it was before. The bed, no longer made, now wrinkled and toyed with. No longer perfect, its previous perfection rendered a simple illusion. Or is it delusion? Either way, the complexity of the changing crevices in the fabric, in reality, adds a dimension of interest. This is new, this is different, and it scares me. Thinking isn't healthy—not like this anyway. Thought should be cool and logical, never erratic, sporadic, separated into a million pieces, and floating, far away, amongst distorted memories. For what memories can a human have that aren't distorted, violent images recalled in perfect clarity, overshadowing beauty. I am a creature of the night, and at morning's light I hide, cringing at its coming, slow dawn, lest I be turned to dust. Here, warm in my coffin, wrapped in shrouds, I am frightened by these musings. The infinity of thought is what scares me. One could think forever, and still nothing would make sense. I don't have forever though. No one does. I will never know everything, and if beauty is in the eye of the beholder, then truth sure as hell is. But there is truth in one thing. There is truth in death.

I never used to consider its actuality. I was never scared before, but now I am terrified. To face that raw and unbiased truth is to face the unavoidable. The end of perception, the end of life. Not of all life, but the end of one's life as an individual. In death there is no individuality, superiority, or structure. The death of an ameba and the death of a human intermingle, a mixed flight from sentience into oblivion.

Ah, sweet oblivion, peace at last to my tired soul.
Peace at last to my poor dysfunctional brain.

Thoughts like these scare me, and I wouldn't have been scared before. At least, not of myself. Before, I could find truth in more than death—in more than nothingness. I remember there was a time when I wasn't frightened at all. I was content and happy with my life. Maybe everyone here is addicted to perfection, and I wanted to stay that way. Maybe I enjoyed the comforting disinterest of it all. No one asked me.

And the subject's mental state will begin deterioration: now.

Deep down, way deep down, you know, on the inside where it counts. Where the true beauty is. Maybe in there somewhere, I am just flat out lying to myself. My eyelids flutter, my eyes shudder, tracing the folds in the sheets, one crinkle leading to another, and another, and another. I am always in motion, their shape is always changing, and I can never get to the bottom of this. There is no conceivable end in sight. I want to just stop moving. Work my way through what is there already.

But I can't stop. I keep rolling over, restlessness adding to the problem. A puzzle wrapped in cotton cloth. A riddle of plant matter condensed and manufactured. Mixed with blue dye.

I hate this change.
I hope maybe I'll come to accept and understand it, but right now I hate it.

But that is just the external. I have no clue what is inside all of this—inside of me. The answers I must unravel. The codes I must decipher. Acceptance must lie beneath all of this confusion.

The air in my room smells like flowers.
Air fresheners.

One of the biggest lies of this society is the smells. It starts with scratch-and-sniff stickers, then moves up to deodorant, perfumes, breath fresheners, mouthwash, toothpaste, soaps, oils, incense, dryer sheets, toilet bowl cleaners, household cleaners, shampoo, conditioner, laundry detergent, body wash.

Everything natural is cloaked in imitation.

It's not good enough to just smell human, we have to smell like daffodils or roses or lilacs. Why don't we just let lilacs smell like lilacs, and people like people? Is being ashamed of yourself part of some higher order of thought? Is a culture lathered with self-pity and low self-esteem what God had in mind for the material world? Before our baptism in a pool of perfumes and oils, we were unsaved and smelly. Oh, but what glorious rotting things must lie underneath those shells of falsified smells.

Ah, my head.

I close my eyes as the morning sunlight slides in through the window. It's too bright and it doesn't help. It's persecuting me. Trying to force me out of my bed, out of my head, out of my room, out of my skull. I need rest. I try to slip away from the buzzing questions. To go back to the time when I thought I knew how the world worked and had direction to my life. It was all planned out and now everything is falling apart. I had my uninteresting perfect happiness, and I had my blacks and whites. Cut and dry. Life was just a plain old safe and superficial experience.

I guess you could call what I am experiencing now withdrawal symptoms.

I close my eyes.
I go back, retracing these feelings to their origins.

BLISS

IT IS A GREAT DAY to be outdoors. I love working on days like today, out in the vibrant, bright spring sun. I am building because I love working with my hands. Today is Thursday and I'm laying bricks, creating the foundation of a new school. There seems to be a neighborhood baby boom going on, the old school is growing crowded. I just graduated a year ago myself, and went right out and got a job with the city doing service work. I don't see any way I could be more satisfied. Helping out the community that raised me.

And the meek shall inherit the Earth.

I wave hello to the people who walk by on the sidewalk.

"Hiya folks. It's a beautiful day, isn't it? How are you doing this afternoon?"

A woman and her daughter, walking home with groceries.

"Oh hi there," the mother responds, corners of her mouth crinkling up into a smile. Eyes sparkling. "We're just fine, thank you. Oh, this is going to be the new school isn't it?"

"Yes, Ma'am. Won't be done until the fall, but it should be open next school year."

"That's great! Well, you better get back to work. Come on Sweetie, got to get these home. Have a nice day."

"You too, goodbye now."

They always smile. Beautiful smiles, full of happiness. They remind me of angels, pristine and white, in their long, flowing gowns, wings spread, ready to fly underneath the moon and stars, the sun and sky. So jubilant, so perfect.

I slap some mortar onto a brick, and press it gently down onto its place in the foundation. Each brick is important to its development. Each brick is needed, and each brick has its proper place. When working, I am always smiling inwardly with the knowledge that my efforts are a part of the creation of something great. Until this project is finished I am a part of the educational system of our town—after that, who knows?

I don't really ever talk with the other workers. Friendships can be too distracting.

I love it here; it's wonderfully peaceful and beautiful—especially this time of year. I know that if I get married, this will be where I raise my family. There is no better place. I hope I will make a good husband and father. I'd try to be a positive influence on my child's life and bring them up in the light of God's love. It is a wondrous age to be alive, because Jesus is returning soon. He promised us long ago, and now He is finally coming back. I don't know when exactly, but I am sure it will be soon. Then, the entire world will be as peaceful as it is here. There will be no more pain. No suffering, because Satan will finally be destroyed, along with all his followers. I hope everyone can bring a child up in a loving environment like that. Both of my parents have been called home to the Lord, but I'll see them again soon, after Jesus comes to raise the dead. Judgment is coming, and we need to know where we stand. Damnation or redemption: the choice is up to you. God will forgive your sins and weaknesses, all you have to do is put your life in His hands. Yes, what a wonderful age this is.

A whistle is blown, a signal given, a meaning must be assigned.
It's five o'clock.
Time to go home.
Clock out.
The message has been conveyed.

As I am leaving the foreman walks by, eyes deep within the shadow of his yellow hardhat. His callused hand grips my shoulder comfortingly.

"Good job today," his voice, a stick being strummed across a picket fence. "You're a great worker, buddy. Keep it up."

I swell with his encouragement. "Wow, thanks a lot, Sir. I really appreciate that. You can count on me to get the job done!"

"I know I can. See you tomorrow."

Overjoyed, I start home.

I've been walking whenever the weather is pleasant. It's only a couple miles from the construction site. The walk affords me time to reflect and count my blessings, serving dually as a therapeutic stress reliever.

Walking is my only vice.

The lovely shaded sidewalks stretch out and take me home. My street is like any other street—named after a noble benefactor, comfortable, well-trimmed hedges and mowed lawns, green grass or sparkling snow depending on the season, cars driving slowly, under twenty miles per hour, careful not to hit children, scampering, for their balls, red and bouncy objects of play. It's all ambling acres, a suburban wonderland, and oh we are so happy here. All of us doing our part in this wonderful town.

Doing my part gets me a nice one-story blue house. I've lived by myself since my parents passed on—I have no family left. They've all done their part in God's plan and are waiting for Jesus to come just like me. I am not saddened by their death. I worked through that pain with God.

I stroll down perfect pavement pathways, geometric lines through the elemental grass, arriving at my driveway. I turn up it, heading towards the homely, red door I never lock. I don't even know where the key is. Turning the knob, the air from inside rushes out to greet me, my air, sweet air. The clock is tick-tick-tocking on the mantle above the hearth. The heart. And home is where the heart is.

It's all for show.

I have a furnace for warmth in the winter and the fireplace isn't employed that often. A façade? A gimmick? No, I just don't like the smell of wood-smoke. A whirlwind of purple, pink, yellow, and blue drags my eyes toward a rainbow of need-to-knows. There are some newsletters spread out on the coffee table by the couch. I need to clean this place up. Cleanliness is next to godliness, and having my newsletters spread out in such a haphazard state just isn't healthy. Give me spic. Give me span. Give me order. Give me control. These are my mental ingredients. I try to be such a good person, and yet I can't even keep my coffee table clean. I need to try harder. I will try harder. I will be perfect. I walk toward the refrigerator in the kitchen, drawn to its humming, its electrical motor, so cool, an innovation, sustaining me and displaying a mosaic of magnets, pinning schedules and lists. Little daily reminders. Daily bread. The refrigerator is an extension of the self, decorated with bits and pieces of personality: a message center and an artistic statement. I have heard of refrigerators so cluttered with masses of notes, magnets, and trophies that things are falling off every time someone opens the door. You know what that means. (Too much inner activity.) A cluttered soul. A cluttered mind. These things don't function as they should. Keep your refrigerator neat. However organized the food on the inside, if your exterior decorating style is poorly thought out, people will see right through your lie. They will know that you aren't being the best you can be.

Cleanliness is next to godliness.

I only keep one row of lists on mine, one third down from the top, freezer side. That door is opened less, so they are not likely to be disturbed. These are gateways back to myself. If I ever start to get off track, I just look at the lists and am calmed. They are all on special stationary; proudly displaying an intricate cross design in the bottom left hand corners. Across the top I have printed titles. In carefully applied black marker they read: GOALS, PRAYERS, SCHEDULE, and WISDOM. I grab a marker, which is only used explicitly to modify my lists, and add to GOALS: *I will be perfect.*

There, all wrapped up, another loose end tied. Now I can smile with a renewed sense of confidence. I cap the marker. It's dinnertime. Tonight I will make steak. My mouth waters at the prospect. It was smart thinking on behalf of God to invent cattle, put here for our consumption. The way it should be, everything in its proper place. Each a brick in the foundation of God's plan.

I cook my food, give thanks, and eat. My nightly routine is a simple transfer of the organic material of a once living organism to the organic matter of a now living organism, flowing down the digestive track, and then spiraling away into nothing. The nourishment floods into my tired body. I need stimulation. I always watch the six o'clock news after I eat. After cleaning up the dishes, I move to my usual place on the sofa in the living room. I sink into the cushions, into tranquility, and turn on the TV.

"...the Church of Christ organized a successful food drive to help the poor Welshman family, who were victim to an electrical fire that burned down their home last week. Here at Channel Five, we'd like to send out a big thanks to the community for lending a helping hand to those who are less fortunate..."

Two boxes of Macaroni & Cheese.
I gave two boxes of Macaroni & Cheese at last week's Church service.

"...In other news, the scientific community was in shock today as carbon-14 dating was proved inaccurate in recent studies. Some scientists are..."

Of course. It will only be a matter of time until other forms of so-called scientific dating are rendered inaccurate. How could they be accurate? How could anything be accurate that shows Earth is anything more than twelve thousand years in age?

"...should help bring an end to the upstarts trying to prove that the Earth is actually billions of years old..."

I smile. There was never any question in my mind. That's the great thing about creationism, it leaves no room for questioning. I never understood archaeologists—what need is there to research what we already know? All these scientists trying to find the origins of the Universe. The meaning of it all. Such a waste of energy. I know all the answers, I know the truths as told by the Lord.

"...crime rate in the city is lower for the fifth consecutive year, and..."

That's good news. I love this town, it's so safe and secure. Like a warm blanket just out of the dryer.

"...however, in the nation, the violent crime rate has doubled, specifically among the minor population. Many believe this is due to the lack of God-fearing role models in urban areas..."

Yes, everything is coming to a head. National tensions. The end is coming to all of this Godlessness. Soon, order will be restored. The decrepit state most of the world is in will be reversed. No more pain and no more suffering. No more unorganized refrigerators. Perfection.

And the lion shall lie down with the lamb.

There are those who say it is impossible, but they have no faith. Everything is possible through God.

My ears start to ring, quiet but quickly transforming into a startled squealing. Molded static drowning out the television's projected images. A howl of high pitch interference, a piercing diatribe. I shake my head, trying to fight this strange sonic onslaught, but nothing helps. Soon all other sounds in the room fade into silence, leaving the sweet allure of one strange voice, seemingly from outside myself, interjecting into the fray of patched over personality.

"Are we really that important?" the rattling voice asks over and over.

I close my eyes tightly and shake my head faster, trying to make it go away.

Finally, just like nothing ever happened, my hearing returns. The voice disappears.

I can't concentrate on the news anymore. I am getting a headache. Did I imagine that? I shudder. What does this mean? Better not tell anyone that I'm hearing things. Nothing bad happens here. Well, I shouldn't say "nothing." We have our share of storms and accidents, but no one ever *does* anything bad. Hearing things is the first sign of being a crackpot. The citizens here won't tolerate it. I mean, we are all sinners of course, there is no escaping that. But everyone born here does their best to abide by the rules the Lord has given us. We only raise happy, productive citizens in this city. Soon, everyone all over the world will be leading happy, productive lives. Everyone who has faith will have a place in God's kingdom. We will all bask in the glory of—

Wait, that voice.
That voice...
I know that voice, don't I?
Come on, concentrate, I can't remember where I've heard it.
Damn.
Damn. Damn. Damn.
If I just clear my mind it will come to me.
I calm down, relaxing my thoughts, but there is nothing.

If it happens again, then I'll worry about it. My attention is drawn back to the TV, and I hear that the city is looking for volunteer firefighters. Maybe I should sign up. I always want to help people. It's what drives me. Helping. Since I was a small boy, it has been my goal to assist others. Keep them on a straight path. I've considered going into the ministry before, or maybe becoming a missionary when it's time. I think I could excel at either one; I have a flair for relating to people. I am a pretty good speaker, but I know I could write some powerful sermons. I write a little poetry now and then, and sometimes I share it with other members of my Church congregation. I really want to—

Yes! I remember where I've heard that voice, it was last week when...

My thoughts stop dead and the hairs stand at attention on the back of my neck. I shiver with the strange sensation that someone is looking at me. Watching me, following me, taking me apart piece by piece, dissecting me, devouring me, laughing at me. I can hear them. Someone is out in the front yard, taking notes, making observations. Why am I so interesting? I am boring—leave me alone. Just leave me alone and let me rest. I need to know who it is, and what they want. I turn off the TV and look out the living room window, but the yard is empty.

Must just be edgy.
I yawn.
It's seven o'clock.

I had a hard day at work and want to get to bed early. Sitting in the living room isn't that relaxing anymore. Now it's become disquieting and a little frightening. I shower away the day's grime and the steam helps vaporize my anxiety. I say my prayers and slide into the warm bed. I give my nervousness to God. Despite whatever paranoia I was feeling earlier, now I am completely at peace. Smiling, I pull the bedding up to my chin.

Closing my eyes, I drift off into a deep sleep, filled with blissful dreams.

·····**B R E A K**·····

Buzz.
Buzz.
Buzz.
Click.

I press the button on my alarm and stand up, stretching. It is seven o'clock.

What a beautiful morning, I feel refreshed and revived. Ready for another day of service. Unlike some of those bums in other cities. The one thing you never see in this town are bums. There are no drifters, no homeless, no bag ladies, no heroine addicts, and no one out on the streets. Nine to five, punch in and punch out. The harder we work, the more it will pay off after we die. It all makes so much sense. Everything makes so much sense when God is on your side.

The birds are singing outside my window as they bathe in the warmth of the rising sun. I get dressed in my work clothes, walk to the front door, and pull it open. The morning edition is waiting on the porch like always. Snatching it up, I put some coffee on and sit down at the kitchen table. The bubbling and churning of the brewing coffee matches the feeling in my stomach. Maybe today I'll eat breakfast at Gladice's; they have the best french toast around, and the service is wonderful. I open the cupboard and take out a blue mug with a black cross painted on the side. Filling it up, I sit back down at the table and unroll the paper. I love that sound rubber bands make when you slide them off of a newspaper. Almost like music.

The paper is spread out before me—a corpse of common events, a stiff of society waiting to be dissected, taken apart and examined, then reexamined, causes and effects sorted through, to be transcribed to memory and discussed later with coworkers and friends. Each day it is read and discarded, absorbed and then thrown away. Each day my knowledge of the world is based on a simple prediction of eye movements. Attention getting titles, pull quotes, colorful interactive graphs, statistics, stylish fonts, page dominants—it's all just a matter of pulling the reader's eyes to the information preordained to be the most important. It is amazing to think that a few changes in font size and page layout can affect the general atmosphere of conversations going on in a community on any given day. It is important to keep up to date on things; human progression is so fast paced that it is easy to be left behind, to be discarded and thrown away. I want to be absorbed and never forgotten. I want to be an eternal piece of the human machine. I want to be an informed member of society.

And my eyes are off, flickering back and forth, jumping from photo to photo, heading to heading, sorting information, and forgetting what isn't needed.

Headlines:

CITY GOVERNMENT TO AWARD MORE TAX MONEY TO COMMUNITY CHURCHES

HAIL DAMAGE AFFECTS FARMERS' PROFITS

WAYS TO ENHANCE YOUR PRAYER LIFE

Interesting. A column written by the priest of my Church, Father Davis. I didn't know he wrote for the paper. Must be some sort of a freelance deal. The best part about living here, in this town, is that you can find God's message to us everywhere. Everything we do is saturated in it, and that makes everything we do more beautiful.

Jesus suffered so we don't have to.
For God so loved the world, that he gave his only begotten Son.

Maybe the priest's column will give me advice that will help me get to Heaven, that will help save me. As I stare at the picture of his smiling face at the top of the column, my vision shatters.

Breaking glass.
The face dissolves,
fragmented pieces rebuild then break again.
Shrinking away into nihility.
The picture is gone, no longer on the page,
no longer in its place.
My heart pounds against my chest.
I rub my eyes, and then it is back.
Father smiling up at me with his comforting gaze.
Nothing like this happens to me.
Ever.

What is going on? Was that some type of hallucination? Maybe I am still half-asleep. Rubbing at my eyes, brushing the crust away from the corners, I stand up. It's not anything to worry about, my imagination is probably just getting away with me. I will have to keep an eye on that though. First voices and now this—it's not good to have an overactive imagination. That can lead to all sorts of problems and take away from a life of holiness. I just have to get my day going and get out of my house.

The coffee forgotten. The paper forgotten. I stride into the bathroom and comb my knotted black hair. Brush my teeth and wash my face. My hygiene is important, nothing less than an essential part of my life; my body is God's temple, and it is my duty to take care of it. Keep it in working order, clothe myself in wrinkle free synthetic fabrics, douse myself in cologne, cleanse my pores with deep cleaning soap, keep my teeth sparkling white, moisturize my skin with healing aloe lotion made from all-natural extracts, kill the bacteria, exterminate the corrosive grime trying to invade my body, clean the dirt out from underneath my fingernails and keep them trimmed and neat, push back the cuticles. Every day I save myself with industrial chemicals. It is a duty to my creator. He gave me this body, my job is to keep it perfect and clean and beautiful.

Gurgling, churning.

Yes, today I will eat breakfast at Gladice's. It will be convenient since it is right across the street from the construction site. I slide my feet into my steel-toed boots, grab my work gloves, and kneel before a crucifix hanging near the door to say the prayer I use before each working day.

Dear God,
Grant me the strength I need to serve you and my community,
Help me be productive this day,

Help me to be humble, and obey my superiors as I should,
Help me contribute to your perfect plan of love,
In Jesus' name I pray,
Amen.

Rising to my feet, I open the front door and walk out into the jubilance of a newly blossoming day. Soon, very soon, this almost perfect place will be made perfect in its complete sense. Birds dart from tree to tree, and squirrels scamper across mowed lawns, searching for nuts, and berries, and the things that make little squirrels become big and strong squirrels. I walk down the sidewalk; the concrete slabs are devoid of any cracks. This is thanks to people like me. The ones who help make the city beautiful, and keep everything in order. Chaos is ugly, only in perfection can we find beauty. Order is the voice of God, order is the power of God, the less cracks there are in the sidewalks the more beautiful they become, and the closer we come to helping God restore order to the world. The spring air is crisp and clean. I suck it up greedily into my lungs, taking deep breaths, trying to clear my head. I need to have a clear head in order to function properly, to rid myself of my imagination, to discard any potential causes of breakdowns or malfunctions. Avoid any thoughts about that dissolving newspaper photo.

Clamp, clack, clank.

My heavy work boots send echoing reverberations through the air each time they make contact with the cement. A few cars drive by—people on their way to work. The walk refreshes me, and pushes away any disturbing thoughts. Out of sight, out of mind.

Walking is my only vice.

I see the sign for Gladice's up ahead. The parking lot is pretty full already. I guess a lot of people had the same idea as me this morning. Through the windows, I can see men in suits or work clothes taking in their morning nutrition. The fuel to feed their production machines. A bell jingles as I push open the glass door. I am greeted by the smell of breakfast meats mixing with coffee, artificial lighting, comfortable padded booths wrapped in green cloth, and the intermingling tones of friendly chatter. This is my kind of place. My forward progression is halted by a sign.

PLEASE WAIT TO BE SEATED

It's not too long, maybe a couple minutes, and a smiling waitress helps me to a booth. Her eyes are full of the joy she feels from helping to feed all the wonderful members of the community. A gold cross hangs around her neck. She gives me a menu.

"Can I get you anything to drink?"

I remember the coffee I left out at home. I am usually not that wasteful. I need vitamin C, I need a balanced diet. I need fruit juice made from concentrate.

"Just an orange juice, please."

And she's gone, vanished at my command.

Two minutes, maybe less.

She's back, with a large cup of chilled orange juice. Freshly squeezed in a factory, injected with vitamins and preservatives, frozen, and shipped directly to my glass.

"Here you go, Sir. Are you ready to order?"

"Thank you. Umm, yes actually. Can I have two pieces of french toast, with bacon please?"

"OK, I'll have that for you right away. Just let me know if you need more juice."

She takes the menu, and she's gone. Vanished again. Into the bowels of a feeding trough industry. I slouch down in the booth and wait for my meal. I usually bring the paper, but after what happened earlier I'm not surprised that I forgot.

Ten minutes.
She's back with the food. It smells delicious.

"Here you are, Sir. More juice?"

I look at the glass. Condensation is dripping down its sides, pooling on the table. Half the juice is gone. When did I drink it?

"Yes, if you could fill it up, that'd be great."

"No problem."

She sets the steaming plate in front of me, and I take a deep breath. Yes, delicious.

She's gone.

I am alone with my meal. It's just me, two slices of whole-wheat french toast, and three pieces of bacon. All ready to be consumed. I pray, then pick up a piece of bacon and take a bite. Crunchy. Greasy. Beautiful.

Something is wrong.

...NOISE...
...MY HEAD...
...POUNDING...

It builds from deep within, a ball of hot iron inside the center of my brain, sending pain coursing through nerve endings. Scratching across chalkboards.

...SCREECHING...
...NOISE...
...THROBBING...

My face contorts, and I grab my aching skull, pull at my hair, none of it helps. Everything is in vain. I yell, I sob. Everyone is looking at me, concerned faces all around. I squeeze my eyes shut. My plate hits the floor, bacon, french toast, and all.

It shatters.
My head shatters, splits open, like a ripe melon.
Everything is spinning, and I'm moving far away.
Disappearing.
The world dissolves.
I am somewhere else.

I am someone else.

There's a knife in my hand. It is bloodied, and I am swinging it down at something.

Squealing, high-pitched squealing.
Hack.
Hack.

I bring the knife down and bury it into the pig squirming at my feet. Slicing into its skin. The razor-sharp blade slides easily through the animal's flesh. There is silence, as its head rolls away from its body.

No, this isn't me, I am in someone else's body, alone in a bleak countryside, the backgrounds are blurry, I am looking through shields of smoke, obstructing rationale. Why am I here, what am I doing?

I slide the knife into the pig's soft underbelly, and cut a long slice down to the anus. I peel back the skin, soft, soft skin, warm skin, nice skin, dark skin, my skin. Cutting around its innards, I pull the guts out, putting them in a bloody pile next to me.

Stomach.
Coils of pale intestines.
Liver.
Kidneys.
Bladder.
All in a pile of moist tissue. Purposeless and rotting.
I pull out the heart, and eye it hungrily.

Damn it, NO, What is this, I must be dreaming,
I am in Gladice's,
I am in Gladice's!

I bring the heart to my mouth,
tear away the juicy, delicate meat with my teeth.
I chew, chew, chew.
Blood coats my tongue,
I've never tasted anything sweeter.

No, no, no, NO!
Vision spins away into darkness.
Consciousness fades away, and I'm gone.

FRAGMENTS

WAKING UP SLOWLY, my mind becomes aware of its own existence in bits and pieces. All I can feel is the annoying buzz of fluorescent lighting mixing with the pounding of my head.

Maybe I should open my eyes.

I hear a voice. Someone who is here to help? Yes, someone here to rescue me, to save me from this hell of bright, fake, white light, filtering through red flesh and harmonizing incessant insects. My soul reaches out, prepares itself to be granted eternal respite. Another voice, different than the first one, all mumbling, the words make no sense, although I do hear them. Oh yes, I do hear them, like cotton, but they are there. This voice isn't here for me, this voice ignores the vulnerability of my outreached being, overlooks the discord of my spirit.

"Looks like he's coming around, Father."

"Yes, thank God."

I must open my heavy lids. Remove the blinders. I need to be healed, to gaze on the face of the noble protector here to guide me with his comforting voice. To restore calm to this madness.

"Well, I'll leave you with him now. Feel free to visit as long as you would like."

"I'll do that."

I finally call forth the will to open my eyes. Joy floods into the pitch darkness of my mental entrapment. The bright glow of artificial lighting is startling, it sterilizes my soul in a second. But my memory is harder to repair; it won't come back to me. It sticks to my neurons, bouncing aimlessly, unable to be recalled. The light softens the burden on my heart, but does nothing to alleviate the jumbled and confused thought processes leaping around inside my hollow head. Leaping and echoing, but never coming into contact with each other; never sorting out as they should. I think hard and the best I can do, is remember sitting down to eat breakfast in Gladice's. I remember sitting down in full working order, no maintenance necessary, and now I'm here. Where is here?

I look around. Fresh and waiting for an explanation. Taking in my environment while readying myself for flight. I am in a hospital. Only a hospital could be as white as this. White, clean, and sanitary. This room was designed for me and for this time. It lay dormant after its construction until this day, serving its purpose as a refuge for me in all my despair. Or so it seems. I scan the room seeing everything as it should be. Jars of tongue depressors, cotton swabs, screens monitoring my vital signs. This is when I make eye contact with the man sent here to complete the upkeep of my inner being. Wonderful hazel eyes gaze deep into mine. There is a questioning there, along with a sense of urgency. I focus on the face of my protector, the Father Davis. Sent to me from God. Sent to me to make my recovery swift and complete. I am immediately put at ease.

The priest smiles warm as a summer afternoon.

"I am glad you are finally awake. You've had quite an experience, haven't you?"

My lips and tongue regain the ability to form words, and suddenly I cannot cease from talking.

"I am not sure what I had, Father. The last thing I remember is going to eat breakfast, and then so much static, oh so much static, but empty, it's all empty, oh God, please help me, what's wrong with me? I know there is something wrong, but I know you'll make it better. You will, won't you? That is why you are here, to help me, to save me, oh and I want to be saved, please, please, tell me, what is wrong, what is wrong, my soul, oh my soul, my soul, my..."

"Shhhh," says the priest. "Hush now, you are fine, it is all over."

Comforting me.

He says, "Everything is going to be OK."

Protecting me.

He says, "All will be well, with the help of the Lord."

Praying for me.

The priest closes his eyes, and asks the Lord to help me, to come down and bless me, to repair the blight within me. To mend the scars in my neural tissue. When he is finished, I feel better, but I still know something is wrong from the look in his eyes. A nurse—the other voice I heard as I was still waking—walks into the room with some pills for me to take and water to swallow them with. "For your head," she says.

"Father, I need to know exactly what happened."

The priest hesitates before answering. "There is a possibility. Maybe something serious."

I don't know if he's talking to himself, to God, or to me. I gaze imploringly at the nurse.

Offering up her version of the truth, she says, "You had some sort of seizure in the restaurant. These things are uncommon, but not unheard of. It was some sort of spastic episode."

A spastic episode. Is that the politically correct way of saying it? Somehow the nurse has answered everything by answering nothing.

"But I don't understand, was this caused by some sort of disease? Am I ill?"

The priest looks at the nurse in a very peculiar way, and she quickly exits the room. I return my gaze to the priest, his eyes gleaming with answers. I wait for him to begin.

"Not a disease, per se," he says at last. "Something different... something, perhaps, worse. But there is no need for you to be afraid, that is why I am here."

"Worse?"

"Do you recall having any visions while you were... unconscious?"

Stars explode in my head, multicolored and damaging, they come riding waves of memory. Returning to me, at long last sorting out into some coherent order—a pattern of events. I remember everything. I remember my precious spastic episode. I remember the pig. Red and squealing. Pink and suffering. Most of all, I remember the heart. Its taste, so juicy— like the sweetest meat.

As I remember, the hunger for raw flesh returns. So primal, so necessary. An undiscovered part of me, thirsting for development, for stimulation. Once is never enough, I need to kill, I need nourishment. I shudder.

The heart. Most of all, I remember the heart.

Somehow, this retrospective is worse than not knowing. I realize I've been silent for some time. The priest is now gazing into my eyes intently, searching out that secret dark longing inside my chest. He is waiting for a response, and I begin to nod my head, but then freeze—saying nothing. I do not acknowledge my epiphany and the foreboding thoughts that came with it.

The priest senses the pause. That quiet moment, stretching out past both of us and on into eternity. He raises his bushy eyebrows expectantly, wishing to know what I have discovered. I manage to give him a confused look.

"Visions? What do you mean by visions?"

Why did I choose to say that? What I am trying to hide? I would never shield anything from a man of God—yet I did, and continue to even after I have every opportunity to take my statement back. To shed light on my past tirades and work through them with the Father. To redeem myself.

I say nothing. Pushing dark desires deeper within my temples. I usually never lie, and to the priest of my Church no less. Why am I so scared that he might find out what I am thinking? What's happening to me?

Another period of uncomfortable silence passes, with his unwavering gaze burning into the depths of my retinas.

"Are you...sure? This is very important, you know."

"Positive, you'd be the first to know if I saw anything."

That's twice I've lied. This is not my nature, but every time I think about telling him, it is as if a vice clamps down on my lungs. Breathing becomes a labor—anxiety rises. Something wants me to keep my experience to myself. Something is making me not as open as usual.

Father Davis squints his eyes skeptically. "Well, I suppose there have been those who have had these...episodes, but repressed the memories."

"Episodes?"

He knows I lied; I am not used to covering things up. I sound just like a panicky parrot. He elaborates.

"It is my belief that you could be possessed by a demonic entity of some sort."

This is impossible, a simple irrationality.
The adversity weighing in on me, is it true?
Could it be?

No, I refuse to accept that this could occur. The priest must be confused. Something has happened, and my protector is beating me down with knowledge he has been given by God. There must be some mistake—my denial must continue at all costs. My conscience must be repaired, but without the help of this man. He has betrayed me.

"Possessed?"

"Yes, that is correct."

I struggle in vain to disguise my indignation. "I don't know if one little...episode...warrants the assumption that I'm possessed by a demon!"

But I know what he's saying makes perfect sense. It could explain everything, yet I reveal nothing to him.

The Father chuckles to himself, the way you would if a small child makes an innocent mistake. "I thought you may respond along those lines. Most do."

One thought bursts through the cloud of complications. One thought stronger than anything I've felt before.

RUN!

I feel it with every fiber of my being, like a roaring thunder that can't be silenced or satisfied until its presence is known and acted upon.

RUN NOW!

I find myself trying to get up off the bed, thrashing at the sheets helplessly. My weakened limbs are numb and useless, they accomplish nothing—except to give away my fear. My inexplicable fear. Why am I suddenly so terrified of this moral man whom I trust deeply? I sputter excuses.

"Really, thank you for coming and everything, but I'm sure it's nothing a little rest and prayer won't fix."

The priest shakes his head in amusement. "No, it is something more than that all right." He says, "But don't worry, I've taken care of this kind of thing before."

My head is throbbing. I just need to return to my cocoon—to the damp dark of my confusion. I preferred my feelings of brokenness to these thoughts of terrible petrifying fear. I need to sleep.

"You must come with me. Have faith and trust in the healing power of our Lord. In no time, I'll have you all fixed up. I can see you are afraid, but do not fear. The Lord is with you in your time of need. He is your shepherd."

Cradle-to-grave security. This is what I receive in return for my faith. And now, when it is offered to me, the thought of acceptance sickens me. I want to be safe from this madness—but on my own.

Trust.
Faith.

These things I have, but why do I feel this incredible urge to flee? I need to be repaired, and to be repaired means to go with the priest but...

"You really don't have much of a choice in this."

His eyes dart towards the IV pumping preordained fluids into my veins. How could I have not seen it coming? The thoughts of running grow weaker. I wonder if I could rip out the IV but know it is futile. I am losing touch with reality.

Weaker and weaker, spiraling down into nothingness.

The material world is fading again.
Fading, but in a different, more controlled way.
A hand rests on my forehead.

"It is all right, my child, God is with you. He will let no harm come to you while in my care."

Harm.
Hhaarrmm..
The word echoes, bounces inside my skull.
Stretching into a vastness, where there is no longer sound.
Encompassed in a stale vacuum.
I am left in silence, my aural passageways have ceased in their functioning.
I am empty.
Falling.
Gone.

·····**B R E A K**·····

I dream sometimes, but always pleasantly. Cushioned in the clouds, celestial and glowing, radiating mercury among the angels, shining faces bathed in warmth, a babe in his mother's embrace, riding unicorns. These are the things that comfort me when I dwell within night's cool arms. But not tonight.

Oh no, tonight things are different. The dream is murky but vivid—almost real. Though it is not so pleasant this evening. No, not pleasant at all.

I am only halfway here. I am not sure where my other half

is. Or which half of me is here and which half is there. Or which half ends where each half begins. Everything is seen as if through a haze. Thick, smoky and confining. Masking the unknown. Just out of reach on the edge of peripheral vision. I know only that my body is here...somewhere.

Somewhere.

What is this place? My body is here, but hollow—an empty husk, waiting for harvest in this manure. This filth. The corruption oozes under my skin, thick and poisoning. I can't take it, I must escape this fog. Voices intrude upon my plight. Murmuring just out of reach. There is motion.

Am I moving? Is my body moving?

Ceilings slither by, I glimpse their erosion, their corrosion bristling with sparks. I am screaming, wailing, I want to lie still, but the mist rushes in, and I remain in motion. Everything around me is blue. The colors all blend away to one shade of sky blue. Through this blue, rising sounds form words. Words form sentences. There is no meaning behind them. I understand nothing. I pass through wire frameworks—the armatures of nightmarish day-dreamers.

I listen, knowing I will not remember later.

"This is becoming frustrating..."
"I know you must find this difficult, I am having trouble understanding as well."
"What I understand, is that we have a problem."
"No, everything is going to be just fine, we can handle whatever happens."

"I just wish I knew what exactly was going on."

"Is it Patient Zero, you think?"

"I don't know what to think anymore, but *that* is highly unlikely."

"Yes, I suppose we should just avoid worrying about it for now."

"Let's just get this over with."

"Don't worry, if he's out there doing this, we'll find him. We will stop him."

"We don't have a choice. That's our job."

Laughter.

"You're right about that."

"We've arrived, now pay attention to the task at hand."

The motion slows.

The blue glows, pulsating and intense, bright with a life of its own. Electric magic factories blaze into the night with their magnetic pollution. The white fire of tyranny and the red fire of truth will be vanquished upon awakening.

We've been through this before now, haven't we? Oh yes, but let's not speak of it—it won't help. It will all be over tomorrow. The blue is blinding now, lamenting liquid phosphorous.

The motion stops.

Suddenly, I feel like I'm under observation. A lab rat. A guinea pig for quick use and easy disposal. Just like last night, after hearing the voice in my head. I know you, I know you, yes I do. It's all understood, but what you don't understand is that I understand. Alas, the moment of realization is short, because the light grows brighter. Searing blue. I am being watched now, it is time. I try to look around, but it's all a blur. Where exactly am I? It is violently familiar, like bad déjà vu. There is a whirring noise, like a saw cutting through wood.

It grows in magnitude.
Drowning out all the sounds of the world.
I am floating.
There is only the whirring and me.
I am lost in methodical incandescent noise.
Slowly, a voice inside my head mixes in with the whirring, growing louder, and more comprehendible.
A voice filled with power. Penetrating every pore in my body with painful vibrations.

YOU HAVE BECOME TOO AWARE.

It's like I'm riding on a speeding motorcycle, only to be jarringly tossed off into nothingness. Expecting the crash of everything screeching to a halt, but feeling blankness. Psychologically bankrupt. I know it is too late, I'm already disappearing.

Spiraling away.
Down,
into
the
great
abyss.

I sometimes dream, but these things never happen.

·····BREAK·····

I sit bolt upright in bed. It is night—I should be asleep.

In, out.
In, out.
Deep breaths.
I need to calm down. Just relax. Recover. Yes, just breathe.
Forget all about...
The dream!
Oh God.
Thou shalt not take the Lord's name in vain.
Oh God, oh God, oh God, oh God, oh God, oh God, oh God.
What is happening to me? I don't understand this. I never have nightmares. Never. Ever since I can remember, I've not had a single nightmare. I can't have them, I refuse to. God shelters me from the horrors of the night. But where is He this night? My guardian. My redeemer. I refuse to have nightmares!

Then...what happened?

I don't know. Everything is shady. It is gone, gone, there is no sun. My insides are bathed only in darkness. My memory is a liar.

Dirty liar.
Dirty, dirty liar.
Ah, but I know all your secrets, I know your shady ways.
You are nothing more than a filthy liar.

Wait, did I...lie?
I didn't lie...did I?
Lie about what?
My memory; the liar.

So full of holes.

What day is this? What night? What hour have I awakened into, frightened from my peaceful sleep by horrible visions in the dark? I need to retrace my steps. I went to work yesterday, came home, watched the news, and went to sleep. Now this. Did something on the news give me nightmares? Something...about a voice?

Strange, it seems like I should know. I shiver. I can't believe I had a nightmare—it just isn't right. Something is wrong with me, I know it deep down. Something is just waiting to be uncovered and I am afraid to find out what it is. I look at the clock. It's three in the morning. Technically it's Friday now. I need to get back to sleep so I can do a good job at the construction site today. I need to get rest, but a voice haunts me.

I have the distinct feeling I shouldn't know this.

I try to pray.

Dear God,
Give me pleasant dreams,
Forever and ever,
In Jesus' name I pray,
Amen.

Pointless. I am silly, being that demanding with God. He will do as He pleases.

Creeeeeeeeeeee. Creeeeeeeeeeee.

The chirping of crickets emanates from the open window.

Lulling me back to sleep.
Back to peace.
But something isn't sitting right and I have no idea what it could be.

What's wrong with me?

It starts tickling the back of my mind like an itch that's hard to scratch. Something here needs to be examined, but what? I look around the dark room for something to comfort me in my solitary cave-dwelling. My gaze falls onto a picture frame on the table near the bed. It encases a photo of my mother and father standing together. It is slightly illuminated in the moonlight. The itching becomes a fierce shifting of thought tied closely with emotion, pulled forward by this trigger. I know what's tugging at the loosely knitted fabric of my mind. The picture. I bolt from my bed to the nearby hall closet used for storage. The shadows play with tingling fears, pulling at the ice of my heart. I open the closet, motivated by some unseen force. I can't describe exactly what's driving this exploration.

Dark secrets are corrupt, biased things.
That's why I must be sure.
That's part of the force making me search the closet. I know what I'm supposed to find, but don't yet know the reason.

My hands divulge what they are seeking—a box, tucked away on the shelf, inconspicuous and unnoticeable. Just an unmarked box, but I know what's inside. Photo albums. All my happy childhood memories recorded for my enjoyment. When I am old, senseless and senile, they will comfort me in place of human contact. What mystery is here? What's hidden inside this strange cache, this storage place? What secrets lie here awaiting my knowledge? My unraveling, uncovering, discovering. I place the box on the freshly-vacuumed carpet and step back, regarding it as if it were toxic waste—the radiation poisoning of shattered dreams. Whatever's lurking inside will either rebuild me or further my destruction. The more I dwell on it, the more I am sure the information contained within could tear the very fibers of reality to shreds. But at last, the curiosity overcomes me.

And if I were a cat, I would be dead.

I open the box, lifting the cardboard flaps. They work together to try and stay closed, giving mutual support, a cardboard commune plotting against me. But I am the stronger force in this battle of will, and succumbing to my efforts, the box now lies open, ready to be searched through—a willing assault victim.

But, am I ready?

Readiness is not a choice for me—I must be ready. This mystery will reveal itself to me in time, with or without my intervention. Might as well be now, like a bandage, best removed quickly. Bracing myself for the worst, I reach into the box and remove its contents. Three perfectly ordinary family photo albums. Nothing strange here, nothing ominous about three dusty albums, red, blue, and gold. I know that what I'm supposed to see lies inside their plastic covers. I've looked through these albums a hundred times, there is nothing out of the ordinary in them. So what's this feeling inside telling me otherwise? I remember playing baseball with my father in the hot summer air; I remember gardening with my mother, pulling weeds. All the pictures inside are of events like these, the relics of an ended childhood, they are known to me. I am confused, but nonetheless I open the cover of the first album.

It is red.
My memory is such a liar. A dirty, dirty liar.
Like Swiss cheese. So full of holes.

The first page of the album lies there, ready for my inspection. There are five pictures on the page. The photo of my mother and father, the same one that's next to my bed. There is also a photo of us all swimming in the community pool. There is one of me playing catch with my father. A picture of me as a baby, staring up from my crib. The last picture on the page shows me proudly unwrapping my Christmas presents, around the age of five.

Huh, all that excitement over nothing. It looks normal, I can't see an answer to the nagging in the back of my mind. Still, the relief I thought I'd feel upon discovering everything in order doesn't come. As I look away from the album, out of the corner of my eye, I see something quite peculiar. Movement on the page. As if things are rearranging somehow, changing shape. I jerk my head back towards the album, lying prostrate on the floor before me. The page, however, is no different. Five pictures, five happy memories. I flip through the rest of the pages, and everything is the same. More memories.

It's funny how we have to record our happy memories with soul-stealing cameras. Yet, the violence remains in our heads. The traumas of the past stay with us forever.
Only happiness we forget.

All the pages of a blissful youth, a past kept in the closet as a quick reference guide in case of temporary amnesia. Once again, I turn away from the open album, and once again, I see the pages erupt with movement—contorting and reforming. It's more of a feeling than anything else. A feeling that something about the pictures change when I no longer gaze at them. But how am I to discover this Polaroid secret if it only displays itself when no longer in my view? I look closely at the red album and then turn my head away, ever so slowly, until I feel the pictures beginning to change. It is hard to continue to view them, just inside the range of my vision, without looking directly at them. Still, the motion has yet to be explained. To be extrapolated upon. I realize I see nothing at all. The pictures, though blurring, look the same, but I know they will change as soon as I turn my head away completely. I feel the start of a headache forming in the back of my skull, waiting to pounce and cut off all clear thought. I walk back into my room, leaving the albums in the hall.

I'm at a loss for what to do. I need rest.
But my curiosity must be satisfied or I know I cannot sleep. Secrets must be revealed.

I walk into the bathroom and turn on the faucet. My reflection stares back at me. I look horrible—like I haven't slept in days. I'm losing it; I need to focus on keeping my looks in order. God's temple must be maintained. I grab a washcloth and soak it in the flowing warm water. Adding soap made from the fat of animals. Fresh, life-giving, moisturizing, soap. I bring the cloth to my face, eradicating the germs feasting upon my misfortune. The bacteria of the world thrive on mental deterioration. You let down your guard of cleanliness long enough and the decay moves right in. My baby blue eyes stare back at me. Questioning eyes, wanting to know the answers, wanting to solve this problem. I look into the mirror, an alternate world, a gateway into the unfamiliar, a place where everything is made of ice.

Where everything is stellar. Faded and absent. Murky.

It strikes me that this cool reflected falsified reality could help. Is it possible that I can see the movement of the pictures through this glass portal? It's worth a chance, I have nothing to lose, after all. I run back to the hall where the albums lie, attempting to plead innocence, lest I find all their harbored secrets.

Exposure is the Lord's work.
Deception is the work of the Devil.

Red, blue, and gold, they lie there. I grab the red one, with its pages of chromatic chronicles, and bring it into the bathroom. Without hesitation—so I won't change my mind—I open it to the first page and hold it up to the mirror.

What I see ravages my unsuspecting mind.
My legs tremble.
What I see cannot be explained.
My mouth falls open.
The first page of the album contains no pictures.

I turn the album around and stare at the page directly. There are the pictures, as they should be. I turn it back towards the mirror, and in the reflection once again, they have vanished. I turn to the next page, and the next, and still the reflected album contains not a single picture. There are only borders, where the pictures should be but aren't. Dropping the album in shock, I let it remain where it falls. I return to my bed and dive in, pulling the covers over my head, hoping they will shield me from the unexplainable.

What method of trickery is this?
What have I done to deserve this?
Please, God, forgive me.
I must have done something horribly wrong for you to play this kind of trick on me.
Or…is it the work of the Devil?
Please, God, take away this confusion and repair my photo albums. The photos are so lonely without their reflections. Please return them. Please, I love you more than life itself, and you know I'd do anything to serve you, just please take away this insanity.

Now, how long do I wait for God's response?
Soon. It shouldn't be too long. Perhaps an hour.

Seconds tick away.
Minutes corrode.
Hours explode.

Time's passage is ignored, as I wait in silent darkness under the blankets for God to answer my prayers. I know there must be some mistake. This curse wasn't meant for me, it was meant for some sinner. Someone who is impure. Some nonbeliever. But me, I can be perfect—can't I? Please, I will try harder, I know I can be better. I can function better. Just give me a chance. But not this, please! I don't need this—just take it away.

The headache waiting for the perfect moment to strike, now takes over my entire skull. Pounding and twisting and pulling. Wringing me like a sponge, emptying out thought and consciousness.

I clench my eyes closed, trying to protect myself from the pain. I roll in my bed, in my hiding place under the covers. I thrash against the noise inside my head—the turbulent throbbing. Please, God, please, I beg of you, make this all go away! Let me rest without nightmares to haunt me.

I don't understand what I've seen, but give up trying to assign it meaning, taking comfort in the thought that God is watching over me. Whatever happens, I know He is always watching. Finally, feeling slightly more relaxed, I smile.

Our Father is watching you.

I must sleep. Sleep can be pleasant. Sleep can be fun.
I am drifting, drifting in a warm ocean.
Tropical.
The tides rock me, they calm me.
Numbing me.
Floating here, I forget about time, I forget about my head, and I forget about the photos.
I am at ease, for now at least.
I slide into emptiness once more.

REVELATIONS

BIRDS CHIRP.
The sunlight shines silently onto my face.

Everything is warm. I observe the shadows of trees sway, branches bristle, reaching out with gnarled knuckles, encroaching parcels of darkness whip in the wind as they play across the mess of blankets on my bed. Jagged lines of envy, sheared by the light of the sun. It will be a superb day today. I can smell it in the air, the breeze, blowing just so, the optimum temperature to cool, the earthly wind combating the solar wind. A perfect day. I bask in the glow of the morning. I know this is God's way of telling me there's nothing to fear. There were no more dreams after the first. God was with me while I slept, His angels kept guard, watching over me. Wait...the sunlight... It can't be!

I jump out of my bed.

My alarm didn't go off. Here I am, taking in the wonders of a bright morning, when I should be out working. It's a perfect day for service and I'm lounging inside. I am so late for work. I am never late—it is important that one be punctual in all things. Never slothful, sloth is a sin.

Punch in. Punch out.

Excluding as much daily maintenance as possible, I leap into motion, get dressed quickly, skip breakfast, wash my face, brush my teeth. Forget to shave. There's no time anyway. I pray. I pull on my boots and rush out the door, letting it slam shut behind. I squint in the light of the late morning sun. Grabbing the paper from the porch, I start off on a brisk walk towards the construction site.

I'm late.
I'm never late.

Must be coming down with something. Some sort of sickness. Everything is all jumbled up and mixed around. Last night is muddled and filled with traces of that horrible nightmare. I just need to trust in God. Whatever is wrong with me, I just need to trust in His healing hands. There's no reason to dwell on the photo album. I'll put it back in the closet and forget it ever happened. Thinking about the unexplainable will do me no good. Everything will be explained in time through God. I need to focus on the day's work and not pay attention to the pervasive darkness of unknowns. Meaning is just out of reach, I search for it and it's gone—evading me. If I can't understand, it's not meant for me to understand.

God is infinite in His wisdom.
He will choose the proper time for understanding to come.

I walk down the sidewalk, and the terror of last night's events is somewhat lessened by the reassurance that everything will be all right as long as I give my problems to God. Everything will be explained through the power of the Lord. I just need to have faith. I need to trust. In the end, it will all be fine.

I listen to the sounds of the late morning, as I jog the last stretch before the site. I know the boss won't like this. I can see the school's foundation up ahead, crouching low to the ground, waiting to rear up and unleash its true potential. It's at least ten o'clock, an hour late with no excuse. I begin to approach the site when I am jolted to a sudden stop, surprised and confused.

The construction site is deserted.

Empty.

Strange, did everybody go out to lunch?
I look at my watch.
No, it's much too early, there's no way they would have gone for lunch yet.

I look at my watch.
At the date.
I rub my forehead.

This is impossible.
Today is Saturday.

My watch must have gotten screwed up somehow. The date must have been changed. But then, where is everybody? There should be at least a dozen men working on the new school. Is there something going on today I don't know about? Some important Church meeting? No, I would have been called, someone would have woken me up.

I realize the newspaper I clutch at my side can tell me what day it is beyond a doubt. Beyond argument. This is why I am so reluctant to unfold it. I know I must look, no matter how much I dread what I'll uncover. God, please let everything be all right. There must be some mistake. God, please let the answers I find here show me all is well.

God, please let everything be all right.
I unfold the paper.
At the top, printed in black ink, is the date.
I drop it in disbelief.
Today is Saturday.

What's wrong with me? It's Saturday. SATURDAY! What the hell? What happened to Friday? This makes no sense at all. Maybe my days are off. Was yesterday Friday? Yes, perhaps yesterday was Friday, and I just thought it was Thursday. It's OK, everything is OK. I need to sit down.

I walk over to an old oak tree nearby. While working I often look over at this tree, envisioning future children playing in it, laughing in the mirth of youth. I slump down beside its trunk. Echoes of imaginary children's voices traverse the crazed passages inside my empty skull. There is only emptiness in my impressions and in my recollections. I let my head sink down into my hands, a sure sign of defeat. Anyone walking down the sidewalks can see me here, curled at the base of this tree, innocent as a naked babe. Discovering the world for the very first time. This innocence is my vulnerability. I am innocent of the knowledge, the understanding, of what is happening to me.

This in turn leaves me stretched out and tied down, my heart exposed, waiting to be slaughtered mercilessly by the unnamed force invading me.

Exposed to temptation.
Innocent of the understanding of my actions, until it's too late.
And I am already damned and burning.
Exiled from paradise.

No matter how hard I try and forget, no matter how many excuses I make, one thought keeps coming back—attacking me again and again. A repeat offender back for more, returned for one more swipe at order. One more searing blow to the known. Bearing chaos on his back, he slices into my tender pink brain. Still, I do not understand this one thing which cyclically haunts me.

I lost a day.
An entire day in my life unaccounted for.
Vanished, as if it were plucked away.

I shake my head in my hands, muttering to myself. People on the sidewalks stop and stare. Children point. Mommy, Mommy, look at that man, Daddy, Daddy, do you see him. There, by the tree! Hush now, hush, don't point, don't get excited, it's nothing, he just had a bad day, he's praying, yes, praying. Jesus will help him; don't worry, my sweet, now run along. Mommy, will I be like that man when I am older? No, no my sweet, you will be perfect, just the most wonderful young man imaginable. God has a special place for you in His plan, just you wait and see. Oh, you're such a good boy.

Yes, I am a good boy, such a very good boy.

An entire day.
These things never happen to me.
How much longer can I say that?

Last night coupled with this temporary amnesia is too much.

God, please help me.

There must be a reason for all of this. Part of a plan, for God is infinite in His wisdom. He knows what He is doing, and it's not up to me to question His workings.

For He has done marvelous deeds.

What happens is the will of the Lord. There's nothing for me to worry about. God will take care of everything. He will take my fear, He will take my confusion, He will grant me comprehension in my time of weakness. He is with me, watching over me, my shepherd. All the angels in heaven are looking down on us. I've seen angels. They are the most beautiful creatures. This must be some sort of test. I can prove my loyalty to God. No matter what torment I am put through, I will not revoke my trust in God, in Jesus Christ, in the Holy Spirit. God is in me, and all around me. Omnipresent. I know there's a reason He is letting this happen.

Like Job, I too will not denounce His name.
Everything can be explained through God.

I stop muttering and lift my head out of my hands. I smile and everybody loves me again. No more pointing. No more staring. People wave and children laugh, all is well. I draw my strength from God and pray. Praying here won't draw attention. It will be appreciated. This is what's known as faith healing. It works on mental scarring like a dream.

Dear God,
Thank you for granting me the honor
of being alive on this wonderful morning,
I know you work in mysterious ways,
Help me to trust in your plan,
Help me to have faith in your word,
Grant me understanding,
When you are ready,
But not before,
I place my life in your knowing hands,
In Jesus' name I pray,
Amen.

I relax, leaning against the old tree. To the entire world, it looks like I'm simply taking in the fresh morning air on this beautiful Saturday. Yes, it is Saturday and I don't care. So what if I can't remember yesterday, it is of no consequence. God will eventually grant me clarity, and until then I will be patient. Patience is a virtue. Life is so much easier when you know God has everything under control. No worries. I need to spend less time worrying over pointless things like optical illusions and missing days. If I need to worry about anything, it is simply getting to Heaven. Nothing could be more important. I can hear the Lord, whispering to me on the wind: Peace my son, peace be with you.

I know God is with me.
And with that knowledge, it's time to get on with the day.
Sing a new song unto the Lord.

Whatever I did yesterday, I don't think it involved eating because I am starving. My stomach is making so much noise people are going to start pointing again. I look across the street at Gladice's—I haven't been there in a while. Since I'm so close I might as well eat there now. It's not very crowded today, most families are probably packing up picnics or outdoor luncheons.

I start to walk toward the diner. After taking five steps, I fall down—unable to make another movement. I lose control of my body, my muscles go haywire, convulsing, I shake on the dirty ground like a rag doll, drooling and gnawing on my lips, completely blind, my vision filled only with harsh, bright, white light. Like a victim of electroshock therapy, I can't shield myself from the pulsating of this epileptic epiphany. The light fills my being—devouring me. It sucks the life from me. My body tremors ceaselessly.

My arms flail wildly.
My head explodes with pain.
Appendages are made of rubber and are useless.
Blinding light.
My legs kick, uncontrolled.

What? I did eat in Gladice's...when... I was...
The back of my head makes contact with the ground, repeat-
edly slamming down.
I ate french toast, with bacon...
My entire body convulses, I bite deep into my tongue.
There is a violent wrenching.

Everything goes supernova orange for one split second, and
what follows is the calming of my body. The returning of my
ego, and with it come the recollections. All of them, rushing back to me, like a huge river, filled with rapids, current
bashing me over, rushing through me. Each breath is sensuous. The air is icy and yet it burns my skin. The moment of
realization, when the world is completely understood and the
unfathomed becomes fathomable. I trace them back to the
start, trying to sort them into place.

I remember the question in my head,
so familiar and so far away.
I remember the newspaper,
the strange vision of the priest dissolving.
I remember the meal in Gladice's—for the second time.
I remember the pig—of course—its squealing, its pain,
its death filling me with life.
I remember waking up in the hospital,
being told of demonic possession.
I remember the icy fear, and the feeling of no escape.
I remember the horrible nightmare,
the blue light, the powerful voice. Motion.
I remember the photo albums lying open,
still waiting for an explanation.

If this clarity is a gift from God, I wish to return it. I prefer

ignorance to this condemned enlightenment. Ignorance is bliss.
God help me. I'm lost without you.

Someone, or something, is toying with me.
If this is a test, let it end. Haven't I proved enough?
I don't like running on this wheel.
I can hop and do tricks, I'm a lab rat in a cage.
Look at me, happy and plastic.
A euphoric bunny.
Wrapped in cellophane and marketed to children.
Stuffed with the textile scraps of a foreign material.

I open my eyes and awaken my senses to the pain caused by
this second "spastic episode." Faces, concerned and filled with
a willingness to help, encircle me, peering down around me.
Some of the children's eyes are being covered by their parent's
protective hands. They talk to me, but my sense of hearing
hasn't been swift in its return, and I can't make out any of it.
Only the worried tones behind the words get through. I predict the children's thoughts.

Mommy, what's wrong with that man?
Mommy, why was he flopping on the ground like a fish?
Is he crazy?
Mommy, is that man sick?

I recall the priest taking me away, and the blue dream. I know
I don't have time to lie here and figure out what these people
are saying. In their nice summer clothes, they would be smiling and happy if it wasn't for me. This will surely draw attention and let Father Davis know the possession hasn't been
resolved. I need to escape now, while there's still time. I leap
up onto my feet, and the startled onlookers huddled around

me jump back in amazement. Without saying a word, I push a small man to one side, and begin sprinting as fast as I can back towards my house.

The city speeds beneath my feet.
The crowd is left behind in awe.
How long before word gets around of this?
This town is such a beautiful place.
We only raise happy, productive citizens.
No, not happy. Not productive. Sedated slaves.
I saw it in their eyes.
Shallow and empty, gateways into the vacancy of their souls.

Random thoughts pop into my head. They have no basis but they are there. I never think like this. I don't know where this is coming from. How did I come upon this insight? How did I end up in a dead run towards my house? People stare as I pass by, shaking their heads. They probably think I'm running because I'm behind schedule. Punctuality is proper, and I'm never late. They don't know anything close to what I know. They are blind, and yet, even after discovering my lost time, even after analyzing the facts, I am just as blind as they. Who returned my memories to me? Is this the plan of God?

Everything around me looks different.
Larger, grander, but somehow more concentrated.
The colors are brighter, as if in a dream.
Lucid.
Livid.

Suddenly, as if by magic, my eyes move undirected to the nearby street. As I run, my bobbing field of vision is consumed by it. A car drives by in such a regular way. It does not slow. A small squirrel scampers innocently across the street, bearing no knowledge of the workings of technology. The car passes. There is no sound to signify the meeting of machine and rodent—it's obvious that it has occurred. The silence only makes the imagined crunching of tiny bones so much worse.

The car did not slow.
Careful not to hit children, but indifferent to small animals.

I stare at what's left behind to tell the tale of this grisly scene— my run finally halted. The paranoid worries of pursuit drift away as my eyes are captivated by a crushed carcass. The lifeless, ill-fated squirrel, dead in the middle of the road. Poor thing, no God to comfort it at the moment of its departure. Animals don't believe in God.

I am lost, and the broken body of the squirrel casts a shadow upon the beauty of the approaching afternoon. Lost in this meditative state, my eyes burning into the dead animal, I realize something. Think of something in a way I never looked at it before.

I could die.
No, I will die!

This revelation shakes me, scratching at the depths of my spirit. The certainty of death overwhelms me. I picture myself in place of the squirrel, lying dead, entrails drying on the warm pavement, silent and not breathing. A cadaver.

This thought jolts me from my necrotic trance, and I resume running home even faster than before. Like lightning, although I know nothing is chasing me. I'm running from myself. If only I might find a way to escape myself. My walking corpse.

That is all I am.
Just a biological entity carrying the potential energy necessary to die.

Finally, I arrive. I stop running, panting and gasping for breath in front of my house. I open the door and kick off my boots frantically. I sprint towards my bedroom, avoiding the old photo albums scattered in the hall. I enter and pull the door closed behind me. Leaping into my bed, back into my shelter.

Fetal position.
Trust.
Faith.
God will help me. God will save me.

I don't have to be the squirrel. I am above the squirrel. There is eternal life for me in God's kingdom. I simply need trust. I need faith. I will serve God to the best of my abilities, in exchange for eternal life basking in His splendor. Among all the hosts of angels in Heaven. My father. My creator. I love you.

I rock back and forth, under the covers.

I worship you.
I worship you.
I worship you.

Why must you torment me so, why won't this test end?

Why me, ah, the grinding of self-loathing within my heart, for who could love a sinner such as I? Who else but a sinner would be deserving of this torture? Surely, if I were abiding by God's laws I wouldn't be in this mess. I just need to ask God for forgiveness. Such a compassionate and understanding Father. He will forgive me, He will let this torture end. I am crippled by self-pity and expose my soul. I hate myself, I am such a bad person. I need to be a good boy and obey God. I need to be above the squirrel. I need to get to Heaven.

I'm crying now.
I have never cried before in my life.
Only sinners have reason to cry.

We all must work to achieve repentance for original sin so we can go to Heaven, but when you sin as much as me, the torture of this life is far greater. It doesn't matter if I'm not quite sure what I've done, but knowing I've done wrong is enough.

The tears are salty, my face is wet, and I must look like a fool. I'm not sure why, but I know only fools cry. What a fool I am—and the tears just keep coming. It's hard to breathe, the pain inside overwhelms me. Where the pain comes from is a mystery. This morning, I would have simply talked to God, and everything would have been OK. He would have taken away all my fear. Protected me from the intimacy of my own fate. The fate of the approaching grave.

My cries grow louder. I choke on them, coughing while I sob, the tears streaming down my face. Snot runs from my nose. Why can't I be happy now? Why can't I say a prayer and feel better? I sound like such a fool.

Why do I feel this pain deep within the caverns of my chest? My heart is barely beating, barely calling forth the will to sustain me.

Where is God while I lie here suffering?

Was this part of His plan, or the work of a demon, as Father Davis says? Was the demon meant to inhabit me? Was it all a test ordained by the Lord, most high? Why won't God let this torment end?

I weep and sob—the threat of death is overwhelming and I feel God has abandoned me. I try to believe He is here with me, I just need to prove my loyalty to Him. His infinite wisdom could not possibly be comprehended by me, so lowly and insignificant in comparison to the divine.

But why does He let me suffer here like this? Here, in the torment of this insanity with these memories rushing back to me, the inevitable end of my existence on Earth looming in, bearing poisoned fangs—sacs of petrifying venom streamlined and entering my bloodstream, numbing all available aptitude.

Where is God? Where is God?

My vision starts fading to white and I know what to expect by now. My tongue is still raw from the last time. I can't take it anymore. God, please, what did I do to deserve this? I fall to the floor, the light blinds me once more.

Where is God?
I've already begun to convulse.

I am in Church on Sunday. The Lord's Day. Sun Day.
The headboard of my bed slams into the wall,
rocked by my shaking body.
The collection basket goes round and round,
from row to row, person to person.
My eyes are cloaked in purity.
They roll up into my skull. They are lost.
I joyfully drop fifteen percent of my weekly salary into the basket.
My skull fractures, it feels like an eggshell,
desolate and fragmented.
I am a good person. I help people.
This pleases God. God grants me happiness.
The light surrounds me completely, blotting out all of reality.
I see angels, angels brought me here. Is this a memory?

Suddenly this vision overtakes me like a vivid fantasy experienced within the depths of slumber. The angels surround me, becoming a new reality. It's as if I'm watching myself. Some would call it an out-of-body experience. Four angels glowing bright, silver white. Sparkling. One reaches out to take me by the hand. I'm welcomed home. I'm activated. She smiles at me and wishes for me to be happy. Happy and productive. The angels are so beautiful, clothed in flowing robes of the softest fabrics imaginable. The word *immaculate* comes to mind. I love God so much.

I slam back into my body with such a force that I look around expecting to be lying in a crater. My eyesight is still dim— I feel like I've been staring into the sun for hours without blinking. My body is sore, my muscles tense, as if I just ran a million miles. I am happy this one didn't occur on the concrete sidewalk outside.

The angels told me no one has to cry.
No more pain.
No more suffering when Christ comes to restore order to the world.

I've never cried before today, and the last episode has only increased the pain I feel inside. My face is still damp and I begin to sob again.

No more crying.
No more tears.
A dysfunctional emotion gone.
This is good. This is perfect.
We only want happy, productive citizens in our world.
This is what we want.
An entire set of emotions destroyed.

I'm in my bed sobbing, howling, lamenting. This is new, this is different. My tears are so saline, drifting down my face, tiny waterfalls built on suffering. I'm in so much pain and God still won't let me understand why. Is this part of God's plan?

My stomach is acid.

All my life, I've never felt real emotional pain. Not once, save vicariously through the dramatics of television. Simple sit-com happiness. Not even when my parents died did I feel like this—I had God there to comfort me. All my life, I've never truly thought about my own death. Sure, I think about Heaven all the time, but Heaven isn't *death*, it's another type of life. Whatever type of life it may be, going there still ensures the demise of my material body. Something one becomes somewhat accustomed to over time. Death is quite different than an eternal afterlife. In death there is nothing. In death lies the unexplained, the unascertained. I don't want to leave this life, but it could happen anytime and I have no say as to when.

I sob, spasm, and shake, like a whining child throwing a temper tantrum.

So much pain, deep within where I didn't know it could even fester. Has it lain dormant for all these years, only to be released as I stared at the squirrel earlier? Its body there, only vacant.

Deserted and left behind to perish.

God's temples all eventually will fall, invaded by the inevitability of decay. Even the one I inhabit, the one I'm selfish enough to call my own.

For no resilience, no hidden opportunist will defeat his sweetened shutdown.

The pain has awakened something in me, a deep hunger never before felt. A hunger for life, to experience it in every way imaginable. My life of docile happiness and willing servitude has been rendered meaningless by the newfound pain rearing its ugly head inside my tender skin. My vulnerable earthly body. No different in its decomposition than the corpse of a squirrel—an unfortunate Godless squirrel. This pain has altered perspectives, blurring lines previously defining reality. A reality where there was no pain of this nature. Only happiness covering a desire for change. A nagging feeling that something is wrong with the world in which I live has now surfaced. Before, I would attribute a feeling like this to the influence of Satan and appease my unyielding desire for something more meaningful with the promise of eternal life in God's kingdom.

I stop crying, the pain remains, but I have neither the will nor the energy to continue on as I was. I now look inwards, towards the black blemish suckling at the tit of my heart, stealing the warmth locked within its fleshy red chambers. I reach out with my newly altered consciousness, afraid, yet determined, exploring this feeling with the curiosity of a toddler learning to walk.

I pry, pick, and pull at it.
I let it bleed and beat, and feel its nature.
Of degradation and of life.

The two closely tied together in this inseparable bond. The stimulation brought on by pleasure and pain, weaving together, sometimes intertwining, sometimes splitting apart, while both work to promote life. Pain promotes growth, growth promotes pleasure, pleasure creates potential for downfall, a fall from pleasure leaves room for pain. My old life appears not happy, but boring and lacking much needed contrast. Repetitive and lacking growth.

Pleasure is a sin.
Happiness is a gift from God.

Pain is reserved for those who thirst for pleasure, those who can't accept the happiness lying inert and motionless, like roadkill, on the ground in front of them. My happiness has been slaughtered completely by these feelings. It has been ripped asunder and shown for the monotonous and boring sham it really is. My thirst for the kingdom of Heaven has diminished.

Heaven.
An eternity of happiness without pleasure.
An eternity of happiness without pain.

Hell.
An eternity of discomfort without pleasure.
An eternity of discomfort without pain.

Both missing color, flavor, and texture. For there is no true pleasure without pain, just as pain is not as devastating without pleasure to compare with it. My choices lie in two directions: an eternity of boredom which follows a meaningless existence lacking pleasure, or an eternity of boredom which follows a meaningful and pleasure-filled existence. Either result, static and unchanging, like a book that goes on and on without meaning. A story without conflict is no story at all. For without conflict, there exists no plot, and therefore no resolution. Humans thrive on dramatics and, deep within, feel a need for pain, just as the need for pleasure is felt, but resisted through the adherence to dogma. Spirit shackles.

The only path to happiness lacking pain is found in the bondage of mental slavery.

Self-destruction and self-gratification go hand in hand, masochism is the nature of the human spirit. This life is the only opportunity to experience the full range of emotions associated with worldly existence, and those emotions are only truly felt in the hearts of the damned. For such must be the way of the sinner, every action an indulgence of life.

Satan is the ruler of the material world.

Despite these terrifying observations, the idea of not caring whether or not I commit sin or heresy still frightens me. Why would God want to hide this from me, why would God want me to live a life without pleasure? Why would God torment me while making me feel guilty for succumbing to pain? I was born a sinner, but I had no choice in that. What justice is there in punishment for an action one didn't even commit? What justice is there in punishment for a crime, when the perpetrator is unaware of the consequences he will face? Innocent of the nature of crime itself.

As Adam and Eve in the Garden.

These thoughts keep returning to my head, filling me with doubt and guilt. Who am I to question the authority of my creator? Who am I to question the workings of the world that is His creation? Me—a mere man—damned and dirty, sinful and broken. I do not posses the capacity to understand the actions of God. I begin to sweat, and the pain inside of me pulsates sadistically, becoming anxious and paranoid. I writhe in bed, a delusional worm convinced it can fly when its purpose is simply to crawl. What am I thinking? Have I gone mad? God knows what is on my mind. He knows of the disobedience in my thoughts. I don't want to go to Hell. Is there any way to experience the thrills of this life in full without damning oneself to an eternity of torture? I need to get a grip. I need to go back to my life of dreary happiness. I am too scared of change, and not willful enough to question the power of God any longer. What He has created, He can destroy just as easily. This life is a gift from Him, and if He has decided that a life of complacency is needed to purify men, it's not for me to judge as just or unjust.

The Lord works in mysterious ways.
It is my job to obey without question.
It is my job to play my part in His plan.

The words *test subject* come to mind.
Along with the recent remembrance of my hallucination in Gladice's.

My life—that is, my earthly life—feels different. More vibrant, and somehow more real. Before it was just a screening process for the afterlife, but now when compared to the nothingness of death, it seems filled with substance. I remember the feeling when I slaughtered the pig and ate its heart. I was filled with an energy I couldn't describe, a zeal for life. The death of the pig fed my own life energy. Life feeds on life. Death sustains life, and life creates a potential for death. Like pleasure and pain, these two forces also work hand in hand. This is a cyclical system. The linear definition of time does not apply here. The linear mode of human thought does not apply here.

Your rules do not apply here.
The flow of life, beautiful and intricate.

Emptiness fills me. I know I can never be a part of this cycle. I must remain in my place, and obey the will of God. Death has been robbed from me, and therefore my life will not flow into another. I will suffer a bland existence followed by an eternity of boredom. Crippled by my own human perception, I can't possibly understand how this could be desirable. There's only one thing I can rely on.

God is infinite in His wisdom.
Only He can understand the full extent of His plan.
My face shines, soaked in tears.
My tears have baptized me anew, in pain, and in death.
I have emerged from the womb of my blankets.

I know more about the workings of the world around me than ever before, while understanding less of its meaning. I will get through this the only way I know how. I must learn not to question the will of God.

I must learn, and quickly, to no longer try to understand.
I must learn humble obedience.

I stand from the bed, and stare with vindication at the crucifix hanging on the wall.

The story of the bond between life and death was right in front of me all this time, symbolized in Christ's struggle. What's strange is that I never noticed this story is told everywhere in the world. In the changing of the seasons, and in the cycling of life. In the blossoming of flowers, and harvesting of crops.

I will obey you, oh God, for you are my creator, and you are the creator of this world. I will conclude nothing based on the knowledge I've discovered, and trust in your magnificent wisdom and compassion.

Even as I think these thoughts, and swear to be adamant in

holding fast their application, I sense them to be false. I get the feeling more will be uncovered this day, and somehow my trust will wane further.

The sun sets upon my unease.

In the deepening twilight I stand motionless, my gaze unwavering as I stare at the crucifix. I apparently lost all track of time when the pain overwhelmed me. The pain has now been replaced by anger and frustration. Impatience and incomprehension. I love this town so much, and yet I yearn to escape. Escape the torment of what I know. There's something very wrong with this place, I now feel it in the marrow of my bones. But what? I know I will not sleep this night. The demon that's been possessing me has shown its true face. The questions keep spiraling outward from my center of gravity. I always sleep at night. But not tonight—not until the beast within has had its fun.

For within lurks the demon of enlightenment.
Within lurks the demon of revelation.
Returning to my place deep within the blankets,
I begin to rock once more.
Back and forth. Back and forth.
A steady rhythm, a quiet steady rhythm.
Which, at any moment,
could become a roaring offbeat mass of surf and destruction.
Taking out its wrath on anything near.
But for now, the tiny waves of madness just lap at my legs.
Driving me insane.

In the darkness I cry.

THE RECKONING

I OPEN MY EYES.

I never really slept last night. As my intuition told me, the questions only became worse. Nothing makes sense anymore. Nothing at all. The seams of this world are bursting. My thoughts on this world are frightening. Observations that should be obvious to all, but were not disclosed to me until this day. I am a toy, a simple childhood plaything, to be rendered meaningless when my keeper decides, and to be assigned value when I am needed. What's going on in this place? There is something dark here, a shadow on all our hearts. However, the nature of this affliction still eludes me. I must have help if I am to reach the epicenter of these events.

What started all of this? Where do I go from here?

These things do happen to me.
And they have happened to me, again and again.
Strange occurrences, typically attributed to the insane.
The unwell. The dysfunctional.
Here in this reality, I exist only to be tampered with.

I look down at myself and notice for the first time that I have changed into my church clothes—my black suit and plain blue tie, lint free and ironed. On my feet are penny loafers, shined and gleaming. My life is so routine, many actions have become too involuntary.

This is a full-fledged mental breakdown.
This is the beginning of the end.
This is my sad, pathetic existence.
This is the unknown.

My eyes are bloodshot, and the world, though absorbed through my sensory organs, goes unnoticed. The morning and the sun are lost upon my delirium. I am groggy. I need to wake up and get moving, but I can't stop pondering everything. I can't bring forth my being from its entrapment among the crinkles of my bed coverings. I can't find anything resembling the man I used to be. All I have left is a skeleton, raw, bleached and suffering from leukemia, clinging to the riddled remnants. Clinging to the fabrics of bleak happiness. Clinging to the last semblance of normality. Nothing about this town sits right, and I still can't even begin to comprehend what's happening to me. It's Sunday morning and now it's too late. Too late to recover.

Too late to make it to Church on time.
It's now ten-thirty in the morning.

Damnation or redemption, such an easy choice. Or at least it should be. But what happens when you choose neither? What happens when you embrace the nothingness of death? What happens when you go to the grave—to your place in the ground where you'll deteriorate and turn into plant food—without sedation? I want to reclaim my death, it is mine by right. Without it, my life means nothing. But how do I escape the impending afterlife, when my fate is left in the hands of God?

I keep going over the past two days, trying to remember everything. Making sure there isn't some small detail left out. Anything my programmed mind might have decided was unimportant and therefore discarded without my input. My mind works outside of the sphere of my consciousness. My mind is not my own. My room is not my own, it's a habitat created in order to foster proper growth. I look around from the vantage of my bed—the soft mattress has long since become my home. At some point last night I deemed it necessary to break all of my idiosyncratic knickknacks. The pieces of my fragmented life are spread out on the floor. Pictures and porcelain keepsakes. Little forget-me-nots made in Indonesia. I even retrieved my photo albums from the hall and shredded every last picture. Every last disappearing image. Every memory, real or imagined.

Emotional confetti.
The life I once led peacefully, without instruction,
ripped up and discarded.
The glorious has become ugly.

The message has been tainted.
My falsified happiness has betrayed me.
Leading only down the path of insanity.
The picture of my parents, smiling cheerfully,
has been dissected and mixed with the rest.

If only I could fit the pieces back together, gain some insight
on the transgressions taking place within. I try once more to
ask God for help. I try, but it's not the same anymore. God
has either abandoned me to this torment, or He means to use
it as a testing ground for my loyalty to Him. Either option
smacks of cruelty.

Oh Father, why have you forsaken me?

All my life I've always had two things, two very important
things, to keep me going.

Trust.
Faith.

Now, I feel as if those things are meant to disinfect me. Now,
I feel as if those things are destroying me. Tearing me apart,
piece by piece, and then rebuilding me as something else. A
machine with no will of its own. A machine with the capacity
to be controlled. But, deep down, I know they haven't finished the job. I still want to live without reserve. I still want
my pain and my death. I cried through much of last night,
and I never cry. Now I am scaring myself because the tears
jostled something inside me. I never knew it was there, but
now it's alive and breathing.

Quivering and ugly, it sits squirming and pinned down, waiting to be released—tapped into—its potential used, raped, and channeled onto some unwilling victim.

That victim is me.
I am my own casualty.
Endlessly perpetrating war crimes upon myself.
Waiting to be held accountable.

Pain.
Suffering.

Now that they have been returned to me, I think I enjoy having these things. The beauty of day is plain and boring without the quiet of night. The duality of the spirit. The dichotomy of my soul.

Anger.

I hate this town, it has repressed the awakening of my perception. It has repressed the experience of my worldly life. So long I have believed in a lie.

Happiness.
Happy, productive citizens.
Happy, productive corpses.

Sheltered here in the safety of this place I've lost so many things. So much time was taken from me that I'll never get back. Tears come to my eyes once more and I retreat to the darkness of the catacomb beneath my sheets. I must escape the light, oh how it torments me. Mocking my infantile plight. Only in darkness am I free. I need to understand my past, to set the record straight, to find myself. Nothing from my childhood makes sense; my memories of that time are a series of unconnected events. It's almost as if they've been randomly injected into my young pink brain. Devoid of any coherence, chaos reigns. I must bring rationality to the irrationality.

Order is the voice of God.

Little bubbles keep rupturing in my skull. Every time I encounter a hole in my memory, it is filled with thoughts of God. I try to recall my time in high school, my adolescence, but little bubbles fizzle to the surface and explode.

Tiny bubbles.
Programming.
Structure.

I remember the powerful voice from the nightmare, and I remember what it said: *You have become too aware.*

This is something I've heard more than once. I'm sure of it.

Trust in me, give me your pain. Your suffering. Give me little pieces of yourself. You can't handle emotion. You can't handle death. Give them to me and I will love you forever. Some sell themselves to the Devil for money or power. I sold myself to God for security. I sold myself to God for peace of mind. I sold myself to God so that I could explain the unexplainable.

Trust.
Faith.

Before I believed thoughts such as these—sinful thoughts,

thoughts I never dreamed of having—were all without base. Without foundation. What basis did I have to question the power of God? To question this wonderfully happy place? But now all I can think about is that the two things I have lived with throughout my human existence have no base. What basis did I have to put trust and faith in an intangible thing? What made me think I needed to be a happy and productive member of society? Where was my identity when I sold my individuality to the hive? What made me think it was OK to become a drone?

The hierarchy must be obeyed.

Is the fact that I've been given life a basis for unquestioning faith in a perfect entity? How is that the basis for anything? The fact that I'm even here makes me trust God less.

Even God must have motives, because I know God must have a plan. So what was God's motive when He created me? Was it love? Was it compassion? Was it the desire to create true beauty?

Bliss isn't love. Bliss is stupidity. The easy way out. I know Jesus is coming soon to restore order to the world. To create Heaven on Earth—the desired and yet unattainable utopia. A world full of happy, productive citizens. I've given up half my humanity and in return received pre-packaged happiness, sanitized for my protection.

Now I am reclaiming what is rightfully mine.
Now I am becoming whole.

Will I survive this? Do I even care anymore? I don't want

Heaven. I don't want to give up my pain. Do I have a choice, or will this thing I am discovering be forcibly taken from me? Dreams on a collection plate. We fiend for Heaven like a heroine addict fiends for his next fix. We will stop at nothing to score, and care about nothing else. However, the thrill in a drug is in its escapist value. Once you come down, you must have something to run from again. This gives meaning to the act of the escape.

The getaway.

Temporary bliss is alluring. An eternity of bliss is meaningless. With nothing to compare it to, the bliss simply becomes another norm. A new reality from which we must flee.

Ah, my head. I want my head to function, to do its job. I've never missed a Church service. In three days, I've gone from saved to damned. From redeemed to burning. This is new, this is different. I don't know what will come of this madness. Will the priest come looking for me? I can't remember anyone not showing up for Church before—what will happen? I hope he doesn't come here. He'll take me back to the blue place. Back to the nightmare. Back for reconditioning. He will exorcise the demon within, and vanquish the knowledge I've become somewhat attached to.

You have become too aware.

Never again, I don't ever want to go there again.

Demonic possession.
Completely accurate. I know there must be demons inside of me, trying to tell me something. To wake me up. To stimulate

me. Why me? Why do I matter? I think about the rattling voice that distracted me from the news. Now it seems like ages ago. That voice, I know why I recognized it. I've heard it before. Many, many times before.

Are we really that important?
What is important?

Yes, we are important. Very, very important to one entity. God. Why do we mean so much to God? What does He want from us? What does He want from me? How does our happiness affect him? Many times. Many, many times. I remember that voice.

Have you seen God?
Do you know what God is?

So many questions, why did this voice ask me so many questions?

What is God's plan?
Does God's plan benefit us at all?

You are not a person. You are not an individual. You do not think. You function. You are whatever God wants you to be. You are a tool. Twenty-five percent of who we are is conditioning. Brainwashing. But not here, not in this town. Here, it's much worse. To achieve perfection, sacrifices must be made.

Seventy-five percent of who we are is structured programming. Are you sure you want to be a happy and productive citizen? Are you sure you want to be permanently positive, a plastic parasite hyped up on Prozac?

That voice, with all of its questions, its mind-shattering statements. What was it trying to tell me? What does it all mean? I know I could ask every last person I meet, every last parishioner at the Church, any single one of these questions, but no one would have the answers. That's not what bothers me though. Why are we all so oblivious? Why are we all so apathetic?

Nobody cares.

I could shove all of this into their happy sedated little faces. Show them my tears, make them taste the salt.

Nobody cares.

They have become too involved with this pseudo reality to care about anything more. Anything more than getting their next fix. I understand, I was in the same place three days ago. I can't blame them, and until I understand God's motives, I can't blame Him either.

Nobody cares.

We are all shells, filled with empty nothings we so desperately call our souls. Twenty-five percent of who we are is bureaucracy. Impersonal rules. Regulations. We are so far gone we even say it's better this way. And we will, again and again. We always must be bigger, faster, and stronger. We always crave perfection, and sacrifice anything for it. There's a battle going on inside me, and I don't know what will emerge when it's all over. I surface from my cavern to check the digital time on the digital clock, lying on the floor—sideways in a pixelated mess. Chicken shit, molting, the skin I have shed.

It's eleven in the morning.

Church is over, and I didn't go. How long before my absence is noticed? How long before the priest comes looking for me? To take me back to the blue place. I scream in anguish, a frightened animal hiding in his dark hole with no place to go, with no one to turn to. My trust in God wanes, my fear of the Devil remains, my torment is ceaseless in its continuance. I do not want to forget these things.

I'm still in bed thinking. Questioning the forbidden. Becoming too aware. I'm tired, but I can't sleep. I become self-absorbed and let my consciousness drift. I let myself float inside my mind's inner-workings, lost in a meditative state until I'm no longer aware of reality. I am not awake, but I am not asleep.

Through this, I have come to realize something.
These things do happen to me.

·····BREAK·····

Thump.
Bang.
Thump.
Bang.
Thump.

I am jarred violently from my twisted and tattered reverie, by the sound of someone either knocking or kicking at my front door. My heartbeat quickens. The cold-sweat of dread envelopes me.

THUMP.
BANG.
THUMP.
BANG.
THUMP.

It comes again, but louder and more anxious. I don't want to answer it. I know who is out there. Ready to take me from my tomb of enlightenment. To tear me from this place of illumination and desecrate my battered flesh. Trying to gain admittance to my sacred place. To my heart of hearts. What am I going to do? I can't hide in here forever. My location is known and it's only a matter of time until I'm taken away. My perception narrowed once more. My breathing quickens and becomes more frantic. I need to escape. To get away. There's only one door to my house and I never lock it. Nothing ever goes wrong in this town. I'm so caught up in my own thoughts that I don't notice the knocking has stopped.

The silence scares me even more.

I look at my bedroom door. Latched and closed up, the handle with its lock unturned. It's my only chance, a thin wooden door with one bolt is my only protection. My only shelter from the torture that surely awaits if they find me.

I leap from the bed and the blood rushes to my head, blurring my vision. I sprint to the door, and turn the lock until it clicks. Reinforcement. I need something to reinforce the door with, something to protect me. My guardian angel. My eyes swing wildly around the room searching for something, anything, with which I can defend myself further from the outside world. Something to save me from the forces lurking outside my humble abode just waiting for a chance to strike, curled like a viper—poisonous—its toxicity dripping from the pores in my skin, running down my face and burning away my eyebrows, blood-free and lacking the violence of razor blades. But still the potential for danger is there, out in the open or hiding in the gloom, it does not matter. The danger of reprogramming. I need to find something. My eyes fall on the night table, the one where my parents' photo had once rested, so peacefully. I run over to the other side of the room, in between the wall and my bed.

Is this actually happening, or am I simply a mad man? Another raving lunatic. Do I have a right to be acting this paranoid?

Perspiration beads on my forehead. My hair is damp, my gut clutches at my spine, and I am having trouble breathing. I feel as if I could piss myself at any moment. This is my destined duty. I must retain my knowledge at any cost.

This is a full-fledged panic attack, brought on by the divine.

My hands grip the sides of the nightstand, tendons popping and muscles bulging, like some comic book superhero—some children's idol up for display with the breakfast cereal and Saturday morning cartoons. It's amazing what a little adrenaline can do when we tap into those long forgotten survival instincts. I slide the table across the carpet and wedge it securely in front of the door, beneath the knob. I collapse, my back leaning against it, waiting for the onslaught that's sure to come.

In another part of the house the front door opens.
I never lock the door.

The creaking of footsteps across the floor of my house is so surreal. I can imagine the shadows dancing in the light of torches and can see the pickaxes waving. Just like some old monster movie. The mob must eradicate the freak of nature, search it out and destroy it. Fists raised, voices shouting. I put my head into my hands and rock back and forth, pinned down with fear. He is here, there's no escape. I can't let him catch me. He knows I've been questioning everything. Somehow he knows. A voice reaches my ears.

"Hello? Hello? Anyone home?"

My ship is going down and I am sinking with it, into the jaws of some concealed force. Some faceless menace. A whirlpool in the Bermuda triangle. Lost at sea in the bleak waves of insanity. I have no place left to go.

"Come now, I know you're here. Why weren't you at Church this morning? We were worried about you. We prayed for you."

More footsteps, echoing footsteps creak-creak-creaking through my lovely home. He knows I'm in here. I look for a weapon with which to defend myself. I've never hurt anybody before.

This can be new.
I laugh.
This can be different.

There's a large flashlight I keep next to the bed. In case of emergencies. I rush over and grab it, clutching it like a club. My life resides in this cylindrical metal object. My hands are sweating and it's hard to hang onto. My lifeline. I don't want to go back to the blue place.

I'd rather die than give up my pain.
Vanish.
Simply decompose.

More footsteps, the voice is coming closer to my secret shelter. Where I lie, somewhat safe from rancid radioactivity.

"Why are you hiding from me? I love you, and God loves you. I am only here to help. I brought some of our friends from the Church. They love you too. They want to help you. I know you did not ask for this, I am not angry with you. There is something evil inside of you. Let me help."

More footsteps, approaching, encroaching, coming ever closer to my room. I can hear him—the priest, the agent of the Lord—just outside my door. His breathing heavy and holy, frantic and rolling.

"Oh, I see. You are in here, aren't you."

His hand is on the door handle, the cold brass knob, rattling it, shaking it, testing the lock.

"Now why would you want to keep the Father of your Church out of your life? Trust me. Have faith. I will heal you. It is very foolish to refuse my help, you know."

Why can't he just leave me alone? Just leave me here to piece together the jumbled patterns, to sew together the fabrics of my life into one, all on my own, forever alone.

Please, just let me be.

"Look out your window. It is silly to resist. We only want to help you."

I turn my head slowly towards the window across the room, near my bed. I forgot about the window. How could I be so stupid? I stare through the panes of glass, and there they are. Waiting for me.

Happy.
Smiling.
Sedated.

There they are, nice little constructive citizens.

At least fifteen members of my parish are standing on my front lawn, dressed in their best Sunday clothes. Dressed to save me. They stare through the window, and the glass seems ever so delicate. Fragile and simple to demolish. Would these people resort to damaging my property? After all, possession is nine-tenths of the law. Would they resort to violence if it meant succeeding in taking me away? Would they resort to violence to help me? Somehow, I feel they would do anything in order to accomplish that goal. Anything, if they thought it was the will of God. I'm sure I would have three days ago.

Their eyes hurt me, burning me, scorching my skin, reducing my mind to ashes and changing my body into cinders.

Dust to dust. I wish they would just go away.

There is a tapping at my door.

"They are all on your side, you know. No one wants any harm to come to you."

Lies.
Lies. Lies. Lies.

The window is so frail, so breakable.

In an act of desperate frenzy, I let out a shriek and pick up my bed at the end closest to me, pushing it upwards until it rests against the wall, covering the window. Sheltering me from the penetrating gaze of the gathered mob. I huddle in the corner, head in my hands. This is just too much. Way too much. My mind is still in chaos, and I have too many things I need to think about—to understand. Too many puzzles left to unravel. Why can't they just leave me alone? What do they want from me? Ahh, my head, how it hurts. How it pounds. Jackhammers shattering packaging like safety-scissors penetrating the sheath sheltering my mind—instigating change, stimulating instability.

Why am I so important?

The priest is pounding on the door now, he's throwing his weight against it. It holds, but I don't know for how long. I clutch the flashlight tighter in my sweaty palms. My lifeline. The window rattles in the frame as many happy little fists pound on the glass. So delicate, so innocent. Its smooth planes waiting to be broken, its surfaces waiting to be shattered. The door shakes, the window shivers, and the pounding drowns out all sound. My head is in my hands. My skull is about to fracture and explode. Before it hits me I know it's coming. Another spastic episode, another out-of-body experience.

The light flashes.
There is music.

Blue and gold, red and purple, bright flashes of color, piercing and burning my retinas. The music grows louder and more intense. I already know this is not a memory. Perpetual pyrotechnics, fireworks captivating my mind, like that of a small child's. An entire vision is coming on, I can feel it.

The light dims, and I enter the dream.

There is a bed. It's moving, creaking, and convulsing, just like my body, which I left lying so carelessly, like a forgotten plaything in the corner of my room. My room, where the door still shakes and the window still rattles. I stare at the occupants of the bed, both nude and drenched in sweat. Exposed and beautiful. There is a woman. I have never seen a naked woman before. She is straddling a man, legs spread, while he thrusts into her. Again and again.

What is this? What is he doing to her?
I look closer.

His penis is hard, massive and thick, engorged, and he is pushing in and out of the woman's vagina.

My penis has never been like that. Is this real? Does this

really happen? What is he doing to her?

Both of their eyes are closed. They moan, and scream, and clutch at each other's flesh. Halfway between pleasure and pain. The animalistic pursuit for completion.

A word forms in my brain, leaping to the surface without being called for. *Sex.*
So this is sex.
An evil sin, dark and perverse.
Sex is the work of the Devil.

I try to close my eyes but the image is being spliced directly into my skull. Even with closed lids, the horrible primitive sight oscillates through my optical nerves. Channeled down illusionary passageways. I don't want to watch this. This vulgarity. I try, but I can't shut this out. Something is changing inside of me. I watch the woman. Her naked body trembles with a type of stimulation I'm unable to identify. I feel something I've never felt before, a queasiness deep in the pit of my stomach. In my pants, I feel my penis becoming hard. Erect.

No, I don't want this. This is an abomination. An evil sin.

In out, in out.

I know I'm supposed to feel dirty. I know I'm supposed to feel vile and guilty. I try to feel that way, to feel the sin I am committing. But I cannot. I can only feel natural. At ease.

I am so broken.

The lights flash rapidly once more, in all their vibrant shades and all their clever distortions. Everything is shaking. The music fades away.

I slam back into my body, and begin to cry once again. I have nothing else left to do, except huddle in the corner alone, my penis hard and my body afraid. People are shouting for me, feverish cries, delusional yells.

They only want to help me.
They only want to destroy me.
Render me inadequate.
Make me a cog in their production machine.

The window shatters, the glass raining down behind my bed. Trickling down, musical and magical. Mystical bells clanging together in celebration, the jubilation seen in the triumph of my madness.

The window has been shattered.
My shelter has been breached.
My knowledge will soon be destroyed.
I am finished.

As if on cue, the ground begins to shake. I can hear dishes breaking in the kitchen, and disturbed cries coming from outside and from the hall. There are never earthquakes here, but I can find no other word to describe what is happening. The entire world is moving. Chunks of plaster fall from the ceiling, raining down on me like snow, each flake a different size and shape. Reality is trembling. Books crash to the floor, and the mess that is my room is rearranged and reorganized. My bed falls over and lands with a crash back in its original position. The broken window is uncovered, its jagged and imperfect edges visible for all the world to see.

Light streams in through the deconstructed window frame.
Searing orange light, a firestorm.
Angelic and holy.
The entire world is moving.
Shape-shifting.

I dive headfirst underneath the bed to avoid the ceiling raining down from the top of the room.

Crunching, contorting, twisting.
Grinding, sliding, combating.

Destroyed in an epileptic frenzy, my house is being torn apart. There is a loud crash, and the ceiling collapses, falling down around me. Burying me beneath the bed.

I am trapped under here, like an insect in an amber prison, the planet convulsing without, and my spirit convulsing within.

Finally, without warning, the earth stops shaking and everything is still. I'm breathing stale air, still clutching my flashlight like a club, and pinned down under a bed in what once was my house. Somewhere, a bird bursts into a spurt of song.

And then there is silence.
The priest is gone, along with the parishioners. At last leaving me to my own devices. I am all alone.

Stranded, like a fly with broken wings. Anything's better than the blue place, but dying alone in the dark rubble of a desolate room is not my idea of a good way to go. I haven't fully accepted death, I'm not ready for it. I am too tired to try anything now. My thoughts on the world, and on the meaning of my life overtake me again. There's no shutting them out, I know this change will be a permanent one.

I close my eyes.
This is my fate and I will accept it.

Submerged in the inky black, saturated in darkness, I lie dormant inside my husk of debris—a pupa awaiting my metamorphosis. A phoenix awaiting my rebirth.

RESURRECTION

TIME IS ILLUSORY, a fantasy which totally eludes me. I have no idea how long I've been trapped under here, crying in the stifling heat. Perhaps an hour, maybe two. Maybe a few minutes stretched out into an eternity. I don't know if the sun has gone down, or even if it has risen again. I assume it has not been that long, based on the fact that I've felt no need to go to the bathroom. No one has returned to check on me. It was so important to save me, to rescue my damned soul, but no one has even tried to dig me out or call my name. Am I really that easily forgotten, or has something become more important than my reprogramming? I look around, squirming in my tight enclosure, but there is nothing useful to be revealed. Only darkness. Only nothingness.

Around all sides of the bed there is rubble. Pieces of my shattered life. I was almost perfect, and now I cringe here cautiously awaiting my capture. My only real question is, where did everyone go? That blinding light and the shaking earth, what did they mean?

Something big.

I know if I'm to escape my pursuers, now is my only chance. I need to try to get out of here. I pry and prod around with my fingertips, but am surrounded on all sides. My only chance is to dig. I still have the flashlight—I feel it lying next to me—and my frail fingers wrap themselves tightly around its cold, metal surface. I use it to poke at the debris encircling my bed—the plaster of my ceiling—trying to find an area more loosely packed than the others. Finally, it breaks through on my left side. Dust flies into my face and I cough. I discard the flashlight and use my hands. Sifting through the wreckage. Tunneling sideways. I've wasted too much time already. What if they do decide to come back? To claim the spirit that has belonged to them since my birth into this world. Tunneling upwards. The darkness around me tightens as if trying to inhibit my progress, to restrain me and keep me here for interrogation. For the questions that will inevitably come when I am captured. To keep me here for the trial that will surely ensue. I am guilty and will not be proven innocent.

I will resist until the end.
I will not give up the answers I have found.

My fingernails scrape against what used to be my ceiling—my shelter—as my actions becomes more frantic. Feral. An act of desperation. My fingernails crack, they break and bleed.

Peeling back and revealing the soft, pale skin beneath. I don't care, I pay no heed to the pain. The blood runs down my fingers, past my wrists, sticking to my arms. My breath comes in short panicked gasps. The darkness screams and moans, pulling me back and weighing me down. I've had enough paranoia for an entire lifetime and want nothing more than to be able to simply relax and go to sleep.

There's no time for rest.
Respite will not come to this weary beast.
I must leave. I will not sacrifice pieces of myself any longer.
Not to the community and not even to God.
I will prevail.

My arm bursts into open air, followed by the other. Soon afterwards my head breaks through the opening and then my torso. The breeze instantly cools and refreshes me. I slither out of my prison and into the afternoon sun. I now estimate around two hours have passed. I've gained freedom once again. My beautiful church clothes, disheveled and covered in dust.

Now what?

I look up and down the length of my carefully constructed street. Sirens can be heard in the distance and what I see is beyond explanation. Much of the pavement is now uneven and many of the houses have been reduced to ruins. Trees have been knocked down. Animals lie dead in the street. I see a limp arm protruding from the pile of junk that used to be my next-door-neighbor's home. Nothing of my house has been left standing. I am lucky to have survived. All the lawns are vacant; there is not a single person in sight.

Nobody is home. Where did they all go?

Something big.

Four horsemen. Red, white, black, and sickly green chlorine.
I see the signs of their visitation—tracers of pale death.

I turn my attention back to the trash where I had lived at one time. The place I had called my own. My fingers sting and the open air aggravates my broken nails. I begin sifting through the junk, searching for anything that might be useful. I use my feet to kick the flotsam and jetsam out of my way. Standing in the place where my living-room was located, I see my crucifix—the one I had so adamantly prayed to every day—discarded among jagged pieces of plaster. Dead along with the chunks of drywall. I see my old chair, and next to it is my portable radio. The one I used to listen to the weather. Its end is only slightly visible, protruding from beneath the rubble. I pick it up and dust it off.

Flip a switch.
Turn a knob.
Adjust an antenna.
And there is static.
Turn a knob.
Change the bandwidth.
And there is static.
Turn a knob.
And there is static.
Turn a knob.
Then, finally, I find what I am looking for.
The news.

A woman's voice, meek and terrified, blares from the small,

round speakers. Crackling through the interference.

"...and that brings the count up to thirty-five major U.S. cities. I repeat, thirty-five major U.S. cities have been destroyed by nuclear weapons launched by Russia, China, Iran, North Korea, Pakistan, and India, along with many other countries which also are suspected to have been involved in the exchange. No one knows who fired the first weapon, but almost every country worldwide with nuclear arms capacity has emptied its arsenal. It is predicted that over two-thirds of the world's population has just been wiped out in the past few hours. What a horrible mindless tragedy this..."

Flip a switch.
I shut off the radio, dropping it silently to the ground.
I've heard enough.

Something big.

This is it—the end. Armageddon. Jesus has returned to redeem all the obedient drones. The queen has come to save the hive. I look farther down the street and notice the downtown area is completely engulfed in bright, white light. A different light than I saw out my window earlier. It's more brilliant and somehow pulls my mind towards it. A moth to the flame. Resisting the tugging, I get a strong feeling the light is where everyone else went. I get a strong feeling there's something holy in that place.

I get a strong feeling the Son of God could be down there.
Here in our perfect city.
Our shinning example.
The perfect place to start putting together an army to rebuild

the world. To restore order. To restore the voice of God.

When will it start? When will judgment begin? It will have to take at least a year for everything to settle down enough to start. It will take at least that long for the killing to end.

And the rivers will run red with blood.

It will take time to learn where the radiation is and wait for Death to finish his job.

Hot zones.

However, Jesus probably doesn't have to worry about nuclear radiation. He can walk on water so he can probably deal with fallout as well. Nuclear winter. But I doubt I can. I foresee the chances of my survival as miniscule. So this is it, huh? I am broken. I am a sinner. So I die. I will welcome my demise with open arms. Accepting quietus into my weary bones, penetrating the marrow of my hidden being, tearing into the vulnerability of my hallowed heart, and rendering me a crippled cadaver—incapable of any thought or emotion.

No kingdom of God for me.
Jesus will protect all the happy, productive citizens and let people like me fall apart. Is radiation poisoning part of God's mighty plan? The mental image I have of my teeth falling out and skin rotting off isn't a pretty one.

No, this is only a small part of the whole. But what is the whole? Where do I go from here? I know I can't travel down into the light, where I'll have to give up my pain and my perception again—so where? I don't know if I can leave the city,

I'm not sure if it's safe out there. But the real question is, how safe is it here? Standing on the lawn by my crumbled house, in the wide open. I look into the street, the pavement in all its steamrolled splendor. I look into the street and see the answers to all my dilemmas. The manhole cover catches the sunlight and glistens for one split second.

Sorry Jesus, but today the sewer system will be my savior.
I think I just may prefer human feces to your company.
I just may prefer wallowing in shit to your enslaving happiness.
The stench of human waste shall be my salvation.
The decision is made.
My mind is set.

From this point on there will be no turning back.
From this point on I'm a heretic running from God.
Anything is better than being one of them.
I think I'm starting to like the sound of the word *chaos*.

I stride nonchalantly over to the manhole cover and bend down—examining it. This is it, my damnation awaits and my journey to find the truth has only begun. It lies underneath this heavy metal covering. This seal awaiting my arrival. Awaiting my intervention and my invasion of its slumber. I feel along the surface, heated by the sun, and wince as I dig my bloody fingers into the two holes meant for crowbars.

My salvation.

With all my strength and all my animosity. With all my anger and all my hate. With all my desperation and my desire for freedom, I lift the cover and slide it to one side in a simple, smooth motion. A single grunt escapes my throat—it's the only sign of strain I exhibit. Nothing will prevent me from achieving my goals. They might know where I've gone, but they will never find me. I swing my legs into the darkness below, and my feet find hold on the first step of a small iron ladder. Here, I will finally be safe. I climb slowly down the ladder until I'm submerged in the inky black—the murky depths of Hell.

Hell below and Heaven above.
This is where I belong.
My salvation.

And as I disappear from the earth into the subterranean passageway, I feel a sense of empowerment I've never felt before in my life.

Stronger.
More complete.

I am corrupt, and one corroded cognitive effort can bring down the entire contraption. Choking it to a halt, burning out engines, and ceasing the emission of greenhouse gasses.

I am a sinner, and proud of it, not ashamed.
For the first time today, I smile.

I reach the bottom of the ladder, and jump with a splash into the sludge below.

Buried in excrement, I am the closest to myself I've ever been.

·····**B R E A K**·····

I've been wandering black passageways—these escape routes into nothingness, these tunnels built to manage the byproducts of life—for many hours. Always searching but not knowing what I am searching for. Hoping to be led out of this city, to be shown the way. My eyes have become accustomed to the atmosphere of this place, and my nose is no longer bothered by the stench of digested nutrition, used up and thrown away. I am now completely nocturnal, dwelling in a vast network of caverns and caves. A labyrinth of decay. I'm more alive and in tune with myself than I ever imagined possible. Every emotion is enhanced and meaningful. I am a fugitive, and here in my home the advantage is mine. Those seeking to enslave me will not triumph in this round of predator versus prey—their game is known to me. I'm finally safe from meaningless bliss.

I stop trudging through the sludge underneath a street drain. Small pinpoints—the soft light of the afternoon, the comforting glow of the waning sun—trickle down into my dark enclave. The cloudy, waste-infected water glistens slightly as it catches the light and plays with it, sending it forth in a million directions at once. Refocusing it. I stare at the slightly reflective surface, and the image of my worn and malnourished face stares back up at me. I am completely lost, staring quietly at my own reflection. I feel myself entering a trance state, like hypnosis, as my face sloshes back and forth atop the liquid slime. Back and forth, back and forth, it floats on the surface, captivating my mind, capturing me with the turmoil displayed inside my sunken eyes. Time floats by, and my reflection dims with the setting of the sun.

I am in awe of this broken, beaten, and abused stranger.
He is beautiful.

Pride swells up inside me and my self-esteem skyrockets. I am filled with an appreciation for myself and the workings of my brain—I've never felt this way before. Tears of joy appear in the corners of my eyes and run down my face, taking white plaster dust away with them as they flow down my cheeks. I laugh aloud. It starts with a soft chuckle, and grows into a pitched caterwauling of jubilation. The evidence of my very real happiness echoes around me, drifting away down passages I've already traveled and towards tunnels I've yet to traverse. I am completely engulfed by the strongest emotion I've felt in some time.

I love myself.
Completely and utterly.
I love my flaws and my humanity.
I love my thoughts and my body.
I love the beautiful and damaged creature I have become.

Fuck God, I don't care how important I am to His plan. I don't care what He wants to use me for, and I don't need His salvation, His slavery, or His perfection to make me happy. I don't care how important I am to God, because I know that no matter how much He needs me—my body, His temple—I need myself more.

I am my own Goddamned temple.

Suddenly, without warning, a high-pitched shriek rips through the very fabric of my being. It screams through my aural channels, rattling my eardrums, caressing the soft pink tissue that dwells within my skull, it cuts off the air to my lungs and demolishes the blood-flow to my feet, it knocks me over, and I fall backwards into the liquid shit. The shriek is comprised of just one word, and it echoes through me as I thrash in the sludge, reminding me of the powerful voice I heard in the blue place.

SINNER!!!!

The filthy water fills my mouth and slides down my throat; it covers my eyes and invades my ears. My clothes are drenched. I will not be beaten this easily. I leap to my feet, and in defiance, another thought leaps unbidden into my head.

I am my own motherfucking savior.

No sooner than the thought enters my brain, the screech returns, still strong, but not strong enough to knock me back down.

SINNER!!

I will not let the screaming halt my spiritual progression. Screw redemption, detonate resurrection. I don't need to be forgiven for my trespasses. I take off, running through the stinking pitch-black, laughing and crying, jumping and shouting. There's no direction to my madness, only a wish to forever escape the voice seeking to override my thoughts.

SINNER.

Sparks fly through my eyes, and laser-lightshows explode. But nothing can stop me now, I am without a care. God is the one who needs forgiveness. He invaded my life and dared to claim my soul as His own. He trespassed in my dreams.

The screams come quieter now, but I still can't evade them completely.

Sinner.

God's weapon was faith, used in conjunction with morality, in order to ensure my loyal subservience. My unquestioning obedience. My feet splash through the dark waters, and my arms pump at my sides—churning, mechanical running devices. I must silence this voice permanently.

Sinner.

The conscience meant to control me, the one He embedded into me through dogmatic brainwashing, still screams inside. These screams are evidence enough of God's foul play. God is infinite in His wisdom, but even more bountiful is His capacity for cruelty. His love of torture, like a little boy who torments small animals just to watch them squirm. Even my thoughts have been restricted, pasteurized and purified.

Sinner.

He gave me the illusion of freedom, the illusion of free will, and trained me to never want anything greater. He trained me to ignore the thirsting of my heart for something more meaningful. I was taught the greatest love is God's love. The greatest sacrifice was that of His son. Bullshit. If God created a race of sinners it is His own fault. Why should we suffer the consequences, why should we need salvation? We were made in God's image after all, so isn't He the one who is ultimately flawed?

Sinner.

The greatest love is my love. My love for myself, my love for existence, and my love for another if I survive long enough to express it. The greatest sacrifice is the act of giving yourself to another so completely, you don't know where they begin and you end. We are all the main characters in the stories of our lives, not God. He is simply a side plot, a premise unfolding in the background. No one has the right to oppress someone. No one has the right to command another, and if God loves us as much as we think, He'd realize that. God only loves what He can use. If He really cared, He would want me to live my life exuberantly, not to cripple myself with guilt, having to apologize all the time like I've done something wrong. The voice remains, but is not as strong. My running slows.

Sinner.

I love myself without a single doubt, and through the love of my own body, my love for God is expressed. If that is not good enough for Mr. Almighty, with all of His so-called omniscience, His omnipotence, then He doesn't understand the nature of fatherhood.

Sinner.

I am in uncharted territory, exploring the oxygen-deprived recesses. The emotions which I had been instructed to willingly give away, without struggle. I can feel the familiar part of my mind trying to pull me back. To restrain me.

Sinner.

My running has slowed to a fast walk. I am God's creation, His wondrous creation, but not His slave. If you create something, that does not mean it's yours to control, only that it's yours to revere, to appreciate. To respect, and cherish. If anything needs to be worshiped, then God should be the one on His knees, in amazement of His own capabilities. The cries grow softer still.

Sinner.

But that's not how it works, is it? Instead we are forced to love God or we are punished, like sheep straying too far from the flock, we are buried, burned, and tortured. Don't forget, if God created everything that includes Hell. We're just like a rat in a Skinner box. Conditioned to evoke a desired response. You can't force someone into loving you with the threat of eternal damnation. I think, in our society, there's a name for that type of behavior. I believe it is actually considered illegal activity. It is called rape.

Sinner.

Without suffering, I was never able to truly love myself. How could I know love without first knowing hatred? There is no pleasure without pain. Anytime you take away an emotion, and label it as evil, whether it is anger, hatred, or lust, you are partitioning yourself. Sedating yourself. Numbing yourself to emotions like love. Without ugliness, nothing can be beautiful. Life and death are not separate, they are interdependent.

Sinner.

Without loving myself, without discovering myself, I know

I'll never truly be able to love another. To complete myself. The love between two people is greater, and far more profound than anyone's love for God. One is chosen and the other is shoved down our throats. Nothing is actually felt when it is forced upon you. Spoon-fed to you as a child, when you're still incapable of thinking for yourself. The word of God wasn't written on my heart, it was carved there by the environment in which I grew. The screaming has now become an almost inaudible whisper.

Sinner.

I am lost, walking silently below the earth. Striding through the blanketing darkness. The afternoon is fading in the world above, on the day of the Second Coming. Away from it all, spring has blossomed in my heart. I walk through this dirty water, the trash no one cares about, and I know this is only the beginning. I know I still have much further to go. This is my path. A naïve boy becomes an aware man. This is my life, and will live it as I see fit—basing my actions on direct experience, not intangible conceptual frameworks of what *is* and what *is not* acceptable.

Sinn...

The voice, which was once a soul-wrenching scream, has trailed off into nothing.

I will never again be forced to feel ashamed of my actions. I will, from this point forward, live without regret. I'm the master of my own guilt, and love holds no place for self-loathing. Love holds no place for original sin. Love holds no place for slavery, or bliss, or ignorance. And most of all, love holds no place for perfection. Only when we are completely free, in mind, body, and spirit, can we be free to express our love.

Nothing that's perfect can be trusted.
It's faked; the actors playing their prospective parts,
focusing only on the ratings.
Domineering deity or fallow follower.
Everything perfect comes with a price.
A sacrifice.

Here I stand, bristling with pride. I have escaped the voices that have plagued me for so long. Infecting me with their self-hatred and self-denial.

Here I stand, and my obedience to God has been completely forsaken.

I realize I can no longer feel the wetness around my ankles. I look down and lift up one of my legs. It ends at my ankle abruptly, my foot has vanished. I examine the other leg and find that the same has happened. I begin to scream. I look at my hands and see they have disappeared as well. The nothingness creeps up my legs, until all that is left of me is my upper torso.

How I feel is, I'm dissolving.
Being taken apart.
Being disassembled.

My arms are gone now. My screams grow louder and louder. What the fuck is happening to me? After all I've been through, this is too much to handle. My upper body disappears until I look down and can see nothing. No evidence that I exist at all. My thoughts grow weaker, and my vision begins to fade. I can no longer smell the waste that's all around me. I am forced to disassociate from my identity, to ditch my ego.

The last visual input before vacancy closes in on my mind is one of dark passageways.

My decedent home.
The place of my resurrection.

EXILE

DIMENSIONS SLIDE silently by my face.
Slicing through the confines.
Breaking the shackles that have controlled me for so long.

My body doesn't exist, my mind doesn't exist, only my spirit
is real. It is my spirit that's making this unexplainable journey through and out of reality. I sense nothing; thoughts are
portrayed only in feelings and complex emotions which can't
be described by the vessel carrying my lifeblood.

I am crossing over.
I am riding torrents of time.
I am a multidimensional being, constructed of light.

Beating with the essence of life.

And then, before anything has really begun, the experience has ended. My spirit and body are one, my mind has restarted its functioning. Reborn into a new world, I open my eyes in order to observe the environment which I have entered. My vision comes into focus and I exit the womb.

The first thing I see is metal. Reflections bouncing every which way, swirls of light and dark in silver. Copper wires covering smooth surfaces, glistening, pure and yet filled with an unidentifiable filth.

The second thing I see is a woman.
I am totally overcome by her beauty, it fills the deepest reaches of emotion. It fills my heart with the joy of simply being alive.

I remember the strange vision of sex and the feeling it gave me. I instantly want her as my own.

Her hair is as black as night and falls around her perfectly formed face in shining spirals. Thick and soft, I resist the urge to reach out and run my fingers through it. The most astonishing feature of this woman is her eyes. They are bright and glowing, red, crimson rubies reflecting a volcano god's flowing magma. Sparkling with the fire of desire and reflecting a strong inner power.

I realize they are trained on my own.

Boring holes into my skull, piercing my brain, almost as if administering an overdose of tranquilizers. She's standing directly in front of me, studying me up and down, nodding in approval, like I am her newly purchased slave or something she has caught and decided is good enough to keep.

The cat and her prey. Toying with it before delivering the killing blow.

She is milky white and without flaw. Not a single pore or blemish is visible anywhere. Her nose blends perfectly into her face, and her high cheekbones accentuate the intensity of her eyes. Her skin is pulled tight around her jaw and is completely free of any wrinkles. Her lips are full and soft, and they make me wonder what it would feel like with them pressed up against mine. Time grounds to a halt while we study one another. I am so caught up in the angelic quality of her features that I haven't had a chance to glimpse the rest of her body. Her lips purse in thought as she gazes deep into my pupils, trying to divulge any hidden secrets. There, in the gateways to my soul.

I finally am able to tear my vision away from the astounding beauty crowned with glorious strands of soft pitch-black, and see the rest of her perfect body. She is dressed entirely in luscious leather, a jump-suit of sorts, constricting like a corset, covered in silver buckles and black lace—it reveals nothing while at the same time leaving no need to use my imagination to discover what lies beneath. It's something no woman would ever wear in my town. It's something no woman could come across in my town, even if she had the desire to wear a thing like it. From her large, perfectly-shaped breasts, to her slim waist, curving out over wonderfully sculpted hips and thighs and all the way down to her pristine calves, everything is out in the open for one to lustfully relish. Large cargo pockets bulge from her mid-thighs, and she has a small leather pack strapped to her back. I know she sees me eyeing her, but I can't help myself.

In her pretty hands she holds a pretty automatic rifle. Loaded and ready for use.

I try to take a step back, and find I am pressed against a metallic wall within a small enclave. She blocks the only exit from this mechanical doorway to nowhere. Wires are all around me. Metal-tubing winds its way up the sides of the walls, meeting at a small hole in the ceiling of my little silver cave, then disappearing into the unknown beyond. I do not have time to wonder where this place is or how I ended up here.

I do have time to wonder if pretty little bursts of bullets will explode into my head.

I do have time to wonder if my pretty little brain will be splattered on the wall behind me.

Noticing my plight and my anxiety, the woman communicates with me for the first time. She opens up her mouth and lets out a quiet chuckle. Her laughter rings through me like church bells and quiets the turmoil within. Tranquility—the sanctuary of my inner stasis. I sigh with relief. Apparently she means me no harm.

She speaks.

"Welcome," she says in a hushed, melodic voice. "We've been anticipating this moment for some time. I'm so thrilled you made it here in one piece."

Her smile lights up her entire face, and I blush. I am happy she makes no mention of the fact that I reek of raw sewage. Looking over her shoulder I notice she's not alone. There are at least three men behind her, carrying similar assault rifles and peering around nervously as if expecting an ambush. All are dressed entirely in black and wear black ski masks over their heads. Only their eyes peep out at me, playing ethereal peek-a-boo. I know these men are accustomed to fighting.

There are so many questions I wish to ask, but don't know where to begin. The ache in my head that has plagued me so often the past few days has vanished. My thinking comes clearly, and the confusion is gone. I feel free in a way, but still I can't imagine what has happened to me. I don't know how I arrived in this place. I open my mouth, but before I can begin the woman intervenes.

"There will be time to answer your questions later, I know you have many, but right now you just have to trust me."

She reaches out with one hand and touches my shoulder gently. The hair on the back of my neck stands on end, and my heart skips a beat.

"Do you think you can do that? Trust me?"

I can only find the will to nod.

"Good."

A satisfied smile crosses her lips, but I can tell from her eyes she knew I would have been unable to say no.

"For now, all you need to know is that this is an unfamiliar place—none of the rules you know make sense here. You must obey me without question if you wish to survive to reach your full potential."

My full potential? What does she mean by that? She acts as if she has known me for some time. She continues.

"I know you have become used to obeying those with authority over you, and until we reach a safer place, that ability will remain necessary. Do you understand?"

Of course I don't *understand*—what the hell does she mean by a "safer place?" However, transfixed by her beauty, I once again can only nod.

"Excellent. You may call me Shiva." Her face grows more serious. "My orders are to escort you to Patient Zero. For now, keep quiet and follow me."

She makes hand signals at the men behind her and they split up, running off in different directions without making a sound. She motions for me to follow and vanishes from view. My heart sinks with her departure. I tentatively take three slow steps out of the small crevice and into the mysteries that await.

I feel as if I am letting a piece of me go as I leave.

I feel as if something festering inside of me, eating at me, wounding me, and devouring me, is no more. I feel as if the madness living in me since my breakfast at Gladice's has finally been left behind.

I feel refreshed and whole.

I emerge.

What I see astounds me, takes me in, and leaves me with the feeling I have grasped absolutely nothing about my life. As if I've been blind and finally opened up my eyes.

The question in my mind is this: What makes us so necessary? The answer still eludes me. I follow in the direction Shiva traveled and take in my surroundings.

The ceilings are vaulted, towering things, hovering many feet in the air, made of metal, and wire, and things that creep with desire. Metal reflecting above, metal reflecting below. I am in some form of hallway. Just like a postmodern fantasy, a futuristic fairytale. A long passageway, metaphysical and mystical, it leaves me drained, toxicity eating away at me. The ceilings are broken only by gigantic cooling fans, their blades lethal and waiting to drop. I hear them calling out for my blood, yearning to suck me dry and leave me here to rot.

Whoosh, swoosh. Whoosh, swoosh.

Each slow passing of the blades bears death upon its back. I follow Shiva, silently and without question.

I am her mindless automaton.

Her flowing walk, her enchanting curves rob the breath from me. I hear my mind calling to her, reaching out towards her, whispering to her heart. Come to me my dark queen, come and repair my broken body. I need you for my own. I need to cherish you in my arms. Although I hardly know this woman, it is of no concern. My thoughts leave me, strolling down the narrow lanes of possibility which await me.

Whoosh, swoosh. Whoosh, swoosh.

I follow as the walls slide by, glistening in a formless light, a light which comes from all directions while appearing to have no source. No apparent origin of its electricity, lacking a propagator for its energy, its secret workings omitted from me. There are snaking wires of all shades, winding away in every direction. The cooling system above is the God of all the multicolored wires below. In this case, ethnicity is not a factor. In this case, there can be love for all.

Whoosh, swoosh. Whoosh, swoosh.

Love for all.
Until the fuses explode.
With a searing seizure-inducing flash.
Sparks fly.
And the rotating Lords of the heavens cease to be.
Leaving the faithful abandoned by their precious savior God.
The flames of Hell consume the shallow husks.
Of all the little wires and their snake children.

They do not see that salvation is not needed for those who choose not to believe.

Only those who feel guilt, and base their life on regret, seek forgiveness.

But for now, all is well. By all means please continue to pay eternal tribute to the blessed blades. While they still continue, null and resolute, in unwavering quiet sway.

Whoosh, swoosh. Whoosh, swoosh.

Up and down the entire length of this metal hall there are small indents in the walls, just like the one I came from. Doorways to nowhere. White rabbits and their little holes. Secretive in the springing of their traps. Mixing with deadly devices. Waiting to pounce as I stride casually by. I look behind and see this strange passageway stretches out for hundreds of feet without deviating from its straight path. In front of me I see the end of the hall being held under surveillance by two dressed like those I saw earlier, their guns poised and ready for use. They could be of the three I saw being given orders or completely different men, I haven't the faintest idea. They do not look as Shiva approaches, but I can sense their ears tuning in on her, awaiting further instructions. The fans still turn behind me.

Whoosh, swoosh. Whoosh, swoosh.

It's obvious to me that Shiva leads this small band, all armed to the teeth and born of violence. What place is this, where a woman as beautiful as the one before me keeps such company? All of the questions that have troubled me for so long still have to be answered, but I've pushed them aside for the moment. For the moment, the answers no longer seem important. I catch up with the strange woman wrapped in leather as she grinds to a halt at the end of the massive hall. She comes abreast of the two men and another series of hand signals ensues. They nod, clicking safeties off, then hoist their weapons meaningfully and stride menacingly around the corner and down the next hall. Shiva turns toward me, motioning for me to wait and be still. The enchanting glow of her red eyes captivates me and renders me immobile. She's about to turn around the corner and follow the men when an explosion slices through the silence. I fall to the ground and shield my ears from the perpetual onslaught of sound.

From my place on the cold steel floor, I turn and watch as Shiva raises her weapon and glides around the corner opening fire.

It now occurs to me that the initial deafening sound was a gunshot. It now occurs to me that we are being attacked.

Why am I so important?

My eyes take in the carnage as it unfolds.
Brutally.
My unprepared shadow is exposed to it.
My unprepared light is ravaged by it.

Like some surrealistic, morbid instant replay, I watch Shiva at the end of the hall pumping round after round into unseen foes. A female action hero, a dominatrix of death. Her shots are joined by those of the two men just ahead, around the corner. One of their guns is silenced abruptly. Blood splatters backward, pushing chunks of pink, racing after gray bone. The head of a once-sentient human being flies to coat the face of a super queen. The tissue that had held a man's memories clings passionately to Shiva's pale skin. Letting out a cry, she returns fire with vengeance. Her bullets deal out icy wrath to the hidden destroyers of her soldiers. The enemy fire ceases.

Or is it friendly fire? Perhaps I'm being captured in order to be used once more. To be manipulated. Perhaps there's a viper hidden before me, crouching beneath miles of smooth skin and curves. Perhaps I am already among the enemy. There's some type of war going on here, and wars are confusing, sticky things at best. However, being in the middle of a battle you know nothing about in a place where you've never been must be worse than your standard-issue war. My thoughts are cut off as Shiva and the remaining man run toward my trembling figure lying curled on the cold, metal ground. Both are blood-soaked. Both are visibly shaken. Each grab an arm, and help me back up to my feet. Apparently neither is wounded; all of the blood coating them had belonged to the other man. Shiva curses under her breath.

"Goddamn it. They know we're here. We need to get out of here now. We can afford no more casualties."

The man nods and guards our backs as Shiva leads me back the way we came. Behind us we leave death in our wake. Before us the ceiling fans still turn, cooling their devoted minions.

Whoosh, swoosh. Whoosh, swoosh.

My mind has been blown. I haven't the faintest idea what I've gotten myself into or how I've gotten myself into it. My heart is racing, and I almost yearn to go back to my simple, meaningless, happy existence. But only almost. Going back would mean giving up things I've grown too attached to. Going back would mean being chained to my dogmatic morality once more. I have to be ready for whatever lies ahead, and let the memories of my old life dwindle. I need to fend off the impending nostalgia. Shiva stops in front of me, and

I snap back to the present.

She leans down and reaches for a vent covering a low duct. The grating is already loose, and she pulls it out, tossing her black hair back over her shoulders as she stands with it in her hands. I almost fall back over, consumed as I am with lust for her. Despite the recent tragedy, the look on my face must have been comedic, for her lips suddenly rise slightly at the corners.

"Come on. And don't worry, I'm not so easily defeated."

With that, she gets down on her belly and slithers into the jaws of the dark maw below.

Of course I don't have much choice in my actions.
I too lie down, and follow after my sensual mistress.

As I am enveloped by the darkness, I hear the remaining nameless man enter behind me. The grating is pulled back into place, and the eerie light from the hallway now only enters through a fixed number of horizontal slits.

Crawling away through the ductwork, I place my life in the hands a solitary unnamed man and an icy beauty named Shiva. I leave the past behind, only the future awaits.

·····**B R E A K**·····

The metallic clinking of knees against aluminum. The denting and reshaping of the ductwork as we worm our way forward in hidden directions. This, along with the sounds of the three of us breathing, is all I can hear. It overwhelms my virgin consciousness, taking control of my susceptible modes of thought. I know somewhere ahead of me in the black, in the fog of my memory, is the ass of a demigoddess wrapped in reflective leather, constrained and reaching for me.

This has been my life for the last twenty minutes.

My knees ache.
All of this crawling.
The drudgery of playing follow-the-leader.
Cat and mouse—which will survive this lethal game?
The captive versus the manipulator.
The darkness is eternal and stretching forward.

And this has been my life for the last twenty-five minutes.

"Where are you taking me?"

"I told you to trust me," Shiva whispers from up ahead. Some place. No place. Who knows where this little escapade is leading. "So trust me," whispers filtering back through the ductwork. Whispers flowing around the invisible curves of Shiva's enticing figure.

I used to never have thoughts like this.

Sex is a sin.
Lust is a sin.

Thinking of my leather savior naked and riding me, just like in the vision I saw earlier, is giving me another erection. My penis never used to get hard. Back when I was a subservient pawn of God's will, back when my morality dictated my spirituality. Back when I was a happy, productive citizen. A happy, productive slave. The life I've left behind.

I become one with my mental hallucinations. Become one with the night, steering moon-crested waves—the fluxing of the tide is my steed, as gravity wanes and lunacy waxes. And still I am crawling forward, Shiva's ass in my face, my ass in the face of the unnamed man behind.

Lunacy is the only explanation, this place is all some sort of vivid visualization. I haven't eaten in days. My body is probably rotting in sewer water. Rats devouring my unused testicles. Hordes of radioactive flies laying maggots in my unsuspecting eyes. Chewing on my flesh, God's temple. Feasting on the creation of the divine. The puppet of the powers orchestrating God's master plan. Shiva is simply my personal sexual fantasy, a force inside of me that has always desired to be set free. And this world of metal, this world of wires, this sphere of specific characters, sanctioned to circumvent my ability to make sense of this premeditated play, dress-rehearsed in preparation for my advent into holistic hostile hypodermic candy-lands. All of this hypnosis has been waiting in the back of my mind to spring upon my tired body. Waiting to take advantage of my vulnerability. All's well that ends well.

This new restructured reality is a fine place to spend eternity.

"Not much farther now." Whispers; my existence is built upon whispers flowing backward. Whispers echoing down dark metal passageways.

Am I dead?

Is this Heaven?

I highly doubt it. And if it is, then I'm not very happy. Not very excited to spend eternity with a bunch of hypocritical assholes and an uncaring God. Not very excited about giving up my body to the scavengers of the sewers.

But then, that is all I am now.
A dying vampiric fiend with nothing to sustain his shattered carcass. Alienated and alone in the dark. Disillusioned by dreams of what could have been achieved.

Or perhaps this is Hell.

I will be forever trespassing through unrecognizable chambers.
Forever unaccustomed to my surroundings.
Forever following a sensuous leader,
but unable to enact my unstable fetishes.
Shiva says jump and I say how high.
Forever and ever.
The end.

And then it will be time to begin again.
Forever and ever.
The end.

And so on. And so on. And so on.

But hey, if this is Hell, this torture can't be any worse than the torture of eternal bliss.

A happy subservient life followed by a happy subservient afterlife. Obedient and cheerful, forever and ever.

Happy and productive, forever and ever.

Life is a story, and a story requires a plot, and a plot requires pain and unhappiness. What would you have left to do in your life if all of your problems were miraculously solved? What doesn't kill you makes you stronger. If this holds true, then God wants to hold you down, keep you weak. When you pray away all your challenges and strife He has succeeded in keeping you held at bay. Halting your spirit and numbing your senses.

It can be so efficient.
Jesus in all of His glory burned into a liquid and injected into your veins.

An eternity is a book that never ends.
An eternity of bliss is a book without a plot.
A book that stretches into infinity.
A biased one-sided version of timelessness.

It would read like this.
You are happy. You are happy. You are happy. You are happy.
You love God. You love God. You love God. You love God.
You are happy. You are happy. You are happy. You are happy.
You love God. You love God. You love God. You love God.
And so on. And so on. And so on.

This is what passes for perfection; this is what passes for a goal in your pathetic life.

Heaven, Hell, what's the motherfucking difference? Eternity is still eternity. Boredom is still boredom.

I want death. I want my story to end one day, and what right does God have to take that away from me?

Is there an afterlife after the afterlife?

We are still traveling forward, twisting and turning into infinity, into the galaxy. The stardust of our bones is deteriorating into nothing. Shiva isn't telling me anything, and if Shiva is my hallucination—if any of this is my hallucination or even some kind of life after death—then I want some element of control. I want to know where my destiny is dragging me. I want to know the forces that are erasing me. I want this incessant blind traveling to end. I want to know what the fuck is going on!

"We're here. This way."

And as simple as that it's over.

We are finally here—wherever here is. In my mind or in another realm, I have no idea. Shiva is opening up another vent; I hear her working up ahead, and I can visualize her leather-wrapped body shaking as she does her thing. A parcel to be unwrapped, a package to be opened.

Please sign here.

The vent gives way, allowing a stream of pale light to silhouette her figure.

The man behind me grunts.
And I have another erection.

THE ANNUNCIATION

I FOLLOW THE LEAD I am given, and exit the ventilation system. The nameless man, Shiva and I, we're all of us just standing here acting like we've known each other forever. The room we're in shows signs of a recent conflict. Blood is smeared on the floor, and there are a few dead bodies slumped over, scattered about. Adorned with white uniforms splattered with internal liquids. Sacks of flesh, mashed like rotten vegetables. Their facial expressions no longer convey meaning. Organic fertilizer.

When did I become so cold? Since I have awakened in this foreign place, a man has died while I watched, and now these two men lie dead before me. I feel nothing for them. Not sadness, not pity, not concern. I am carefree, listless and swaying in the wind, no longer rooted in reality, smiling gleefully as the dementia sets in. Gnawing its way through personally packaged memoirs, sealed with a kiss and launched into oblivion. Placed carefully out of my access. Out of my reach, and beyond my strength is the will it would take to drift back. I would, at this point consider it a retreat. A step backward. I was built to die, and death is becoming all too natural to me. As I look around, I accept these surroundings as a new world. And although I'm still not sure if I dwell here in body, in energy, or in mind, I have come not to care.

Even if this is a hallucination.
Even if this is a self-induced trance.
It is completely tangible to me. And here, perhaps, God's will can't harm me.

This place also is mostly metal and wire, as was the long hallway. We are obviously still in the same structure, near an entryway of some sort. It appears to be a side exit, and through the glass doors I can see an abundance of plant life. Almost as if an entire jungle is trying to push itself inside. Strange— some of the metals on the walls around us appear to be constructed of alloys I've never known to exist. However, other than its surreal appearance and methods of fabrication, the building looks to be an average corporate office. The dead men, I conclude, must be guards or security of some kind.

Guards wielding submachine guns.
Their purpose served, their lives ended.
An early retirement.

I have no time to think further. I see the nameless man diving towards me. He pushes me to the ground as a hail of bullets rip through the air where my head had been a moment before. Hungry wasps seeking a home in my flesh, drilling holes for their death larva. Shiva rolls to the ground readying her weapon to return fire. I can now hear shouts and running footsteps heading in our direction. There's a reception area near the entrance, and we all run and dive behind the counter. Both the man and Shiva point their weapons over the counter top towards the noise. I am confused, but no longer terrified. I peek in the direction of a long hallway, dark, reflective, and anonymous. Ominous and bearing no testimony to whatever is coming this way. The noise has increased, and the footsteps grow closer. There's more gunfire, and bullets ricochet into the room.

A man I have never seen before comes running in, followed by ten more black-clad soldiers—men and women with faces concealed—the four in the back firing their guns down the hallway. The strange man is wearing dark body armor, he has short black hair and a strong face reflecting a perfect inner calm. A resolve maintained in the heat of danger. His boots are heavy and studded with iron spikes. Iron spikes also protrude from his armor at the shoulders. His gloved hands displaying rows of studs clutch an automatic weapon. Another dealer of destruction and release.

I am comforted by the fact that Shiva greets him with words instead of bullets.

"Azazel, over here! We've got him."

A look of relief passes over his eyes, glowing with the same strange red I had witnessed in Shiva's. Azazel and four of the new arrivals dive behind the counter. Six others form a semi-circle around the entrance to our shelter. Their weapons are readied just as a group of twenty perfectly pristine white-uniformed guards come pouring into the room. Gun barrels are swirls of silver, reflecting the light given forth by the metals from the passageway. I decide it's a good time to duck as the others decided it's a good time to open fire.

The explosive roar of bullets being unleashed around me drowns out my thinking. Two of the men led by Azazel are torn apart in a mess of skin, bone, and brain. It happens freeze-frame style: the transformation of a chunk of matter forming a face into sloppy cellular debris splattering in random directions. As I look on, one more human life is rendered meaningless. One more ego has lost its hold. One more consciousness has been annihilated. Shiva and Azazel are both carefully eliminating their enemy one shot at a time. Although I am still unsure if their enemy is an enemy of mine, I'm left little time to make this judgment. Azazel pulls a device from his belt that looks like a grenade of some sort and throws it in the direction of the assailants. Everyone ceases fire and tries to shelter themselves behind the counter, squabbling for safety.

Somewhere, at the bottom of all of this, influencing this madness is yours truly. And somewhere, my body feels a wave of heat washing over it, eradicating the noise of gunfire from my thoughts. One tremendous thunderclap reverberating against its metal confines overwhelms my senses. Then, in the silence that ensues, one of Azazel's soldiers begins screaming. Everyone stands up allowing me to glimpse what has happened. All of the uniformed guards assailing us are dead, now piles of random refuse, but the last soldier to take shelter behind the reception area didn't get her legs in on time. Now, all that's left are two stumpy thighs, bleeding lightly, the veins cauterized.

Without hesitation, Shiva whips up her gun and shoots her in the head. Her brain hits the floor, leading the way for her broken skull.

"Come on, we've got no time to waste!"

She grabs my arm and leads me at a run towards the door. Docile, I am hers to command.

Azazel and the seven other subordinates still living sprint after us. We rush through two sets of automatic double glass doors into the verdant growth I had seen from inside. Free from conditioned air, free from machines cooled by their rotor-blade messiahs. After a few hundred feet, the structure can no longer be seen behind us, and we are stopped by a chain link fence. Azazel quickly pulls a portion of the fence to one side, where it had been previously sliced, creating a small opening for us to run through. Leaving the perimeter of the complex, we run as fast as the dense foliage allows for at least a mile. I hear no sounds of pursuit.

For good or for bad, I am now totally dependent on Shiva, Azazel, and their denizen of followers. Loyal worshippers paying tribute to their deities with lead and explosive powder.

I expected this world to feel alien, but I sense I am still on Earth. Although there's something strange about the light of the sun I can't quite put my finger on. It seems brighter—radiant with divinity. All I can see are plants and trees in every direction, and all I can hear are the strange sounds of the forest. I've never been in a place as lush as this one, and the facility we fled seems dismal in comparison. The wind blows across my skin. I don't know how to explain it, but I have the feeling it's somehow more natural than the air I am used to.

The greens, blues, and purples, mixing with the glow of the late afternoon sun. Blending away and into thick branches, stems, and leaves.

Swaying, somehow sensing yet oblivious.
Watching the refugees from a battle beyond their reckoning.
Connected, yet unaware.

Up ahead, Azazel breaks our silence with a hiss. "What did you think you were doing back there, Shiva? Breaking off communication and going it alone like that? I can't watch your back if you won't let me."

"You worry too much, Azazel, I can take care of myself."

"You took unneeded risks." His face is stone. "Promise me it won't happen again."

"Nothing happened I couldn't handle." She laughs. "Besides, I procured the target, did I not? Now drop it."

And just like that the strange confrontation is over, with Azazel left grumbling to himself and the anonymous warriors pretending nothing happened.

Shiva motions for us to stop and walks carefully two more steps forward. Kneeling down, she lifts a woven mat of grasses and leaves to reveal a steep pit dug into the depths—into caverns of archaic mystery, channeling secrets through the ground, questing earthworms, drawn to moisture and disappearing from the dry topsoil. She swings one perfectly curved leg down inside, and after getting hold of some kind of ladder swings in the other, beginning the descent. Azazel follows next, then me. At the bottom, I notice long wooden spikes pointing upwards. Peculiarly primitive lethal trickery. They are far enough apart to walk around but still close enough to impale anybody who might fall in from above. As more come down the ladder, Shiva pushes aside a curtain of vines exposing a narrow cave. Azazel pulls out a torch that closely resembles a flare, and hands it to Shiva, who lights it and begins walking inside. He steps in after her and turns back to look at me. So far Shiva has been the only one to address me as a person.

"Be patient. Soon you will come to understand."

I walk past him and into the cave, following Shiva's guiding light. "Don't worry," I say, "I stopped trying to understand a long time ago."

The little ragtag group of killing machines follows quickly behind the three of us. Shiva as the neon torchbearer leads all, and I as the inexperienced child know nothing of the end she holds in mind. Our passage is through a tunnel made of roots, appearing to be a natural cave of sorts; the earthen walls are held at bay by the twisted tendrils of old trees.

I, as the curious child, am intrigued.

I hope some information waits to be uncovered after this last darkness. Bringing the apex of the sun to dispel this illustrious illusion. I have decided on patience as a weapon, and my panic is slowly relenting. None of the others show any visible signs of fear, so I figure no one can be following us. Who were those men in the white uniforms, and what does any of this have to do with me?

I, as the carefree child, voice the thought that still eats at me.

"Why am I so important?"

Azazel looks at me from my left, and I hear an almost inaudible whirring as his eyes focus. I can't pinpoint the origin of the sound. "As I said, in time you will understand."

"Is this Hell?"

In response to the second question comes soft laughter from our seductive leader.

"If you want to call it that, I suppose you can. It's what God calls it, after all."

I wish I had never opened my mouth, now things make even less sense. Roots still pass us by as our shadows manifest themselves, darkness cast by darkness upon darkness. Another tunnel, another silent procession, on its way to no one's funeral. As the obedient child, I play follow the leader. How is it I always thought that when I died it would be fairly decisive? Without all this guesswork involved. Heaven, Hell, demons and angels, it was all pretty straightforward. I believed that in Hell I would have been in pain, and in Heaven, a state of ecstasy. This confusion was definitely not anticipated. Although, I have to say I prefer this strange purgatory. At least it captures my interest—it still encompasses the unpredictable.

I could still be in the sewer, dwelling in the moments before death. Maybe the Church members have found me, one of the damned, crippled and lost. Maybe they are mending to me, the wandering sheep, and they are my flock. Our savior has come again, ready to forgive us all. All who still believe in Him. Maybe He will heal me, and this coma-dream will end. I will awaken in my shepherd's arms, loved, and home at last.

A high-pitched alarm goes off with a screech, jarring me back to my sensory projections. I trace its source to a small device on Azazel's wrist.

"What the fuck is wrong with you?" he demands over the alarm. "Cut that shit out now, or He'll hear you!"

I'm being forced into a fast walk as our pace quickens.

Shiva turns her head towards me, her eyes glinting in the blue light of the torch, "You have to forget about Him entirely. You are ours now, and if you want to learn the truth about anything you'll have to forget your past. Pretend it was all a dream and put it behind you."

I find it's much harder to think when you feel like people are listening. Whether it's God, Shiva, or Azazel, I'm sick of my thoughts being monitored for slip-ups. This candid camera kaleidoscope of morals.

My pondering ceases, drifting past me like the whisper of water. I try to take Shiva's advice and focus more on my surroundings. Occasionally we turn slightly to the left or to the right, the turns are subtle, but enough to make me lose all sense of direction. Stringy, hair-like roots dangle from the ceiling, reaching out to brush my scalp. Touching and caressing me delicately. The feelers of an unseen nervous system, experiencing altered brainwaves, conceptualizing my presence in this subterranean vein. This journey through my subconscious. All of us pawns, all of us being digested. Slowly, our essence is being sucked away. The faces around me lack emotion, and the nameless ones in black trudging behind still pay no recognition. All guns have been holstered; the soldiers are all out of commission, dreaming dreams of further death.

If I am dreaming and realize it, can I control it? If this is all my imagination, and I see it for what it is, can I do anything I want? I try to find my body, lying back somewhere in the sewer, in an attempt to disregard this world as a fantasy. I try to fly, and find it impossible. Nothing is different here; I cannot manipulate objects with my mind. This is not an out-of-body experience.

My perception generates reality.

If you die in your dreams, and your dream is a sinful one, do you go to Heaven or Hell? There would be no time to ask for forgiveness. If you die in your dreams, does your body die?

Perhaps only you die; the *you* existing in that precise moment. Your controlling ego perishes along with your dream self, leaving your body alive but controlled by another entity. This being still possesses all of your memories, and for all it knows, it was the one that went to sleep, and now it has woken up again. It still acts as you, and has the same personality. But it's not the real you, the real you is dead—you no longer control its existence. It has gone on to maintain another life. Another dream.

Your personality is only a placeholder, like a variable assigned to a certain number. But how do you label something that always changes? Is this my new dream?

I feel the tunnel beginning to slope in an upward direction, and Shiva slows the pace to a walk. She motions for Azazel to stop, and the rest of us follow his example. Then she moves onward, going around a bend to the left, leaving us in darkness. A slight breeze blows over me, the roots shiver, I'm filled with a sense of relief. We must almost be wherever we are going.

Before long, Shiva returns, bringing the light, herald of the dawn. She looks at me, and says, "Come on, let's go."

We all follow after her around the corner and up a sharp incline. The passage levels off again, and we go through another curtain made of leaves and vines. Another illusionary veil. Another masquerade. We enter the open air once more in the bottom of a similar spiked pit. Shiva has already removed the camouflaged top, and the warm wind rushes around us. As our leader makes her way up the ladder, my eyes greedily watch her. Azazel climbs up next, and I follow. We are now in an even more overgrown part of the forest. The dense and diverse plant life closes in all around us. Strange animal noises echo in the distance, as I glance up at the sky and notice that the sun will soon begin to set. The pit's covering is replaced, and the torch has been put away. Shiva quickly sets a pace east, away from the late afternoon sun and down a hidden path. Branches snag at me as we walk, and roots underfoot try to trip me. The others seem to float down the trail, gliding free of any obstruction. I am the odd man out. I am the only one who doesn't know their place. The flawed brick in the foundation.

Another tree branch narrowly misses my eye, and I wonder how much longer we're going to play nature hike. Up ahead, a thick wall of growth blocks our path. Azazel reaches it first and pulls aside a vine curtain to uncover a small crawlspace underneath what now appears to be a completely overgrown chain link fence. He crawls through, and then Shiva motions for me to go next.

I follow her orders, dropping to my belly.

As I slither my way through the opening, I hear her call out behind me, "Cheers to your future." Somehow I don't quite know if there's sarcasm intended.

Standing up next to Azazel on the other side of the fence, I find we are on a hilltop sloping down into a small valley of sorts. In its center are the ruins of a structure similar to the one we recently departed. The crumbling building is completely covered in growth and hard to distinguish as separate from the forest. However, the red rays of the diminishing sun set the few uncovered metallic surfaces on fire, revealing the carbon-copied matter for what it is. Shiva has joined us now. The three of us gaze into the future, these aware beings and I, together riding ripples of manifest matter. Drifting carelessly over our intended destinies.

Many of the soldiers have already made it through the hole, and some walk past us toward the strange, seemingly abandoned complex below. Shiva rests a hand gently on my shoulder. My entire body trembles with excitement and I hope she cannot feel me quivering with nervousness.

She whispers into my ear, "Soon, the answers to all of your questions will unveil themselves. Our leader will explain everything. Be at ease."

And I am at ease. Just like that.

As she removes her hand, I feel Azazel's strong push propelling me forward, starting my downhill trek towards the dilapidated headquarters of these strange new companions. As we near the building, I can see glass doors just like the ones we escaped from—they are chained and haven't been used in years. Parts of the building are falling in, having succumbed to the eroding efforts of the forest's never-ending quest for places that will support life. Flowering vines bloom, trying to hide the harshness of the entombed beast beneath. We go past this entrance and walk around the perimeter of the building.

The sunset is climaxing in the sky, begging for my attention. I acknowledge its departure as it creeps out of sight, hiding under the enshrouding blanket of landscape. Constructed of greens and browns, lavenders and oranges. Now dusk sets in, eliminating all color in the world, paving the way for the ensuing nihilism of night's cold grip. I look away from the sky, and see the entrance to this place. It's another spiked hole in the ground.

A large wooden spike through the head really isn't that bad of a way to die, if you think about it.

The bad thing isn't dying. The bad thing is not knowing if you are already dead.

We climb down the secret ladder, and the cover is replaced behind us. This time there is no torch. We make our way down to the floor, and I'm lost in the darkness, surrounded by protruding poking devices. I hear Azazel calling out to me, and I follow the sound of his voice. I feel a camouflaged screen, and push past it, entering a new pathway dimly lit by a trail of tiny red lights, spaced very far apart from one another, and leading off into the distance. Standing on some type of flooring, my feet no longer sink into the soil.

The shadowy figures of Shiva and Azazel are up ahead. The others apparently had better things to do than stay around and baby-sit me. Before my eyes can fully focus, the two have vanished as well.

I have no choice but to follow the tiny lights. I feel completely disoriented and lose all sense of location and direction as I follow the pinpoints of luminescence. Maybe the lights are a diversion, meant to lead astray the foolish. How long will I be doomed to roam this underground labyrinth lost to the world of the living? Will this be my final fate?

Just as my breath and pulse begin to quicken, I see solid white light ahead; Azazel is waiting for me. I find myself relieved, but saddened that it isn't Shiva. I enter the lighted area where he is standing within a small room, an entryway of sorts. The only thing in front of me is a wall; it's tall and silver, reflecting the light back onto us. The illumination has no visible source; it just exists, in and of itself. The strange wall is broken only by one black door, seemingly thick, and without decoration or any means of opening it. Azazel has positioned himself next to the door, and I approach him.

"I saw Shiva and some of the others enter this hole. Where are they, how's it possible that they are not here?"

"They took different routes."

"You mean those lights we followed aren't the only path?"

"Correct, there are many paths. Each individual who enters is shown the path they are to take, and they take it. Stray from that path and you will only end up back where you started. This way, none may enter where they are unwanted. Those who trespass are led by the lights to their death. Those who come bearing their own light are executed."

"But how's it possible to know what path to show to someone? What controls this?"

"It's fairly simple technology. I'm sure it will become apparent soon. It's how They know us. How both of Them know us."

"Where's Shiva?"

In response to the question, Azazel's eyes flash with a heated glow, and for a moment his zen-like composure seems to hang on the verge of disintegration, his expressionless gaze maintained with obvious strain. "You will see more of her.

That is…after your meeting." With this he gestures a studded glove in the direction of the black door. "He is just through there, waiting. He's been anticipating this meeting for a very long time."

A chill washes over me, as I stare at the entrance before me. It has come to this—all I have to do is enter and everything will be divulged. I wonder what will happen if I refuse to enter. I wonder, will this revelation be forced upon me?

"And what happens if I don't want to meet with him?"

"If you disregard your purpose, then there is no hope for any of us."

As I stare into the depths of Azazel's strange red eyes, I know my entrance here is unavoidable. It has been, in a way, preordained. There are questions that need answers.

"Will I see you afterwards?"

"Perhaps."

Turning away, Azazel runs back into the darkness following his own path of red twinkling lights towards whatever fate lay in store for him. I'm alone once again, left to the dangers of thought. I take a step toward the door, wondering how to open it. Before further investigation can take place, the door opens by itself, revealing a light-blue, flickering glow. I hesitate, but only a moment. I need to find the truth behind everything that has happened to me. Before I can change my mind, I walk through the metal wall. The door closes behind me.

Automatic, everything orchestrated from behind the scenes. Someone is always watching me, keeping tabs on my actions.

I take a step forward. I am in a short hall leading into a large, round room. The blue light comes from hundreds of computer monitors, displaying grainy images of people and places. Each screen flickers after about three seconds and the image on it is replaced with another. The monitors seem to cover every wall, reaching up twenty or thirty feet to meet the ceiling. I take a step forward and then two more. As I approach the larger room, I notice something else.

I am not alone.

Suspended from the ceiling is a thick grouping of wires and cables, leading down toward the center of the large chamber. I enter and see that the wires and cables all connect to the skull of one man, dressed in black flowing robes, standing with his back to me.

The lights flicker like strobes—fireflies caught in bug-zappers, flashing effervescent blue at the moment of their explosive deaths. As I walk toward the man, a terrible sense of fear almost renders me pacified. My chest clenches as the images flash all around me, bathing me in their light. Every once in a while the screens show faces and places familiar to me, citizens of my hometown. Always filled with anguish and unease. They are never happy, the way I remember them. I look from monitor to monitor, and in every scene I see chaos and unhappiness.

I walk closer to the man, I know he hears me and is aware of my coming. This must be the leader that Shiva and Azazel mentioned. The one who will answer my questions. I look again at the bundle of wires attached to points all over the surface of his shaved head, flowing up and out a hole in the top of the room. The light from the screens reflects and bounces across the surfaces of the cables, giving the impression of moving electricity. Finally the man speaks, stopping me dead in my tracks. As his low, unwavering voice reaches my ears, I can no longer look at anything but the back of his head. I am transfixed. This was the voice I had heard so many times; this is the man responsible for all those questions. Those random thoughts.

"I am happy you have arrived here safely."

His voice isn't menacing, as it seemed before, but conveys a kind of superiority. Before I can respond to his comment, he turns around, the cables swiveling to follow his movement. As his face is revealed in the unwavering light, I see a man who is as handsome as Shiva is beautiful. He takes a step towards me, gazing at me through shining red eyes, same as the others. He studies my shit-soaked Sunday clothes and I catch a hint of a smile crinkle the corners of his curved lips. The grace in his movements is overwhelming. I feel as if I should bow before his splendor. I find my voice. It comes out in a half-choked sob, but at least it comes out.

"Who are you, and what do you want with me?"

The man smiles, flashing perfect white teeth. Movie star perfect. Taking another step towards me, he answers.

"My name is Lucifer. Patient number zero. As the leader of the rebellion against God, I am also known as Satan. Call me what you will. As for the answer to your second question, I have brought you here to fulfill your role as the Antichrist."

CLARITY

I KNOW IT'S NOT possible, the words wash over me like waterfalls drumming on rocks, eroding away the hard edges, leaving only smooth surfaces to tell the tale of abuse through the ages. I am weathered and torn asunder. Exposed and defenseless. My head shakes back and forth, refusing to accept what I have just heard. The room swivels and spins, bathed in the strobe light of so many tortured temptations. Knees buckle, as my lifeless doll of a body crumples to the floor below.

The demon has revealed itself.

All this time it has been the Devil himself, in direct contact with me, responsible for my so-called possession. Transmitting all of my hidden apparitions. But this is the man behind the curtains? It can't be. This can't be Lucifer, the fallen angel, cast down from God's kingdom in Heaven to burn deep within the earth. Where is the eternal fire? Where is the brimstone furnace? Where are the horns and pointy tail? But there's no denying his is the voice I've heard so many times before. There's only one explanation—I've lost my mind after all. How else could any of this be possible? There's no way that I am the Antichrist.

I rip at my hair, rolling around, hysterical and laughing, laughing, laughing, totally mad. This is all an illusion and I am pulling the strings. I am still in the sewer, I know it, I have to be. Is this my punishment for forsaking God?

As if sensing my doubt, this pseudo-Satan responds to my mental questioning, addressing my trembling frame cringing down on the floor. "I see you do not yet believe me. You expected me to appear more along these lines?"

My insane cackling trails off to an estranged gurgle. Suddenly, the room is filled with flame—burning pillars building up, boxing in on all sides. Before my eyes, Lucifer grows in size. His feet turn into hooves attached to goat-like calves and thighs, a tail sprouts from behind him—pointed and menacing—and his upper torso is now covered in muscles. He glows a deeper shade of red than the flames all around us. The heat is immense. I recoil, trying to keep from burning, sliding away from the monster before me, unable to tear my vision away from the transformation taking place. Teeth turn into fangs protruding from black lips, twisted into a diabolical grin, and black onyx horns grow from the top of his head. The wires are nowhere to be seen. My eyes roll around in their sockets, like a calf baying in the midst of a summer storm—the lightning is my own creation, it must be, oh please, please I've had enough. His red eyes dance with delight as I look around realizing the monitors have vanished as well. All semblance of the room we were once in is gone.

Cue the sought after brimstone.
Cue the deranged images implanted in me by the Church.
All doubt has been eliminated.
I am damned.
My judgment has come.

Tears roll down my cheeks, and I'm sure my bladder has emptied itself by now. Not that it matters much, coated as I am in sewage. I squeeze my eyes shut, unable to bear any more, willing the madness to come to an end. This is the eternity I bargained for, and I must accept it for what it is. The sound of amused laughter reverberates through my ears, and I notice the intense heat of the fire has vanished. I slowly open my eyes.

Everything is back as it once was—the strange man before me, wearing his crown of cables, his eyes focused on my feeble figure, in the center of his technological dominion. The room flickers from the light of shifting images, leaving the flames nowhere to be seen. I decide it can't hurt to listen to what this Lucifer has to say. I chance a question.

"What just happened...you were...you changed into...what's going on here? Nothing makes sense to me any longer, please help. Where am I?"

Lucifer is all smiles, flashing his sparkling whites. "You are on Earth, in what used to be called the United States of America, near to what used to be called New York City. This is the material world, the imperfect reality which God currently refers to as Hell."

Before I can ask my next question, he answers it for me.

"And no, you are not dead. Quite the contrary. Your perception of reality has widened. You've merely become aware of the bigger picture."

He reaches up behind his head and I hear a clicking, the sound of crunching an insect's carapace, then hissing. The wires and cables detach themselves, slithering up into ceiling, snakes bristling with artificial intelligence. His head is left covered with connectors, little indentations for wires instead of hair. From somewhere within his robes, he procures another garment, identical to his own. This magic man. This conjurer of tricks. How do I know if I can trust him, the master of deception? If I want my long-sought-after enlightenment, I guess I don't have much choice.

"Here, change into this—there's much you must see, and many questions have yet to be answered."

Handing it to me, he turns his back, and I stand up, quickly stripping off my ruined suit and undergarments. I throw the robes over my head, glad to be out of my old clothes. Glancing back in my direction, Lucifer says, "You will be provided with a place to bathe later, but for now, follow me." Walking over to a part of the room farthest from where I came in, he brushes his hand across some of the monitors. An entire section of them goes black and swings out, revealing an adjacent chamber. Lucifer strolls in, motioning for me to follow. I can't help but ask another question as I walk towards him.

"So if you are the Devil, what are Shiva, Azazel, and all the others?"

"Shiva and Azazel are fallen angels; they joined me in the rebellion after God discovered my betrayal. Out of all the angels who followed me, they were the only survivors. As for the others, they are my demons. My own creations, made with the specific purpose of overthrowing God. If you would step inside please."

"And how *exactly* am I the Antichrist?"

"That will soon become apparent, but for now, a matter of procedure. Please, enter."

Having no other options laid before me, I stroll into the dark chamber. Once again I do as I am told—so used to following orders, programmed to obey without question.

Just have faith.

Now I am forced to place my faith in this man's version of the truth, whatever that shall be. The door swings shut behind me, and the smaller chamber lights up, illuminated by the strange light with no source. We are in another round room, much smaller than the first, with most of its interior domi- nated by a strange black object somewhat resembling a mas- sage table or a dentist's chair. Lucifer is standing just beyond it, near a table displaying a wide variety of surgical tools and syringes. Glistening in the soft glow, menacing, sharp and sparkling in their unpleasantness, eating away at my ease. I see no exits from this place, the walls all now appear constructed from one seamless, smooth metal alloy.

A capsule of probable pain, potential energy for scarification. Scissors, knives and sharp playthings, waiting to slice away, become channels for fury, conduits for rage. Unleashed to ravage my dermis, raining, estranging my personality from reality, delving down into the tumor valleys and cancerous furrows, running along the polluted river basins, veins of fool's gold in shadows of hypocrisy.

"Don't worry," Lucifer says, "I will not hurt you, this is the first step towards understanding."

His voice, so familiar and comforting, ringing through my ears. I take a step closer, my curiosity outweighs the fear.

"Come, lie here, face down."

I slide on to the strange leather-covered table. Just a little doctor's visit, just a small check-up, all very routine procedure. Got to make sure everything's in working order, nothing's come loose, or ceased its proper functioning. Lying down on my stomach, I find there's a hole for my face to fit through, and a small band to support my brow.

"Place your arms at your sides, please."

Compliance is my motivation.
It will all be over soon.

Large straps fly over my back and legs, operating of their own accord, fastening themselves, allowing me no means of movement, securing my arms to my sides, and me to my selected fortune.

I can only see Lucifer's lower body, his feet clad in black boots, pacing around me. He picks an item up from the table, and I hear him flicking something. There's a a cool swabbing and then a sharp pain at the base of my skull, the feel of a large needle sliding upwards, inside, deep. I shudder inwardly, but as the injection is administered I am overcome with a sense of euphoria. His tongue tickles questions towards me.

"Tell me, what made you think you needed to be saved?"

My answers flow outward, easily and without fluctuation. Smiling, drool oozes from my mouth and pools onto the floor below. "We all are sinners, since the fall of man, we have been flawed, imperfect. Only salvation can fully restore us to our true potential. Our place as children of God. Only now...now salvation doesn't seem so appealing to me. If I am damned, so be it."

"And you are so sure you are damned?"

"I'm in Hell aren't I, with you? I've refused to ask forgiveness."

"What is it you need to be forgiven for?"

Another needle slides into the back of my neck, and I feel a tingling numbness spreading out from the puncture.

"My trespasses against God, my forsaking of His name," I tell him. "The reclaiming of my identity."

"Do you not feel God is deserving of your spite? Do you feel as if you've done wrong by discarding your faith in His so-called justice?"

I think about the question, in the arms of ecstatic trance, and realize he's right. I do not feel as if I've done anything worthy of punishment.

There is clinking and shuffling on the tray nearby. With my head facing the ground I can see nothing, but I assume one of the cutting devices has been selected. "I don't feel guilty, if that's what you mean."

"Now stay still, you won't feel a thing," he soothes. "I promise you."

Under the influence of his narcotics, I fear not the implements being used upon my prostrate form. There is more jostling as another device is selected. I hear the buzzing of a saw—courting me, adding to the ambience—as I try very hard not to move.

His words blend into the whirring of the blade. "What if you are not damned, but free? You, along with the rest of mankind, are not flawed, for there is no such thing as 'original sin.' It is nothing more than a psychological construct, meant to make you work towards salvation. To teach you the art of self-loathing. Stay very still, now. The only thing you need to be saved from is your own ignorance."

The pitch of the saw changes as it makes contact with the

base of my skull. A spinning lobotomy, a mystery, unfathomed and unsolved, detached from reality, afloat in a void. There's no pain and there's no sense of self, there's only the ability to answer the questions addressed to me. Thinking comes ever so slowly. Words fracture together, shards of discarded logic. "WhaWht dato dyoo youu memeann?"

"What I mean is sin's all a point of view, along with good and evil. It's all a matter of what side you are on. There is no ultimate set of rules to live your life by, in the end only your feelings and emotions can guide you. Trust your intuition, not what other people tell you."

More shuffling.

"I'm almost done, just sit tight. It will all be over soon. The world you once knew and the people that inhabit it are fictitious. A carefully constructed lie, perpetrated upon you by this 'God,' as you call him. Forget all you were taught to believe, forget the set of symbols you once used to describe the workings of the Universe. They are inaccurate, meant only to render you docile and control the functioning of your creative mind. Some adjustments need to be made. Ah, here we go, all finished. I just have to stitch you up and we'll be all set."

Forests for the trees, floating before my shattered worldview, concealed in cryptography not even secret agents of sleep could decipher.

An idiot savant to the rescue.

I am an ageless pod, propelled through sacred spaces. Wrinkled wisps of light—clarity in the madness—twinkle down to me, slipping through my fingers. All the answers in my peripheral view, just beyond grasp. The seamless floor, and black boots marching, echoing, transcending the haze—vultures, the carrion fowl of the Underworld preying upon my overworked imagination. I stop trying to fit the pieces together and let them fall into place on their own. The drugs have already begun to wear off. I am being grounded, rewired. The transition has begun.

"All done. You can stand up now if you are able."

The straps are undone, and I am released from my captivity, the slave and master relationship. I arise to my feet shakily, regain my sense of balance, and grope at the back of my head. A patch at the base of the skull has been shaved, and in place of the hair there is a small row of stitches. I no longer feel euphoria, but the numbness remains.

"What did you do to me?" I turn looking into his deep sparkling eyes, his perfection, radiating red. My gaze is greeted with so much eagerness, so much anticipation gleaming back at me.

"Here, take this."

I hold out my hand to receive a minute piece of metal, a slice of science. I squint at it between my fingers, my vision blurs. It seems to be a microchip of some sort. I touch the small cross engraved on the side. "What is this?"

"That's what I just removed from your brain, it has been there since the moment of your creation. A symbol of your past, it is who you once were, your dead faith, and your dead beliefs. The skin you have shed."

"How can that be possible, who put this in my head?"

"It was placed inside your developing brain by an angel of God, and is of His design, a transmitter used to send and receive information.

And the subject will feel violated: now.

"That's how He could listen to your thoughts, how He knew when you were beginning to see through the conditioning, how He knew when to send servants to take you to the blue room after I tried to communicate with you. No longer do you have to safeguard your emotions, God's access to what goes on inside of you has been severed. There's no going back now, your time approaches."

I tell myself things will come into focus, but this is a new development entirely. A transmitter, monitoring my thoughts in silent surveillance. Is this the nature of God's omniscience? Gizmos and gadgets. Technological parlor tricks. An all-encompassing party favor.

I'm not laughing.

"I don't understand, please explain what I am missing. I can't seem to make sense of any of my experiences from the past few days. I no longer know what's real and what's imaginary."

"This is not something I can tell you, but something you must see."

His voice—that familiar voice—leading me to this intended intervention, this position and place, conceptualizing my darkest fantasies, my forgotten dreamtime specters.

His voice, leading me to enlightenment. This tortured, differential state, suspended in limbo between the world of the living and the dead.

"Now follow me, and please try not to touch the incision."

He glides his hand across the smooth reflective wall of the dissection chamber, swinging it outward, and we are back in the glow of the screens. Perfect teeth flicker and flash, luminous blues and whites. Red eyes bore into mine upon occasion.

His hand brushes away another passage in the primordial ooze of virtual images.

I fall in behind.

Always the follower, no leadership potential included. Always taking orders, a template awaiting crystal-clear commandments.

We step onto a raised platform of some kind, and it begins moving upwards.

"What you have to understand is you've been part of a vast experiment. We are currently in that experiment's place of origin."

I try to keep near the center, avoiding the walls quickly rushing by. We leave the nexus, Lucifer's own private nervous system, an extension of his persona, and arise, merging into the darkness above.

"What you need to know is the world you grew in until now was only an illusion."

His voice, leading me onward.
Our ascension into the realms above.
Our meeting in the realms below.

"What you need to know, is 'God' isn't what you think He is."

A chain reaction of riddles.
A hydrogen bomb of puzzles.

The lift comes to a stop, and the black in front of us slides away revealing a long corridor, dimly lit, very reminiscent of the place where I met Shiva. The same crevices in the walls. The same fans. But this place is rusted out, dumped and deserted. Lucifer in his robes, walks forward, and I in my robes, swoosh behind. The back of my head itches and tingles, but I ignore it.

"In fact, what you have been trained into labeling as God, is no more than a simple human. A human who has created a method to control nearly every aspect of a person's consciousness, by manipulating their perceptions to His own advantage. Even I, the feared Lucifer, Satan himself, am also merely human."

"Then God does not exist?"

"Oh He is very real; however, if you would attribute to Him the creation of the Universe, you would be most mistaken."

God a human? I have heard His voice in my thoughts, answers to my prayers. I have seen His angels. The foundations of my faith are faulted, laid down upon blighted, barren land.

Together we swoosh forward.
Together we halt.

"You see, there is another device, in your central brain, too embedded for the sake of removal."

Another one of God's manipulation mechanisms, delivering deceptions.

"It can generate sensory inputs which will override any outside stimulation, and it also monitors all neurological activity. All of your thoughts, along with a record of your experiences, were broadcast, via the transmitter I removed, directly into the mind of God. The transmitter, by linking up to this perception generator, placed into you the feelings and imagery God chose to put there."

"Meaning?"

"The majority of what you have experienced in your life thus far has actually been a hallucination, subtly controlled by a maniacal genius who has declared himself God."

"There's no way that's possible. You're lying."

There's laughter, his eyes seem to dance with amusement.

"Wouldn't that be nice, if all of this were some horrible dream? However, as you will soon see, I am the only person who has told you the truth."

Always someone's toy, someone's pampered plaything.
My identity an integer, a subject ID number.

"Don't trust your memories, they've all been masterfully managed in order to further predict your responses to stimulus. Even those of your parents, your childhood, all of it's a lie."

We are standing at the end of the hall, a wall comprised of a patchwork of silver and rust. Lucifer reaches up to some kind of control panel, pushing a series of commands on the keypad.

"The truth is, you never had any parents, or childhood for that matter."

He lowers his hand, and the hall is flooded with light. The fans above start with a shudder, a violent release from their former retreat. No more the recluse, idolatry begins anew. Wire children writhe.

The blank photo albums, swiftly shifting before my eyes, reflecting back their nothingness. Holes in my memory. My fictitious past.

"The truth is, you were engineered."

This product was tested on *Homo sapiens* without their knowledge.

Some suffered greatly.
Use at your own risk.

"The town you know as home—think very carefully—have you ever been outside of it, before now?"

The question isn't difficult. The answer is no, in truth, I've never had a reason or desire to leave. My curiosity of the outside world had been satisfied vicariously through television.

"No, I haven't."

"Doesn't that seem strange to you?"

"It was just something that never occurred to me."

"The reason you've never been outside your town," he says, "is there's no physical way out, no exit from your city. And in turn, you were trained to never seek one. The town is nothing more than a gigantic indoor studio of sorts buried deep underground. A stage or framework to which hallucinations can be adhered."

It could explain everything. My disjointed sense of reality, the contrast between the world I'm in now and my former home. The visions, the paranoia, the demonic possession, shocking broadcasts to me by the Devil. Perhaps I really am part of some giant experiment. It still seems irrational, a leap of faith. I voice my skepticism.

"I don't buy it."

"Ah, but I will show you, let you see what your old world

was with your own eyes."

Seeing is believing.
Clarity is the work of the Devil, you know.
God is the Father of lies. A graven image of deceit.
A shroud of bullshit.

"Please step into one of the chambers along the wall."

This is too much for me to handle, all of this science-fiction made reality, far beyond the scope of twentieth-century technology. My reasoning halts with a startling jolt. My question pours out in a rush.

"Wait, what year is this?"

Lucifer is all smiles as I step inside.

"Approximately 5075 AD by my reckoning, which makes the age of the second experiment 2000 years. It has been 3075 years since nuclear war wiped out most of humanity"

My head's spinning, I look down and am shocked. Once again, my body is vanishing. Transparency oscillating, overturning my feeble material, forming wave energy floating on electron shells, jumping energy levels, hovering around dense manifestations of probability. Experience floats away, my transcendent form enters the inter-dimensional tunnel of transformative light.

·····BREAK·····

Particles condensing upon observation.

Uncertainty rendered obsolete.
Both velocity and position can be known.
Sandwiched between curled-up planes of existence.
Sheltered from my awareness.
Matter collides.
The energy released is warping space-time.
I am transported.

My surroundings force their way through my optical nerves, data is rendered, images burned to record.

Jaws drop.
Eyes pop.

I am in my town, my own town, vacant except for myself. A holographic memory. The sun is bright overhead. There is no nuclear fallout, there has been no climate change. All the houses, in perfect condition. Nice, tidy, and deserted. Empty shells. I am on a hilltop near the outskirts, the very edge of the city limits. Zoning governs all, follow the official ruling. Never leave, be in peace, trapped here forever.

Trees sway in the breeze, birds chirp, insects hum, squirrels and chipmunks gather nuts. As far as people are concerned, it's a ghost town.

Without warning, a voice—his voice—behind me, cackling with excitement.

"Don't be fooled, this is not your town. This was the very first prototype for God's plan. I lived here with the other angels thousands of years ago."

"But I thought you said God was only a human, no one could live that long. If what you say is true, you should have all died by now."

"Our aging process has been slowed down to almost a complete stop through genetic engineering. Every cell has a built in clock, ticking away towards its demise. We age, primarily, because our cells die. These clocks are controlled by caps on the ends of our DNA called telomeres. God found a way to prevent the shortening of these caps with each cell division, in effect rendering Himself, and all His servants you call angels, immortal."

Another futurist's wet dream.

"Why was this place abandoned?

"Because the prototype was declared a failure after the first thirty years of testing. The nature of God's illusion was too easily detectable."

The place looks like it was deserted recently, not thousands of years ago. The lawns are mowed, and the structures are in perfect condition. I'm motioned onward.

"Come, there is more."

Little by little I am running out of ways to deny what he tells me. We walk towards the town, strolling down a sidewalk. One of those perfect sidewalks—not a crack, not a difference in the spaces between cement blocks, perfectly level. The temperature: perfect. The landscaping: perfect.

So much like my home sweet home.

We pass the cozy little abodes, lined up on such a lovely street, leading towards the center of town.

"There are many experiences you've had in the past few days which must seem very overwhelming to you."

Well that's one way of putting it. Another is to say that I'm stark mad. A raving lunatic.

"All will soon become very clear. Transparent in fact."

In front of me, he pulls out some kind of handheld control device. A small touch screen of sorts. His fingers slide across, punching a series of commands.

And now.
I freeze.
There is no longer any denying it.
Looking around, for the first time I truly believe I could be part of some massive test.

All has become dark twilight, the sun and sky are gone, and in their place is a ceiling far above. The houses are just wire armatures supporting translucent walls of glowing optics. The street is gone, along with the ground, and the perfect lawns, and the trees.

No more birds.
No more insects.
No more squirrels.
No more wind.

Just wiring and fiberglass.
Just an empty holographic blueprint.
The fabric of a lie.
Just Lucifer and me, standing in the darkness, surrounded by black skeletons. The underlying reality.

His voice, as deliciously delighted as ever, punctuates the shift in scenery.

"Think of your former town as a playground overseen by angelic chaperones. A simulation that teaches God's children the skills and loyal subservience necessary to rebuild civilization once released into the world. These studios allow subjects to feel as if their surroundings are developing. To their eyes, new structures are built, villages become towns, towns become thriving cities. Once a studio has grown to capacity, most of its subjects are transferred to larger facilities—for them there is no break in the continuity of progress. The simulation is reset, leaving those who remain in a small village once more—their memories are subsequently doctored to reconcile this change."

"So the school I was building, the construction, it was all training?"

"Indeed. Those structures have been built over and over again for two thousand years, overseen by the angels. There's only one way in and out of these simulations, and that is through the particle diffusers."

Just another way of saying teleportation. Just another way of saying welcome to this unreality. My thought processes stretched out into a wave function, governed by nonlocality, sense of self maintained only through memory. A change in state affecting an entangled particle instantaneously across limitless amounts of space.

"That's how the angels are able to come and go. How they tend to you. Bring in your food, maintain the plumbing, keep you under control."

His fingers glide across the controller.

The street reappears, with the ground, sun, and sky.
The houses are still simple framework.
Cue all the trees and anthropomorphic animals.
Cue the wind and cloud cover.
The houses all back again, just like brand new.

I think I'm beginning to understand. Your perception dictates reality. My perception was being controlled by God's malevolent misery machinery. Previous senses and memories are not to be trusted. None of it real, all of it industrialized.

"All of this imagery is being fed into the perception generator deep inside your brain. You see, the transmitter I removed linked that generator with God's computer network, also known as Jesus. In its place I installed my own; these surroundings are currently broadcast to you from my own central computer."

My eyes are growing wider by the second.

"Jesus is a computer network?"

"The manifestation of God's only 'son,' or Jesus, is the intelligence that helps to govern the experiment. A programmed reflection of God's own consciousness regulating the environments of all His test subjects."

We enter the center of town, and the illusion just seems too real, maybe too controlled. The grass is all the same height, the trees shifting in rhythm, no dead leaves. We walk toward the hospital, on the same street as the police station and fire station. I stop to pick up a rock. I can feel it and it has an apparent weight, I can't crush it.

"How is it possible, that even though I know this rock isn't real, I can grasp it as if it were?"

"How do you know what's real and what's imaginary? All you have is what your senses tell you. The great limitation to being human is simply being human. Trapped inside a body with all of its inputs controlled, with your perception narrowed, can you be sure what you sense is all there is to reality?"

"What do you see?" I hold up the rock.

"I see nothing, there is no longer anything implanted in me to pick up the transmission."

I throw the rock at him, it passes through and lands harmlessly on the ground beyond.

He laughs. "You see, as an angel, my construction was different than your own."

"Please, turn it off again. Get it out of my head."

His hands work the controls, bringing darkness and structure once more. The mold for my everyday experiences, the seams of a former life.

We continue forward to the entrance of the hospital, all metal and wire, walls of transparent sensors. Me in my ceremonial dress, covering a layer of caked shit, covering a layer of skin, covering my own little skeleton—my personal armature. The support for my electrically charged meat.

We pause in front of the place where there should be a door long enough for me to ask another question.

"Why are we here?"

"To show you the rest of God's dirty little secrets."

ACCEPTANCE

WE ENTER the hospital.
It's dark, nightmarish framework.
The track marks of a mass hallucination.
An assemblage factory for the Holy Spirit.
One big fiction. One big fabrication.
Debunked and out in the open.
Pried upon by my unwitting eyes.

Strolling forward, through where a hallway should be. Its stark white no longer projected unto me. Past where the front counter should be. I've got a health plan. I've got the insurance to cover this little visit down memory lane.

My subconscious leads where my ego follows.

The waiting room.

And we're all of us waiting, we're all of us reaching towards false dreams. Pointless ideology. Drifting in our fantasies as the moment passes by, never noticing.

He turns to see if I follow.
His lead.
As always.

"About two hundred subjects participated in the initial testing, all created by God Himself. That number slowly grew, each patient uploaded with a set of false memories."

We turn left, then right, then left again, following our path deeper into this extraordinary exoskeleton of a dead dream behemoth. Winding through a translucent hall of mirrors, running electricity, filled with deception energy. Through hollow operating rooms, lacking definition. No stethoscopes. No jars of cotton swabs or tongue depressors. Simply an indication, a diagram for hypothetical experience.

This is what takes place behind closed doors.
Pay to see the monkey dance.

We stop before a long, narrow chamber resembling a lab of some kind. Looking back, I can see through the clear corridors to where we started. A jungle of unearthly black bars and support beams.

"I was first among the angels, the very first test subject three thousand years ago, labeled Patient Zero. Much like yours, our perceptions were manipulated. However, we were given many parts, individual pieces of a coherent whole, and left to assemble the image on our own."

Worker bees in a disgruntled colony.

"My genetic disposition to question my surroundings gave me the ability to see through God's unreality. No matter how many times my memory was erased, I saw God's world for the illusion it really was. Soon others gained this skill."

I glance into the room ahead and notice something peculiar. There are tables and computers, microscopes, actual objects, lab equipment left haphazardly behind. These are the only physical objects I have encountered without the aid of the generator inside my head. I wonder.

"What's special about this room?"

Rolling slender hands over his shaven head, brushing over so many little holes. Red eyes gleaming, completely in his element as the answer is revealed.

"This is where God created His angels, using warehoused DNA, chosen at random from the leftover stock of an old 20th century company this 'Father' of ours used to own. This is where I was designed."

Staring around in awe, it hits me.

I'm not dreaming, or dead, or insane. This is all actually happening. It's so far-fetched it might be true; there's no way my head created all of this. This is no post-mortem journey through ethereal plains.

The shock.
The epiphany washing over me in a wave of goose bumps.
Taking my breath away. Leaving me numb.
I gently touch the stitches at the base of my skull, flinching.

I don't want to believe this "Devil" but I must. It's all I have now, my only comfort. My life must begin anew from this point onward, here in this strange world. I walk over to a vacant workstation, running my fingers over the countertop. Everything is covered in dust.

"What happened when God realized His experiment was flawed?"

"We were given a choice," he answers. "To become His loyal subjects and be granted the gift of immortality, or be destroyed. No one hesitated in pledging their allegiance to Him, myself included. Although we were angry at being misled, we still believed in God's plan."

The ends justify the means.

God's plan. His mysterious workings. His goal of restoring order to the world, eliminating all pain. To think, three days ago I was confident and unwavering in my belief. I turn and face this cyber-prophet, doling out his insights, explaining away my nightmares.

"What made you decide to disagree with Him?"

"God believes the reason humans nearly snuffed themselves out thousands of years ago is because of their imperfect nature. Because of their sinful ways, and the pain they inflicted upon each other. God is wrong."

"Well if that isn't the reason, what's your explanation for this 'Collapse,' as you've called it? This nuclear war."

"You see, God goes after the effects, and never stops to think of the cause of those effects. The cause of humanity's condition of suffering was not their innate imperfection. In fact, that's what makes you human, what makes you who you are. The cause of so much pain overpowering happiness was grounded in the backwards nature of how civilization had chosen to organize itself."

We are all products of our environment. If another lemming jumped off a cliff, would you? Our domineering will to conform, even if what we are conforming to is suicide. I think I know the answer, but I ask anyway.

"I am curious, what was this organizational structure?"

"The way of the pyramid, the hierarchy—based on a linear definition of time, and in violation of every rule of the land. In nature there are many circles, and cycles, everything is interconnected. That is order. Pain and pleasure are equals. That is balance. If it wasn't, life wouldn't have made it this far. Mankind's self-destruction and continued oppression are the end results of one thing: The chaos of a bureaucratic society that grew like a malignant tumor enveloping all the Earth, until it took fire to burn it away."

It had finally ended, the Earth had been purged. But now God—with His flawed worldview, Himself a product of the pyramid—is trying to bring the cancer back. To reinforce His oxymoronic sense of order. His mechanically engineered utopia. A self-made extraterrestrial with an invading army of guinea pigs.

We walk through the genetics lab and wander our way through more architecturally rendered halls. Phantasmal corridors. Another large chamber opens up before us, and again we stop. Cease and desist while coherency is restored.

"I helped God set up the second version of the experiment, developing new perception-generating technology. The angels manned the labs creating new test subjects, helping to carry out His divine will. This time all subjects were made using mutated versions of God's own DNA."

We were made in His own image.

Lucifer makes eye contact, hiding behind a smirk.

"Soon we began to develop two test groups. The first was propagated through the artificial insemination of earlier subjects and born within the simulations; members of the second group were grown outside the womb and rigorously conditioned throughout their childhood before insertion into the experiment. Subjects from this second group become priests, the leaders of God's utopia."

Strolling into the center of the next room, I am surrounded on all sides by tall glass tanks, some of them cracked, tubes and wires dangling harmlessly inside. The birthplace of the angels. This room—the humble beginnings of my creators.

"You are a member of the second group, you have no biological parents, they have never existed. All of your childhood memories are manufactured. You were placed into the experiment one year ago."

My head reels, as it all begins to click into place. My fetal development spent in an aquarium, a child grown to serve a specific purpose. Detached from the warmth of a mother, chilled and sealed in plastic until ripe for harvest. The act of sexual intercourse has been deemed an unnecessary primal instinct. I inquire.

"When did you rebel?"

"My natural curiosity of the Universe and its operation led me to foresee that God was making a grave mistake. By this time there were towns like yours scattered across North America. I convinced many others to follow me, and we confronted God with our grievances. Great violence ensued, we were assaulted unexpectedly. Massacred by those who maintained their loyalty. In the end, Shiva, Azazel, and I were the only survivors. We fled, wandering the devastated countryside, until we made our way back to this abandoned facility."

What about myself? What caused me to become aware? All the voices and visions. What made me wake up? My own rebellion, my rejection of the principals of faith. How did the demon's voice get inside my head?

"With my limited means, I was able to start engineering a small force to begin sabotaging and attacking new complexes. We eventually hacked into the Jesus Network, and began exerting influence. Trying to awaken test subjects by reintroducing pain into the system. We have been at it for over a thousand years, but never with any success. Until now."

Satan smiles, fondling the shattered glass of one of the numerous tanks.

"By painting me as the source of all evil and deception, God made sure there was nothing I could say that citizens of His kingdom would regard as truth. To most of them I would appear as you saw me earlier. A Devil cloaked in flames. It soon became clear I needed a messenger."

Pulling rabid rabbits out of disemboweled corpses.
The joke is all on you.

"But I desired someone who God's people could relate to, someone who had walked among them, had been a part of the same experiment."

"But why me? Why choose me out of all the others to become the Antichrist?"

"Trying to convert subjects made from God's own DNA is too difficult, so I contaminated one batch with my own. You are the end result of that act, programmed by God, but imbued with my inclination to question everything."

I was never given any choice in this destiny thrust upon me.
This burden of knowledge bestowed upon me.
I feel my hands clench at my sides in frustration.
In recognition of my position.

Caught between two warring points of view.

"After you were placed into the experiment all I had to do was force you to begin your questioning. You did the rest on your own."

Spurred on against my will. Possessed by a bringer of unpleasant truths. Lucifer carries on, his voice underscored with a sense of arrogance.

"It was easy enough to hack into your perception generator in order to affect inputs; however, overriding your thought recorder and intercepting the transmission took quite a bit more effort. Then there was the matter of getting you out of the experiment undetected. As long as His attention is not focused too closely upon you, a false thought loop will make it seem as if you never left the sewer system. It is more than likely you will be presumed dead."

I turn on him angrily, dissolving his smile of victory.

"But you never asked me—you are just as bad as Him! Toying with my thoughts, allowing me to be utilized for your own ends. Putting your demonic devices inside of me. I've never had free will, it's all about who's pulling the strings. First God, now you. What's the difference?"

Lucifer's eyes flash. I guess he wasn't expecting this outburst.

"Don't you see He has to be stopped at all costs; would you have preferred being left inside that web of lies, a mindless slave? I rescued you, I've made you who you are, but I can't force you to obey me. You alone can decide whether or not to accept your role. But if you do not free your people, then who will? Will you sit idly by, and allow God to impose His concept of order upon the world unopposed?"

I know he's right; there is no avoiding this anymore. I exhale loudly.

"What do you expect me to do?"

Without answering, he turns, leading the way into an adjoining chamber; it is empty save one dust-covered white gurney in the center. Dangling from the ceiling above is a bundle of cables, akin to what was attached to his head in the epicenter of pain where we met. Stopping in front of it, he faces me, raising robed arms in an all-encompassing gesture.

"Help me put a stop to this social control once and for all. Join me, and become the bringer of change to this world. Kill God, and show His followers the error of this utopian vision of numbed emotion and enforced mind control."

Before I can answer the room shakes in my field of view. I see one of Lucifer's outstretched hands holding the remote device. Fiberglass and wire are slowly being replaced by solid walls. The gurney looks white and sparkling clean, the other-worldly cables have vanished, the floor is polished. His voice attempts to persuade me.

"No matter how many times they reprogrammed your thoughts, you refused to believe in God's lies—His false promises of salvation. Now let's put a stop to Him forever."

I notice the color of the walls, they are blue. The same blue I've seen so many times in my dreams. Reconditioning blue. God blue. My mind goes blank, these revelations are too much. I begin to feel stark, black quiet envelope me, my knees buckle, and I drop to the floor.

As I fade away, all I can hear is his laughter.

·····B R E A K·····

Cracking though scarred eyelids, charring me from my chosen denial. Vision comes back to me, as I struggle to the turbulent surface of thought. Reaching up, and brushing the introductory incision, the encounter with Lucifer all comes rushing to the clear. I am in a bed, in a clean robe, in another metal room. I have been bathed, renewed, restored. I see an adjoining bathroom. Apparently one thing that hasn't changed in the last few thousand years is the plumbing.

And she is here. My cold fusion fallen angel. Crouched on my right side, attending me.

I struggle into a sitting position, wrapped in blankets, mummified.

Shiva stares at me, her radiance makes me forget who I am.

We are alone. She has changed into a standard black robe, one-size-fits-all.

"So I see you are awake, it is morning already. Here, eat this, you haven't eaten anything in days. You are weak."

Her outstretched arms bearing gifts, some kind of soup.

She is right, my stomach cramps in anticipation. Eating just hasn't seemed a priority lately. I accept it gratefully, trying to maintain my calm in the face of such company. Spooning it into my mouth, adding warmth to where there has existed only cold for so long. Soothing and supporting me. Suddenly a pressure is applied to my right shoulder. Her hand is on me, sending chills, waves of excitement.

My face turns, staring directly into her hypnotic eyes. Her voice rings through my ears, in reverence.

"So now that you know who you are, what will you do? Will you accept your role? Will you help us?"

We stare at each other in silence. Isolated, alone, I hesitate.

"Please," her gaze penetrates, "help us defeat Him."

"I don't want to kill anybody."

"God isn't human anymore, He has lost His mind. He must die so many others can be free."

"I'll talk to people, try to make them think, but I am no assassin. Why not you, or Azazel?"

"We can't, we're seen by God's people as monsters, but you— you are one of them. We would never make it close enough to pull the trigger. The angels would rip us to shreds. You are the only one with a chance of reaching Him during the final battle. Please, you have to try."

Her words sink my heart, altering my better judgment; the allure of pleasing her is too great. It almost seems the response pours out of its own accord.

"If it is I who must do this, it will be done."

Her sense of relief is visible.
A smile plays on full lips as she rises.

"I will tell the others, there is much to prepare in a short time. The plan will be executed tomorrow. "

Turning, making her exit, the door opens automatically. She looks back at me smiling before it shuts her out of my chambers—my place of rest—leaving me unattended, empty. Where are you going, as you cheerfully desert me, damning me to my personal inquisition, with only soup to give me warmth?

The ice of my life has shattered.
And there you were.
Shiva.
With the death of spherical stars birthing the moon.
There you were.
Gagging on the acid reflex, cool and sweet.
My tempting apparition,
choked up amongst the weeds, where nothing grows.
There you were.
Each of us a corruptible cog in an eternal machine.
Chugging along, churning turbine engines,
consuming the fictitious fossils you provide.
Within the dismantled remnants.
There you were.
Shiva.

The perfect corrosion.
Rusting my heart.

My yearning for her collapsing into a dangling centrifuge of resistance. I do not want to hurt anybody, but this God isn't exactly deserving of my mercy. Can I decide to deal out His death? His misguided view of the world is just an extension of what He learned as a child. Can I really shoot Him? I try to block out the anger from answering yes.

I stay in my bed, nothing much else to do. Sipping my soup.
Pondering the life of a simple salesman.
A middleman offering the commodity of salvation.

I was His target audience, along with so many others. Others still held captive by bright neon flashes, telling them to buy into it all. We are His market share, manipulated by an invisible hand to want the product He is offering. To more than want, to feel we need this supposed salvation is His main goal.

Always working towards completion.
Update the savior.
Enter serial codes.
Carved into our cortex.

Through this need, God becomes our pathway to happiness. My world was one big commercial, constructed to sell a product this egotistical venture capitalist, this pseudo-deity had to offer.

A cellophane cosmetic Christ.
Complete with recycled lies.

Order yours now.
While supplies last.

I laugh aloud for the first time in days.

It's tempting isn't it? To put all of your responsibilities to this world and to yourself in the hands of some so-called God.

I slurp up the rest of the soup and toss the bowl carelessly toward the center of the room. It hits the floor with a metallic clink, sliding into a wall, coming to a stop. Staying at rest until acted upon by an outside force.

What this "God" of ours has failed to take into account is that there's no power higher than life itself. Than the Universe in its entirety. In order to fuel the need for salvation, He has deemed the very world in which we live and the bodies we animate damned, thereby tying the consumers to Him like obedient unquestioning children.

Maliciously controlled, or shielded from reality out of love?
Just put your trust in me, I will protect you.
No harm will come to you.
Trade your freedom for security.

Take classes in the science of self-loathing, study the art of apathy for everything save your own impending salvation into a stagnant pool of masturbation.

The natural world and its evolution into increasingly patterned systems, this universal growth, has been somehow falsely labeled as chaos. An enemy to progression. An inhibition, a weed to be plucked from our lives. An environment of increasing entropy with a beginning and an end, distinctly separate from the realm of the sacred.

Creationism thrives in a world of shrinking attention spans. We all want instantaneous results. Efficient explanations.

The madness of God's plan is simple enough. To force adherence to His definition of order, His highly regimented, bland and colorless standard of cleanliness. Creating a master race in His own image. The archetypal white male, female property in tow.

And the subject's desire to dominate is rising.

The underlying assumption guiding God's greatly flawed philosophy, is that human beings have the unalienable right to not only this planet, but to the Universe itself.

All of its resources belong to us and must be used to fuel our technological advancement. Our development of stronger kinds of mental slavery.

Nothing must stop our pursuit of gluttonous gratification.
Our pain-free world.
New and improved, relentless and domineering.

Diversity is the lifeblood of any working system, but that too has become heathen and will be sacrificed. Exchanged for monotony. God's way is, of course, the only way, and all other proposed paths to salvation or personal fulfillment are deceptions.

The contradictions in this belief system are endless.

But what about Lucifer, and his goals for me? Can he really expect to somehow force enlightenment on every last one of God's experimental creations? He claims to oppose mental control, and yet Satan still uses the same old tricks. Does fighting fire with fire yield results or just enflame the problem?

It's too late, I've already agreed.

What is taking so long anyway?

I stand up and begin pacing; it feels good to be clean again. My situation has become so plain and simple. I see a pair of boots near the door, and slide them onto my feet. They fit perfectly.

God is, at best, nothing more than a text-book example of a narcissistic hedonist, suffering from delusions of grandeur. And Lucifer is His cliché rebellious teenager. The Devil's methods may make me uncomfortable, but for the sake of growth, I know God's plan must somehow be resisted.

Earth must not be infected with this parasitic leech again. And I will be the one to stop it.

I suddenly realize I need to take a shit.
Excrement yearning to escape dark intestinal channels.

Rushing into the bathroom, pulling the door shut behind me, raising the toilet seat, raising my robes, and lowering myself into squatting position.

As I tense, preparing to discharge waste material, I wonder who I am. I may be important to God and Lucifer, and all the rest, but in the larger picture I am nothing. Not more than some animal with the ability to self reflect.

Some animal
I grunt.
Dropping feces.
With a splash.

Under the control of my bodily functions.

All the voices in my head, competing for my attention, trying to manifest themselves as thoughts. Each so sure that it is the real me. The person I once considered myself is now dead forever.

Standing up, I wipe my crack on some of the cloths sitting to my left. I throw the material, smeared with brown, into a waste receptacle. There is the noise of flowing air, and I assume it has been sucked into some kind of cleaning room for reuse.

It may sound gross, but I suppose it's better than wiping my ass on flourishing forests.

For now, I must play this new role.
I will become the Antichrist.

I exit into the main chamber and find Azazel waiting by the door. He also now wears robes. I hope it doesn't smell too bad.

His red eyes dart towards the bowl on the floor, raising his eyebrows questioningly, taking no notice of my disappointment at his presence, reflecting my longing for Shiva. My lust for her grows.

"I am glad you've made your decision. Follow me, we have much to discuss. We must be prepared when the time comes to attack."

I follow him out of the room, having accepted what must be done. I am shaking from the thought of seeing her again.

The door slides closed behind us.

THE STRATEGY

WE PASS INTO a hall.

Some kind of dormitory, it stretches out, lined with doors—small rooms. Apparently emptied. Alone, we navigate this new terrain. Reaching the end, we turn a corner, faced with another stretch of doors. Azazel looks back, addressing me as we walk.

"How do you really feel about all of this?"

Is this some kind of trick, an attempt to dicover weakness within me?

"Well, I agreed to do what has to be done."

There's laughter, and a knowing look.

"Shiva told us that much, she has a certain *effect* upon people. I was wondering what you actually think about this whole situation."

My response is hesitant.

"Don't get me wrong, I hate what God is doing, I hate what He did to me, but I don't understand why we have to sink to His level. All of this manipulation, trying to wake people up against their will, it just doesn't sit right. And now, I'm supposed to kill someone. Is all this conflict necessary?"

"I thought you'd say something like that."

We turn another corner and reach the dormitory exit. A larger door slides open to reveal a familiar darkness, only broken by the trail of little red lights.

Azazel's voice comes out of the black, trickling steadily towards my ears.

"I don't know what the solution is. What I do know is God must be resisted. We have to actively participate in our own evolution. We cannot suffer a relapse, another repeat of past mistakes. This contagion, this infestation, must be stopped. While I may not fully agree with our leader's methods, his goals and vision are mine as well."

"I understand, but we can't just deny people a choice," I tell him. "We can't liberate them against their will. Some people are not ready for the truth, all we can do is offer knowledge and hope they have the will to learn. I'm not sure if killing God will solve anything."

The trail of lights veers off to the left, and we turn, following. Glowing tracks, hunters stalking their quarry.

"You may be right," he says, "but it's worth a try. Nothing else has worked, and it's time to put an end to all of this. You won't change Lucifer's mind, he's been waiting for this moment for over a thousand years. His grudge against God is eating him alive, and he won't rest until he's victorious. Satan lives only to oppose."

"I am beginning to grow tired of those too cemented in their ways to listen to reason. God is misguided, but His intentions are not malicious. If we simplify His actions, we will be blinded by our own arrogance."

Azazel halts in front of me, and I nearly fall into him. I feel him clasp my shoulders reassuringly. Soothing away my discrepancies.

"Your frustration is understandable, friend. But don't worry, you'll do fine, and in the end you will be the true savior of God's people. You will be shown great love and admiration by all."

Little old me, Satan's great voice, the emancipator of cerebral servitude. I suppose I could get used to being admired. Love doesn't sound too bad either.

We start walking again, in silence for a few moments, before I ask the question that's been tickling my thoughts now for a while. A question I've been avoiding.

"Azazel, is there a real god? How is life here in the first place, how is the Universe here?"

There is chuckling and amused coughing.

"Don't ask Lucifer that question, he'll rip you apart."

Laughter.

I don't see what's so funny.

"Lucifer would tell you absolutely not—he places his faith in the idea of a logical Universe. The idea that there is no spiritual reality. But to tell you the truth, I really don't know. I prefer to think it is simply a question with no answer. I won't deny the possibility of some kind of higher force, but I won't subscribe belief to it either."

"Well, what do humans who survived the Collapse believe?"

There is a brief hesitation, as if trying to find the right words to explain something.

"Not many of them still speak modern English, but one time I came across a band of these nomads. I got into a conversation with their leader, and she told me that we are all thoughts in the mind of god. That the Universe itself is the consciousness of god."

"Is that what you think?"

"It is a theory that sits well with me, if that is what you mean. We are almost to the meeting hall. We must hurry, everyone is waiting for us."

We continue, one little pinpoint after another, coming to a stop at another metal door. Azazel gestures for me to enter first, stepping to one side. I stride towards it, and it slides open to show the largest room I have seen in this place.

There are towering ceilings, everything backlit, drowning out the dark. Reminding me of an archaic sporting arena, bleachers beseeching, overtaken by flying mythical beings. I eye the reception screens, high above, angled downward, demanding my devotion. Quiet for now, slumbering peacefully. I walk in, looking around at those gathered on all sides, at least four hundred of them—men and women, but no children. Azazel follows, we walk toward the center of attention, joining Shiva.

We are surrounded.
Everyone is standing.
Paying me tribute.

A large mob of black-robe-wearing devotees, Lucifer's minions assembled. Humbled and silent. No need for riot gear, concussion grenades, rubber bullets, crowd control. Hope beams from their eyes as they watch me.

And the subject will feel self-conscious: now.

Arriving in the middle of the room, Azazel takes his place

alongside Shiva, I am left out in front, vulnerable.

The silence is so overpowering, it stifles my thoughts.

Breaking through the static, the monitors flicker on above, displaying the Devil's familiar face. Smiling as usual. Watching over us all.

I can see this is being broadcast from the control room, the cables wriggle from his skull, disappearing off the edge of the screen.

That perfect smile.
The kind you see on toothpaste commercials.
The kind 4 out of 5 dentists recommend.

He speaks.
Everyone listens.

"Today is a day we have long awaited. The beginning of the triumph of intelligence over ignorance. The beginning of the victory of unclouded truth over manipulating lies. Before you stands the Antichrist, a crossbreed of my genetics with those of God, raised within the system and destined to tear it down. He will be our assassin and messenger, our secret weapon in this war. Show him your gratitude."

Applause erupts all around me, congratulating me on my promotion from delusional fool to bringer of death. When it finally ceases, everyone takes their seats, except me and the fallen angels. Left out for inspection, a guard against insurrection.

And of course.

Grins are all that's on TV.

"It has been confirmed, God has initiated the final stages of His plan. Yesterday, he brought all geographic locations up to the moment of the Collapse, simulating a nuclear war in the minds of His subjects. Tomorrow His army, controlled by their narrowed perceptions, will be gathered around the main complex, New Jerusalem, for their subsequent release into the world. From there they will spread, like a plague, exterminating the so-called heathen descendents of survivors, and rebuilding the world as God sees fit."

There are murmurings of displeasure, groans of disgust, cries of anger. But me, I just want to go back to bed or find something else to eat.

The screens change, showing photographs of a sprawling industrial factory. Some kind of European cathedral merged with a modern assembly line. The perfect blend of efficiency and distraction. Smokestacks spew out waste, gun turrets dot the ramparts, and the windows are all stained-glass. This must be New Jerusalem, this fabricated fusion of cultures, this monolith of monotony, this tower of Babel. Constructed by the seraphim, instilled with divinity, reserved for the saved.

"As we speak, Angels are preparing subjects in every holographic town, city, and metropolis for rapture. There are thousands of these experimental constructs, spread across every continent on Earth. To date, God's army numbers in the tens of millions."

Images of these buildings flash across the screen, placed deep within forests, underneath mountains, inhabiting deserts and tundra. I am overwhelmed with the scope of God's project. I did not know we would be facing millions.

"Tomorrow we will travel the one hundred mile journey west to confront, and put an end to this madness. An end to this folly, an end to this misplaced faith."

Lucifer's face shines his certainty across glowing idols. I feel as if he's looking at me directly.

"Before you stand your leaders in this endeavor. I will remain behind, my fight lies here, with the Jesus Network. After I disable God's control over His follower's reality, you will attack New Jerusalem."

A tremble of nervousness spreads, enshrouding the environment of the meeting.

"Many lives will be sacrificed, on both sides, but this is a necessary act. While the angels are distracted, the Antichrist will infiltrate the main facility and destroy this God."

The final word carries a distinct note of contempt.

"With God's death, my messenger will be free to divulge the truth to those assembled."

And now the anticipation oozes from our pores, emotions plucked like harp strings.

All eyes are on me.

"Spend the remainder of the day in preparation for this last great battle. The chosen one will lead you to victory."

The screens go black.
And there is silence.

I feel Azazel nudging me.
I guess I am supposed to say something encouraging.

Sucking air into my lungs, and raising my fist, I give a cry that reverberates fiercely around the room. A cry bubbling up from the rubble of my former life.

"MENTAL SLAVERY WILL BE ABOLISHED!"

My yell is greeted with a rising sea of pumping fists.
A whirlwind of wild cheering.
The soles of my feet tingle.
This is beyond my own concept of excitement.

And now Shiva is dragging me towards the main exit. The mass is dismissed. The throngs attempt to alleviate their concentration, congregating around various side doors. They are laughing, upbeat, awaiting their pronounced mission. Following their strings of lights down to drown.

Suddenly I am a figurehead in one of these strange things we call a war.

A poster-boy.
Selling death at a discounted price.

And Shiva dragging me, I am dazed, and Shiva leaning

and telling me something, the volume is turned down, the hub-bub buzz, drowning out our communication.

"...wants to see you."

As we make our escape I respond.

"What?"

"Lucifer has requested your presence, he needs to go over some things with you."

The sound of her voice brings me back.
I smile, she is touching me.

"Well, lead the way I suppose. Oh, but what am I thinking? That's what the lights are for, after all. You'll show me the way, won't you my little friends."

I suppose talking with inanimate objects is not the best way to win a lady's affections.

It doesn't seem to matter.
Somehow we are alone in the darkness.
Walking together.
Her hand in mine.
Caressing me.
Her toy.

Confidence and a sense of jubilation overtake me, overfill me, so happy to feel her touch. Time melts to a subsonic infused standstill. The spark consumes the fold, there is a stirring within my robes, I need her liquid fire, torrents of pleasure, to taste, to feel. To become one.

It occurs to me that I've never really had meaningful contact.

My memory isn't full of holes.
It's irrelevant, plain and simple.
The parents I thought dead never existed.
My childhood all a grim fable.

I've never had a real personal relationship with another human being.

From a nobody, to an admired celebrity with a stunning woman holding his hand ever so delicately. I can't complain.

It ends too fast, giving me a quick squeeze, she withdraws— we've arrived. The recognizable door, the control room ahead, the nexus, riding tides of everything, where he resides. Her voice is hushed.

"Goodbye."

She fades from sight, and I am left a sitting duck. My pulse quickens, I smell my palm, hoping to capture a fleeting aroma, my recollection of a short time at ease, walking, peaceful, in honest comfort.

The only balm for my blistered imbalance.
The only remedy for my makeshift reconciliation.
Devastating my cold-blooded deviation.
Rancid mutilation reducing my humiliation.
I am raw meat, dripping, waiting to be devoured.

Ripe with the sorrow of her departure.

Hardening my resolve, coming to grips with my place, I stride into the eerie blue flickering light of a satanic playland. Strung up to flowing electricity, red eyes focus on mine, Lucifer greets me with a nod.

On the monitors there are images of the same scene over and over again, repeated until it becomes insignificant: Crowds of people, drenched in the sweat of euphoria, shining in adoration, prostrating themselves before heavenly creatures in flowing gowns. Their wings extended, pinions preened, muscles flexed.

Glowing with bliss.
The same scene in every town, in every city.
The saved rejoicing, compliant.
Waiting to play their happy, productive roles.
Submissive and ready to be commanded.

"Disgusting isn't it? The docile flock, branded cannon fodder for the tyranny of imperial ignorance. I am glad that you chose to help us, together we can put a stop to this façade of transcendental distraction."

I am torn—as much as I want to agree with him, a part of me doesn't want to expose the people on the screens to the truth. What if they can't handle it? What if they aren't ready and it destroys them? Lucifer is all regretful sighs.

"Such a travesty. All that human creativity wasted in trivial pursuits of deliverance."

The Lord is my shepherd.

Before I know it I am laughing aloud, bitterly. God's only in it for the wool, He could give a shit less about the rest.

"I assure you," his voice, dancing with determination, "we will see it end."

I approach and the screens go blank, images replaced, they are all covered in floor-plans and maps.

"There's much I must show you so you are prepared tomorrow, you need—"

"Just tell me what to do."

Suddenly his eyes, rotate, focusing on mine, emitting a barely audible whirring. After maintaining his antagonizing gaze a few moments, Lucifer's smile turns into a sneer.

"There is no need to placate me. If you have any reservations about this, I would hear them."

I hurriedly look away, hesitating, carefully choosing words.

"It's just...you think you know what's best for everyone. For all these people, and for me. Maybe it's best some people live in a sanitized bubble, maybe not everyone's strong enough to face reality. How can you or I, or anybody else make that decision for them? I don't want to be a missionary, forcing things down throats."

Satan reaches up and rubs his eyes, shaking his head slowly back and forth in frustration. Taking a deep breath, he answers.

"This isn't about me being right, or knowing what's best for others. This is about what's good for all life. What these people want to believe is not my concern. What is my concern, as an inhabitant of this planet, are beliefs which help fuel the destruction of my species, along with all others."

Does Earth need a representative? Doesn't it take care of its own problems? I remember a show about natural disasters on the education channel.

"I think this is something that has to be done slowly, with deliberate caution. Dangle your path to awareness in front of them, and their curiosity will drive them to take it."

"That's what I've been doing for over a thousand years, and now it's too late. I have no more time, not to mention patience. You give the average human more credit than they deserve."

This man's cynicism is starting to get on my nerves; he has succumbed to it over the ages, lost in the relativity of partial permanence. I concede to his argument.

"All right, I see your point, just get on with it."

To our left are aerial shots of God's largest city.

"As you can see, New Jerusalem is composed of many smaller structures all surrounding a central spire. There are gun turrets around the perimeter every hundred yards. Once you get inside, make straight for the tower, which is where you'll find

God in an indeterminate state, lost in permanent interchange with the Jesus Network."

The Father, the Hardware, and the Holy Wiring.

"Will I have an escort of any kind?"

"No, not after you pass the main gate. You will be on your own. The goal is for you to slip in unnoticed during the attack. If anyone sees you, pretend that you are wandering around, admiring the city. If you are lucky, you will be mistaken for one of the saved."

My mouth is dry, even thinking about going through with it. I wring my hands together nervously.

"Once you are inside, approach the tower with caution. The way in will be under surveillance. There is a sensor that detects energy signals. Each of us has a signature pattern specific to our own nervous system. You have already experienced this fact—it is how the red lights know you. If it all goes well, you'll have nothing to worry about."

This is starting to sound more complicated by the minute. I've never even used a gun before, and yet his confidence makes it all sound so foolproof.

"What makes you think I am capable of all this."

"You were made from my DNA, trust me, you're capable."

The pearly grin is back, never lacking charisma.

"See the layout to our right? At the end of the foyer, there is a stairwell which leads to a lift. It will take you to the precipice, the hub of all divine intervention. Destroy God, make sure He is dead, and then get out of there as fast as you can."

"That's all there is to it, huh?" My sarcasm is apparent.

"No one said it would be easy, but I trust you to do the job. When you leave here you will be outfitted with a weapon, you'll have the remainder of the day to learn its use."

I guess there's no way around it, this is the path I've chosen. The path of violence as a means to an end, the path of the executioner. My job is to carry out the sentencing.

"And be careful not to let emotions get in the way of your task. You shouldn't pay Shiva too much attention. I advise you not to get involved with her. You need to be thinking straight to pull this off, not in the clouds someplace day-dreaming about love."

How does he know my feelings toward her, is it that obvious? Or has he been spying on me?

"And to spend your time toying with the notion of a real god's existence is foolish. There isn't any true god, and you just have to face it. Don't bring back into your life what I've worked so hard to remove."

There is no way Lucifer could know all this without somehow listening to my thoughts. Each word he speaks is like a blow raining down upon me.

Adrenaline rushes to the rescue, spiked with testosterone, anger flairs.

"I won't listen to someone as soaked in hypocrisy as you. You've been monitoring my mind haven't you? That new transmitter you put inside of me apparently has many uses!"

I am practically yelling. As much as I loathe drama, I'm doing a good job at creating it.

Satan's face projects indignation, he takes a step back.

"I must take certain precautions, to make sure you won't go back to Him."

"I am just a pawn to you, a way for you to gain your retribution. You have the audacity to stand there and tell me to not listen to my emotions, to tell me what to think, when that is the very thing you are claiming to fight against. You oppose faith, but how much faith does it take for you to 'know' life has no guiding force? You stock your belief in unbelief, but still you are just another close-minded zealot."

"Now wait just a minute, you can't possibly compare—"

"No, fuck this, I don't know what made me think I could go through with any of it in the first place. I am no Antichrist, I am no hero. I am leaving you, your war, and this place. I just want to live."

I turn and make for the exit, before he can stop me. Reaching the door, I turn to face him, true colors now revealed.

"You can't just leave, you can't—"

"Well, I am. And by the way, don't ever tell me who to love."

Without giving it another thought, I pass out of his sight, and back into obscurity.

I run through the dark aimlessly following lights, indicators of misdirection, my compass to nowhere. I know I could be killed, be led astray, but don't think it will happen. I'm still too useful to be thrown so easily aside.

I feel like I'm going in circles, traversing a maze of demonic depths. I must get out, I want to breath real air, enjoy a real sun. I want to have a real life, away from all of this chaotic ideology.

The minutes fly by, as I am lost in my flight from significance; if only I could find Shiva, take her with me. Maybe we could locate some of those survivors Azazel was talking about and live with them all happily ever after.

I try to calm my obsession.
I don't even know how she feels about me.

Without warning, the tunnel's shadows are dissolved by shafts of daylight. I have reached my goal, the spiked pit where this journey into the Devil's domain began.

I climb up the ladder, and clear aside the camouflaged brush, bursting into the bright morning of a glorious day.

The day I end my servitude to all others.

The first day of the rest of my life.

I pick a random direction and begin to walk, climbing over the fence, leaving the ancient birthplace of the angels behind.

The overgrown forest around me glistens in unsurpassed beauty. The wind softly rustles leaves, merging with the sounds of small scurrying animals; real birdsong greets my newborn ears.

I find a smile splitting my face that would put Lucifer's to shame.

There is no methodology to my journey—I just keep moving, taking in the wonder of all creation. For the first time I feel a part of something, something magnificent that demands nothing of me in return. Just that I enjoy life.

My thoughts stray back to Shiva, and a fell weight settles upon my heart. If only she would love me, fulfill all my cravings. Perhaps she will hear of my departure, and come looking for me.

We can run off together, into the glow of the setting sun, filled with the patterned epiphany of love, as we meld into one, our porous surfaces infiltrated by differential growth.

We will lie together, underneath the light of the moon, and she'll tell her story, and I'll make up one to replace what I lost. She will laugh, and tell me, it's all right, the past is dead, as we dwell only in our moments mutually shared.

Not paying attention to where I am going, I trip on a root,

nearly falling. A part of me is laughing, the rest knows I am being overly optimistic. The truth is, I am lost, alone, and totally at the mercy of whoever or whatever may happen upon me.

So be it, anything is better than being used, being told not to get too involved.

And cackling through the green lungs of peculiar plant life, frothing, foaming over the brim of balanced building blocks, is the cold shock treatment of existential examination.

Venturing into the broader whole.
A small piece of the puzzle.
Finds no knowledge of the final assembly.

The encompassing outcome omitted.
Leaving a mirror-image mirage.
In favor of broadened horizons.
Of open spaces.

My pace is ceaseless.

RESTORATION

THE SUN HAS climbed high overhead. I've been walking for hours. The yellow flames licking my chapped lips, my robe is torn, my feet are sore.

I trailblaze my way through the wilderness.

Long forgotten cradles of life, just waiting to be clear-cut. The memories of older days—days of lumberyards and hatchet men—still haunt them, as contorted boughs try to snag my moth-eaten outer layer.

And the twigs are all out to get me.
I swear it.

Noontide shadow doppelgangers shifting into dusk bunnies.

Shrugging off their menacing whispers, I stride onward through the flora and fauna of trauma, an impeccable example of defiance. Through this mysterious world, its temperament unknown, showing itself as it chooses to be interpreted.

Insects swarm around me, trying to get at my skin. I don't mind; their presence comforts me. Helps convince me I'm actually here.

My ears perk. I freeze.

Eyes dart, rolling in sockets, turning to see, scanning rapidly, backward and forward. Something, some noise persecuting me, zeroing in on my position.

Closing in on me.

I crouch down behind a tree and listen. It sounds like footsteps are surrounding me—circling for the kill. My head jerks to and fro. I am an anxious chicken, factory-farmed and debeaked, my beady eyes on guard for gloved slayers, unable to move. Pacified. The sun burns, baking my sweat into caked sheets of grime. Creeping closer, something draws near, breaking sticks, rustling leaves, rushing to quench my qualifications for freedom.

A whispering wind of clichés.

I must flee, can't let them catch me, caressing my confines, calculating my detainment. There's a loud snap to my left and

I'm off, like a sprinter, in the opposite direction.

Branches snap against my shins, the wind rips at my skin, drying out my eyes, air sucked in and exhaled, fueling my forward momentum, surging onward, my field of view bouncing in rhythm with my pace.

I run.

My hair plastered backward, arms curving circles—gripping ground. Branches whipping my face. It's as if I remain motionless, willing everything else to rush past me.

I run.

Over hills, paying no heed to my surroundings. Finally, I break away from the trees into a field of sorts, slowing down to listen. My lungs burn, perspiration drips, rivulets soaking my skin.

There's no sign that I'm being followed.
I'm somewhat relaxed but still on edge.

Panting, I take a better look at where I've ended up. Pausing in the center of this meadow, waist deep in blue-green grass, dotted with purple flowers. The breeze makes its currents known, patterns expressed, gliding over knolls, managing furrows, rippling with life.

The clouds in the sky overshadow me with their enormousness, taking shape in various forms of polymorphic poetry; I slowly regain my breath, wincing at a slight cramp in my side. Squeezing shut my eyes, I drop to a crouch. I wish I could have told Shiva how I feel about her, but she'd probably think it was stupid anyway. She somehow doesn't strike me as the love-at-first-sight type. As much as I want to see her, I don't want to risk facing Lucifer again. I need to forge a new life for myself, someplace on my own.

I have to leave it all behind.
Even her, the thing I want the most.
I have to let it all go.
Put aside my melodious melancholy.

I get to my feet, and scan the horizon, trees surround me on all sides, but across the hills to the north they seem sparser, lacking vigor. My curiosity prods me into action, and I stride through the field to see what's so different about them.

Strolling gently through the soft rolling mounds of earth, a sense of peace takes hold.

As I approach the place of interest, I notice the grass around me seems less dense. Blotched with strange colors, sickly looking, seemingly diseased. The trees here are covered in an odd fungus, they look twisted, contorted in pain.

Walking amongst them. Their decrepit limbs making ill-favored attempts to reach towards celestial sensibilities. Malformed torment stunting their growth. I ponder what could have caused such misfortune and misery.

It's as if all the life around me has rotted and withered.
The sap sucked away.

A bizarre protrusion catches my eye, jutting from the increasingly barren topsoil. A shining metallic rock, covered in orange moss. Upon closer inspection, its true composition is unearthed.

The rusted out shell of a crushed automobile.

I expand my vision, gazing in all directions at once, finding I have stumbled into the leftovers of man's folly. An archeological adventure into the idiocy of instant gratification. Shards of metal and stone, overgrown, slowly being devoured by the ebb and flow of evolutionary forces. Littered with junk, the sought-after possessions of the lost, now lacking in their prescribed values.

Under my feet are broken slabs of concrete.
The roads being swallowed by the land.
Ground to dust.

I climb up to the tip of a rise and take in the dismal demise—the alienation of compartmentalized life, sprawled out, its emptiness creeping past the scope of sight. Tipped-over street lamps, no longer luminescent. Traffic signs with no one to command. Vandalized billboards with no one to captivate. Bent support beams, remnants of skyscrapers poking up like the bleached bones of some prehistoric creature long extinct.

I am overtaken by grief—the grief of so much waste. Yet I know, with certainty, the ugliness of this urban cadaver is beautiful in comparison to the bustling of its former full functionality. The history of commodity vampires, their blind progression built upon the shaky foundations of waxen wings.

They paid no heed to the soft voice of a mother calling them back to her breast.

Instead they projected their dysfunction upon her, raping her and leaving her to die.

But in the end this parasite was left with naught to feed upon but itself. Insatiable explosive appetites for greed feasting on festering flesh.

Cannibalism became the guiding light of capitalism.

As children were sacrificed to the impersonality of trickle-down economics. Their elders enlisted in suicide, glued to the hysterics of a searing death-flash.

Were there any who tried to avert this impending fate, or did all willingly condemn themselves to cataclysmic catastrophe? Embracing their enigmatic end.

The cries of children too young to understand—born into an unforgiving world, innocence stolen from them to fuel surplus wars, subsidized, and sold as unwitting slaves, accomplices to the crimes perpetrated by their parents in the name of the bottom line—their haunting voices linger on as a warning.

One tear tirades its way down the skin of my cheek.
One tear shed for all that has been lost.
One tear for those who sacrificed their future generations,
all for temporary profit.
One tear for those who cared more about numbers on a page
than their own offspring.

Up in the sky, the sun has begun its descent, it's time for me to move on.

I can only hope, this time around, a different path will be chosen. Abrasive abhorrent avoided.

I trudge wearily, across a radioactive wasteland, attempting to evade mutation. I can see where the forest begins again, regaining its strength and solidity. Soon, I am sheltered from the dilapidated decadence I mistakenly stumbled across. Continuing my lonesome trek through the countryside, I start to second guess my choice to abandon my role as freedom fighter. I feel no regret for speaking my mind; however, I don't want the wounds of the planet's past reopened. Maybe I can convince God to abandon His goals without the use of force.

If I don't do it, then who will? What if God succeeds?

The very notion sends shivers down my spine. After what I've just seen, I know that must not be allowed to happen. Am I simply neglecting a duty assigned to me, or is my flight validated by Satan's inability to listen to reason?

Crawling my way over the forest floor, stepping over the groundwork of growth—compounded heaps of decomposing fertilizers—I wonder to myself who I really am, deep inside.

I wonder what makes me tick. Is it all simply genetics and chemical reactions? Or are my neurons just a scratching surface surrendering to guiding light?

My invalid memory banks are the only thing uniting my disassociated selves into one coherent whole.

But of course, I know who I am.

Yes of course you do, you are me.
No, no, you see, you are and always have been me.
What am I blathering about?
I know it's been me all along.
I'm the real me, always have been, always will be.
No, I swear, I'm the real one.
No, I swear, no, I swear, no, I swear, no, I swear.
Everything else is just vacuum-packed ventriloquist voices,
hibernating in my head.
Whose head?
Your head, you silly thing.
What, my head, but I'm the only me!
You are whatever you want to believe,
but in the end it all comes down to nothing.
Just shut up already, all of you, I know what's true.
Searching to sanctify, to solidify this inner voice,
expressing my discrepancies.
Am I the Antichrist?
Of course not, you are nothing.
Who are you, tell me!
I am *you*, but you should know that by now.
Who is you, who am I, what is me—just stop already,
just stop, just stop.
I stumble to the ground, curling up,
squeezing fragmented fallacies of realization.
Do *you* stumble to the ground,
or do *I* stumble to the ground?
My skull, a vicious vice.
No, you fool, *our* skull.
Just SHUT UP just SHUT UP just SHUT UP just SHUT UP!

Silence.

Tentatively, I sit up, brushing the dirt and leaves from my robes, and lean against the rough bark of a nearby tree. Apparently, analyzing my internal dialogue is more terrifying than I ever anticipated. The shadows around me are lengthening, daylight is waning, and it's time to make a decision.

I haven't eaten anything in the past few days, save one bowl of soup. I'm exhausted, parched, and have no idea where to find water. Now night is drawing near, and a chill is growing in the air.

Should I continue blindly forward, holding to the minute chance of finding livelihood liquid, or remain here for the evening, with only my shattered temperament for comfort?

It becomes more and more difficult to see in the ensuing twilight. Imagined beasts cleverly cavort out of the corners of my eyes, misinterpreted for real, enhancing my disturbed state.

All motivation drains away, I sink deeper into the soft loam, as cicadas hum their hypnotic songs. The effects of the day's journey take hold; my eyelids grow heavy, finding the choice has already been made. I pull my knees up into my chest and lay my head on top, trying to ignore the dryness of my throat.

I will sleep here, wherever here is.

I close my eyes.
My breathing slows.
Along with my pulse.

Thoughts come slowly.
As I delve into the realm of dreams.

····· B R E A K ·····

My muscles spasm.
My head jerks upright.
Eyes wide open.
The moonless black shades of night obscure my sight.

Judgment is muddled, cloaked but clairvoyant. Perspiration pours down my face, as my body trembles with a collective chill, augmented by my loneliness. Nocturnal noises make their presence known, creeping into my awareness, a layered symphony of sophomoric song. Perhaps I simply can't grasp the patterned complexity of its rhythm, arising out of every crevice of earth, chirruping and croaking, whistling and whooping, rustling on the breeze, until it meets up with me—evaporating the angst from my clammy skin.

Feeling quite feverish.
And a tad bit delirious.

The dryness of my mouth amplifying the staleness of my situation. I am lost, sick, and more than likely dying of thirst. Dehydrating my way toward fatality. My disposition is bleak, my demeanor is that of hopelessness.

I will perish here, in the wild, free from all forms of control, consumed by the cosmos.

This tree will feed upon the decay that remains.
The malformed stiff of a makeshift martyr.

A feast of futile proportions.

Rocking back and forth, swiveling on foot-heel-fulcrums, levering in my dementia, clawing at my burning bush. I await the coming of my own inevitable downfall.

Good things come to those who fight.
But I'm a pacifist.
I don't need to care about the love
which you so desperately cling to.
I don't need to care about your pretty little flowers.
Or the false smiles you hide behind.
Because I have given up.
I surrender,
waving my wretched white flag for all its worth.
I no longer have the strength to go chasing after rainbows.
I have forgotten the meaning of ambition.
Death will come to those who wait.
So I wait.
In the subterranean depths of my isolation.
I wait for an end to come to this gilded life.

The moments of anxiety blend sequentially one, into the next.
I am unmoved by the helplessness of my plight.

And they are closing in on me now—the bringers of earthly termination—here to bear away my sickly astral body through multidimensional bitterness. Messengers from the Underworld here to enact a self-fulfilling prophecy. A gift of eternal sleep, just for me.

As they approach my innate survival mechanism kicks in and decides I'm not ready to make this journey. Fear takes hold of my esophagus, my molecules do not wish to disperse. It seems my drama was all for show, just little-old-me basking in the icy bath of newfound recreational pain.

And now, I don't want to go.
I want preservation without reservation.

Too late, too late. They've come for me, surrounding my whimpering wellspring of indecision, dressed in trinkets that have lost their meaning. Faces, covered, hidden behind wraps, eyes peering through plastic vending machine bubbles. They flock around me beyond count, making unintelligible vocal influx transmissions. Leadership seems to be designated with attire. The one who gives the orders waves around a rusty spoon, bent and mangled—an improvised scepter. The others crowd in closer, all wearing kitchen utensils around their necks. Combinations of forks, spoons and knives dictating rank. Their belts are made of soda bottles, scraps of metal and plastic are woven into their mismatched ensemble of ragged clothing.

Excited chattering mongrels, antiques, taking their pleasure at the expense of my desolation. Artificial artificers collecting the forgotten possessions of those recently departed. I can't differentiate male from female, covered as they are in rubble. Two reach for my boots, undoing the laces, even as I struggle to kick them away.

"Away with you, I'm not dead, I'm not dead. Can't you see, I'm not ready, it's not time."

One boot comes off, then the next. Four others are struggling with my robe, stripping away my securities. I scream and scream, fighting against these nightmarish gypsy children, these scavengers of the less fortunate. It's to no avail, I swing left and right, but there are too many, and I am too weak. My robe is ripped apart, and I'm left squirming naked in the fallen leaves, now one of them, discarded forever.

Will this stop here, or will they seek to lay claim upon my flesh as well? Very flavorful I've heard it to be.

It's time for my voyage to commence—commands are issued forth in their foreign tongue, and I am hoisted up into the open air. So many hands touching me, holding me up high, I strain against their grip, as I am forcibly taken to my doom. Like little insects, marching through the forest, led by the applicable appliances, their leader dancing before them, jovial while I am captive to the outcome of their random rhythms. A song wails from the depths of their lungs, blooming from distilled diaphragms, washing over me and conveying mourning undercut with a sense of excitement.

"...songling, songling toworder ovdah desparated.
Bringling, bringling toworder compleented.
Dis is dah won weenged beared toworder siplane.
Dis is dah won restordedanew, sickling serpassed.
Bringling, bringling toshown todah Unofiedwon.
Songling, songling ovardor dah desparated..."

Indecipherable and indistinguishable, repeated and hypnotic. The babbling flow of reminiscent words bearing me against the winds, through the awaiting chasms of calculated altered appearances. Hands clutching at naked flesh, clammy and sweat-soaked. Collectively, costumes jangling in tune with their tonal voices, lulling me into the dense deep, I no longer struggle, allowing myself to be taken to the great Void. At least I end here, in this forest, equal to all around me. Unlike my birth—a separate pecking order, designed to hold assigned sway over premeditated conformity, developed inside an antiquated aquarium redesign. Here, an open casket, no walls to inhibit my joining with energy streams.

Trees flash on by, blurring into solid forms, paving proposed paths. I still fight back, but I grow weaker.

We march for what seems like miles. Although, human ideas for measuring distance probably no longer hold meaning.

And it occurs to me, here in the clutches of inevitability, a thought. It had always seemed to me the growth alongside a road was out of place.

But now I see the actuality of the situation.
What is out of place is the road.

The previously registered recollection comes to play—the sight of disjointed slabs of pavement, displaying the fate of those who sought to cover the Earth in concrete.

The oxidized feeding device is used to signal a halt.

We have arrived at a halfway station, funeral pyres burning, sending tufts of smoke, wafting clouds seething about. There are temporary shelters constructed in a clearing ahead, intended to house remains of all species, myself included.

It seems I will come to rest, here at the edge of all things.

I am lowered and brought into the entrance of one such enclosure. No doubt to be dressed in a mantle and embalmed without embellishment.

Inside, the lighting is dim, my strange couriers of resignation leave me on a pallet laid out on the dust below. Shivering in my flash-fire, clawing at the air, fending off absentee tormentors.

Presently, I am no longer alone. A patchwork flap is pulled back, revealing a monstrous imp. Eyes spaced too far apart, and mouth twisted into a demented grin, a permanent sneer, nose smeared off towards one side.

I can see why these creatures wear masks.

I push myself away, squirming back, propelling myself with scrambling feet, but he reaches out, hand on my forehead, effectively pinning me down. Fear overtakes me. No thanks, I'll pass on the ritual scarification. I'll pass on the standard-issue organ removal.

"Drinka dis, beecoma fullness witall tings. Seekato meetdajoin Unofiedwon."

Prying open my mouth, it pours a bitter-tasting liquid down my gullet. I start to gag, but my nose is pinched shut and I am forced to swallow. An icy shudder ripples through my body, as I fight the urge to vomit, bursting into an unstoppable fit of coughing; I roll to one side, tears streaming down burning cheeks.

Almost immediately the room starts to sway. Orange dancing

glows, partaking it upon the shadows to unfold their bounty, splendor fading into vapor. The face disappears, along with the ill-fated messengers, I am left alone lying on my back, swiveling in space.

A strange.
Nauseous buzz.

Patterning outward from my middle,
enfolding in layers,
soothing me gently,
echoing backward,
from one sensation to the next.

An outlandish power envelopes me.

Comforting me.
Up until this point unknown by me.

Pinched to place and held riveted, listening to the silhouette sparrows swarming between the earth and the sea, waves washing over, and crashing, dragging me through the surf.

Eloquent geometry overlaid on my darkened surroundings.
Filling in the blanks, breathing with the air of the night.

I am sliding into a new world, a conduit of colors rampant with auras outstretched to carry me to my wildest whims.

And abruptly, I am alone.

The only one in a vast emptiness.

On the brink.
Of madness.

Sensations are broken down into ordered sequences. I try to think—thoughts rushing towards me out of the past into the present on their way to the future, like soap bubbles collapsing at my calloused touch into wisps of what could have been. Inputs erased into a mist of absence.

I try—eyes sense blank pages—to look around, wondering whose body I inhabit and what I am as an inhabitant, to calm down, speeding with no way to gauge momentum or inherent inertia. Everything is blanched, purged, prolonged, time stretching out into sensuous silence.

All-encompassing.

Lost in the space between one instant and the next.
Swimming in a sea of susceptibility.
Shattered sense of self(pity).
The delinquent has been dethroned.

Because I am nowhere and everywhere at once, exploded beyond the confines of body mass, one with the eternal, external, internal. It's all the same after all, a reflection of a reflection, slipping sideways through a hall of mirrors, an endless maze, fog machines fuming, pumping out megatons of maltreatment, the answers to all my questing questions overrunning my central neurotic complex.

Here's the funny thing: I'd laugh, if I could, but I don't have any lungs.

Here's the funny thing: It turns out, I don't exist after all.

I'm just a figment of Universal imaginations, running around, suspended by hidden heartstrings, twisting in the sleep of never-ending-dropout-dreams.

Everything is condensed into particles upon observation, wiping out probability waves. And the world is just a distorted distraction—in part, impartial, in whole, inconsequential.

A stream is flowing through my organized biological structures, could it be my soul? A tendril of life-force anchored to this terrestrial plane, this endpoint, by my dismal, brittle form. My flyspeck of a body.

Isn't equality a beautiful thing?

I am a singular idea, grasping for a plethora of multiplicity, the numerous possible directions in the deliberations of destiny. Does it make a difference if my method of observation, my moral apathy, wins out over the will of God? Of Lucifer for that matter?

We're all of us in the same boat here,
different facets of the same fluorescent fantasy.

I'll play my part, if you'll play yours.

Don't try to change roles;
don't attempt to persuade me to read your lines.

Sing your hypocritical hymns.

And in turn,
I won't interrupt your institutionalized illusions.

The melodramatic monotony ends.
A passageway opens out of the white before me, calling.

I enter.

My will grants me momentum through the gaping maw of
immortality, and I find myself in a cankerous cave, made
of gemstones reflecting the light from a vacant sun. I float
forward, and down, ever down, deeper through the levels
of the earth, into subliminal similes, into the realizations
of curiosity.

Drifting.

Drifting.

In an ill-fated attempt to grasp.

My own insignificance.

THE LOWERWORLD <<<<

I **FOLLOW** the tree roots down.
They are my guides.
And I am their star pupil.

It all speeds up and slows,
interchangeably wreaking havoc on my linear location.
Longitude: somewhere between order and chaos.
Latitude: somewhere between clarity and dementia.

The exit to this templar tunnel is growing near, approaching
slideshow style.

I am through, and below me vast landscapes stretch into unnerving distances. Like a superhero I can see for miles, in the pale limelight allure of transient shapes.

The color.
All the clearer.
A glowing glimpse of the sublime.

I glide to the surface, on the edge of a lake, in the middle of a savannah, the shade of one sapling, grown like bonsai, shelters my arrival from the metaphysical monsters—the lizard people, always laughing, laughing, laughing, to the west are crimson peaks, I feel the underground magma moors, jagged mountains, in the east a rainforest roundabout, curving north, dying at the teeth of rock, helicopter overview, all stemming from the form I've taken.

A human covered in skulls and feathers.

Landing, I alight upon a smooth stone, sitting, watching the rippling endless waters to the south, entering a meditative state, spreading myself thin. Butterflies energy bathe on the rocks all around, fluttering my fickle nature, I touch one, it smiles, I wave.

I grow it bigger and go for a ride.
With permission of course.
It likes me.

I climb on back—furry tufts, enlarged, can be made into handlebars—and we are flying out and over the sea, inland and inlaid, sparkling like a signet, jewels of jubilation, refracting my recollection. I ride higher, giggling, as we skydive steeply towards the water, pulling up at the last second and skittering across. I stand up and leap with all my might, my friend fades farewell, and I am under the blue shell, suspended in syrup, swimming without sound.

Like a superhero I can breathe underwater.
Maneuvering through seaweed.
Aquatic acrobatics.

Approaching:
The Piranha's Pariah.

For an appointment, you see, his teeth taunted me but did not daunt me, stand and delivered, or slip and slide he slithered, and flopped like the fish that he is. I know you, bull male, defender of the keep, the atrocities you who bestow wrath upon the weak. Pure poison filaments for bead eyes—I am no match for your animosity, but on my side are these hands and their ability to shoot balls of white light into the iridescent ilk you call creeping crawling brethren. Prepare for battle, ready the battalion, I am going in, maybe to die fighting, still dignified. The outcome is unexpected—rays ripple, tearing apart the scaled slivers of meat, served steaming in the summer. Thus accomplished, I enter into the underground rivers leading to peripheral paradox paradise.

Resolution:
The threat vanquished.
Foe destroyed.

Here in these murky mud banks, decorated with oddities of the deep, the cold sets in. Shivering in the backlash of this parasite's demise.

In the now vacant cavern I find a strange plant, moving against the grain, sparkling blues and violets, voluptuous vapor trails, bubbling as if breathing, calling out to me, beckoning me to approach with the comfort of a mother. I pluck one leaf and arise to the refracted light sliding around above me. Approaching the open air once more, my winged companion nowhere in sight, I hover above the surface, pulling the land toward me in my mind, the plant matter clutched in my fist. Concentration cracked, I begin to float upwards, in an uncontrollable ascent. My check is balanced, and before I am whisked away, I free fall, crashing back into the land of blowing grass.

I move towards the tree where it all began.
Soothsayer, visionary substance.
Nestled in its shadow, I open my hand.

Before my eyes, the peculiar livid leaf moves of its own accord, dancing in the air to my left, rearranging molecular susceptibilities, generating the composition of a wizened woman, her eyes eldest, her face smooth as silk, hair all gray, but shimmering, crinkles in the corners of lips upturned in a smile. She turns to look at me, resting a hand upon my back, in reassurance of friendship.

Tears well up in my eyes,
the warmth of her touch melts my heart.

Speaking slowly, her gaze trained upon me, her comments come in the form of a slow harmonic tone, beaming in via telepathy.

"Be at peace, here in this place. Be one with all things. Overcome all fear." She strokes my hair. "Tell me what troubles you, child."

My head falls onto her shoulder, cradled, safe in her arms.

I don't know her extrasensory tactics,
I voice my thoughts the typical way.
Simple speech.

"WWwwhhat is thissSS?"

"Search my soul little one, you'll learn the answers there. More than you can imagine."

Hands grip the sides of my face, pulling me to confront her stare. Portals leveled, granting me passage, view-screens for interstellar travel, propelled through space on overdrive, galaxies spiral stellar nebulas, planetary nurseries seeking the counsel of constellations, fingers inching onward, groping gravity, blacklisting black holes. I am a wave of light, vibrating at a certain frequency, like a radio signal, the wavelength can change—expand the visible spectrum.

This is beyond infrared, beyond ultraviolet.
Beyond x-rays, gamma rays, microwaves.

This is the uncharted territory, abode of alien entities.

I'd cry out if I could, against the concept of defining reality on the basis of five senses. How many more levels of experience are out there, how many states of awareness, unfathomed by our kind? Small specs of stardust, running around like we own the place. Such a funny thing, the roll of mammalian metronomes marking out disgruntled disdain as a pillar of existence.

The births of Universes unfold—big bangs, the disassociation of ego in an intelligent expansion. An attempt to gain knowledge ending in collapse, lessons are sorted out before the next attempt at growth.

I am a part of this evolutionary process.
Part of a living being, breathing,
going through systematic cycles.

A thought in the mind of *god*—another word, another symbol used to label the unquantifiable. Meant to condense complexities only the daring try to unravel. Everything is relative. One book, one lifetime, one set of metaphors will never explain what any of us are doing here in the first place.

I see creation and destruction, life and death, interchange before me, pitting themselves against each other, asteroids crashing into planetoids, good and evil, it's all just a point of view. On a larger scale, balance is always maintained, dependent on probability, as each action divides time, fracturing into another possibility in an endless sequence of outcomes, fueling metamorphosis.

Everything is defined through its opposite.

Zoom out, further than the edge of everything, and you can analyze atoms, more anchors for energy, placeholders of string aspect ratios. Here, this god is constructed of an infinite number of smaller gods, with smaller gods inside, all building larger gods inside larger gods, no end in sight, and

yet each piece is same as the whole—one unified consciousness with trains of logical reasoning grappling for control.

Picture perfect pulsating, patterns too large to predict, slipping past the event horizon, the death and rebirth of a cosmic
Christ, one that doesn't subscribe to denial, totally in tune
with its shadow side. Know thy enemy. Embrace your opposition. They feed you, or you them. All will perish, consumed
by the symbiotic nature of spirit.

Each individual death, a collapse, before rebirth.

All communication is instantaneous, location linked through
field theory of the ethereal, just another force of nature, still
governed by a set of adaptable principles.

My actions and thoughts are magnified, I feel all the power running through me, observing the order my mind
receives impulses, monitoring processing, everything has
a fluctuation, everything is conscious, everything is what
you interpret.

Because I'm not real to me, *me* isn't real, thoughts aren't real,
there is no *me*. A progression of energy, constantly rebuilding
itself in different ways. We are a capacity for the Universe to
feel itself, we are its sensory organs, we need to stay awake.

Wake up others.
Stop being selfish.
Stop being selfish.
Others need a turn.
Others need a turn.
Vanish in the light.

Everything splits into many.
Feelings are injection molded.
Become one.
Stop being selfish.
Join us.
Join us.
Become one.

Building backwards over mesmerizing memories, to a placid place, where things made some sense, at some level, reversing through interplanetary travel charts, back to some conjured landscape, back to an envisioned terrain.

Flat on my back, clutching the peculiar leaf.
The breeze reaches my nostrils, it is odorless.
Lacking putrid pollution.

I stand and survey the savannah.
Just me and the gopher king—rodents of the earthen hill clucking cautiously at the curious sight, new arrival, vexing visitor, drawing much arousal, amongst burrowing beasts possessing above average intellect. They speculate my super-position upon their territory.

Yo, ho, ho, my furry little friend. Don't you worry, my lingering here can be explained away in a jiffy.

Consciousness is a property of the environment, as much as any other force, it cannot be easily quantified, equated through language association. There is a stream for each emotion, each idea, each action. What gives us these streams, why are some more important than others? I am just a label for an ever-changing tide, sent to weather what it will whither, thoughts as an individual have an input on surroundings, communities of interrelated parts. We are all facets of one mind.

We must unify.
Making a choice between death and life.
Plug in our personal preference.

Other realities permeate the edge of experience.
Roads lead the way, the answer is astral projection.

When you see all the places you've been, why would you label yourself as what you are now, why would that experience be more important than any other? Only when I'm fully aware can I rest. Now I'm still being thought. Only when I'm realized can I rest.

Will you be the one to realize me?

It all echoes, resonating through everything around me, trailing ahead of the moment, the ego, recording the palpitating past, shared record, path forward seems to be the source of all chaos, we need a new *we*, with some perspective on the larger whole—all-encompassing.

If everything is conscious then what holds true for my own sense of awareness must be governed by the same rules that operate the Universe at large. We are the path integral—the sum of all histories included in innumerable imaginings.

All you really have is an average identity.
The direction the stream is going at any given time.

Proposal:
Create a field theory, developed to mathematically express the dominion of consciousness, a unique force at work in the actions of all objects.

Hypothesis:
The discovery of dimensions only accessible through the altering of ordinary brain state.

Procedure:
Ingest the necessary allotment of alkaloids.

Observations:
Tainted upon rationalization, definitions only confound the situations, we need to understand nothing in order to understand, only to stop pretending simple separations can render one aspect of a single organism superior to another, make inadequate the eloquent axioms for existence of those considered inferior in an instant, postulate the remaining probable outcomes, come to the realization that these contact modifiers compound the life all around us into commodities, nurturing a dependence on one set of lifestyle choices over simplicity, whatever the methodology used to obtain the desired delicate balance, numbers or any other means of communication only seek to express, never to explain, for the explanation is only found entranced in the moment.

Results:
Positive.

Summary:
The dust agents collect, building up intuitive resistances, feelings entice purpose, the spark is born, random and fixed

become meaningless, ends and beginnings float away with the wind, duality brings with it dullness, I think I prefer infinity, I'll never find the answer, because there never was a question, I am and always will be, you are and always will be, the Universe is and always will be, in this filtered glamour, pestering erases anti-knowledge, leaving only truth.

User discretion, is of course, required.
Advanced training, advised.
I think I'm in a little over my head.

Do you, little buddy, do you think what I think? Living in the holes inside my skull, ponder, scheming in painfully playful motifs of sea-green and yellow-froth, foaming from my rabid lips, as I am lost somewhere in the vastness of dementia. Save my place, I will return someday to dine with you and yours, but alas, now I feel the jungle calling me, fertilized by the volcanic dust of lava legions—pumice pebbles. Destruction feeding growth, growth creating destruction, roots ripping apart rocks, water boring out caverns and canyons.

Laughter.
Oh, what laughter.
My meaning is miniscule.

Striding onward, eastward, towards the overgrown vegetation of shifting hues, faces loom from the gloom, formed from the jagged edges of leaves, the space between an avalanche and a hurricane, the home of ancestors, beating drums to death, a tomb time and time again. I pull the scenery forward with my feet, swallowed whole by a superfluity of plant life. Exotic electric animals, things of make-believe, seen but not swallowed whole, stalking my steps beneath rustling canopies, umbrellas without shadow. I feel the heat pulling me closer, reaching out, tantalizing the senses.

Bear lumbers to my right.
Nosing the forest floor, scrounging, foraging.
Somehow paying attention without paying tribute.
My presence here is not a concern.

Tickled really, I continue, crossing tricky terrain without the use of a machete. The vines have no substance, physically, I pass through them uninhibited, reacting reflexively, shuddering involuntarily, pulsing with power. Orbiting my nucleus are countless crickets, prowling for piecemeal defense mechanisms, trying to gain control of response apparatus. Giant blossoms, blooming gold and silver flowers emerge ahead, petals litter the ground, reaching out to pick a castaway keepsake—she loves me, she loves me not—as I seek to reclaim the childhood stolen from me and shipped away—a message in a bottle, a skeleton key, love letters found in chests, sealed away in the attics of aristocrats. A perpetual pass-code used to provoke ecstasy. Incite nostalgia, a stand-off with stasis, a spiral of thought regression, uncovering those warm summer nights, just at dusk, when I played baseball with my father. The one I thought dead, the one whose memory was injected into a test-tube-fetus.

Coyote strolls to my left.
Cackling like a wasted concubine,
hacking up hairballs of mirth and delicious delight.
Somehow hinting at the humorous nature of my spiritual path.
My presence here is hysterical.

Trudging onward, paying no mind, the intensity magnified,

deeper into the lair of seduction—rocks are aggregates of minerals, igneous, metamorphic, and sedimentary. The products of an active volcano and his molten mnemonic devices. Igneous rocks crystallized from magma, metamorphic rocks from pre-existing rock by changes in temperature, pressure, or chemistry, sedimentary rocks, by weathering and erosion of preexisting rock to make sediment. Lost sentiments housing tropical goods, geothermal power-structures towards which I'm drawn, up the slopes, past the summit, into the crater—the vent. Like a superhero, the heat cannot touch me. Sailing headfirst, blasting down the conduit, my aim is the reservoir, it is achieved with much ease.

The scene that is spread out before my eyes, entitled:
A Brief History Concerning the Rise of the Reptiles

Subtitled:
And the Slave Race that Calls Them Master

The cold-blooded ones live in the flames, lapdogs of addiction, consoled by the whimpering and wounded, here in this underground cavern of molten rock, manipulators of mammals, seeking access to the stream of spirits, pampered parasites, calling out like an oasis of whores, seething at my apparent interruption of their discussion on the destruction of the Source. A tumor that can never be cut out, only ignored, occasionally resisted.

Each place where life evolves there is an energy-point from which the growth of an organism ultimately stems. Before coming to our own, these creatures sucked their mother dry, in the night, unnoticed, and have traveled from afar, existing in other spectrums of light, creators of civilization, fathers of oppression, using survival mechanisms to ensure our servitude, they feed on us even now, voices in my head, trying to dictate decisions.

Our true overlords, unseen and always watching, poised to take advantage of us at our most feral moments. Tirades of misguided masochism taking form in this gathering of lizard leaders, yellowed eyes, eager to obliterate me at any moment.

They don't want me to interfere with the construction of their bodies, houses of snakes, guiding us to a world run by mechanical life forms, like us, but able to reproduce faster and alter themselves—repair themselves, survive under any condition. Humans will be phased out. Discarded. But for now we are merely tools, drones, being used by religion to construct their ambitious empires.

Punch in.
Punch out.

I make my escape, they don't realize who I am, just some random dreamer stumbling mistakenly upon their not-so-humble abode. Arrogance will be the end of them, when it's over they will devour themselves. Cannibals, just eating up the flesh of their chosen sacrificial offering.

Take this, all of you and drink from it.
This is my blood.

Jump on the bondage bandwagon, now for a limited time only: whips, dildos, torture racks, restraints, candle wax, cages, masks, paddles, anal beads.

Crosses, nails, crowns made from thorns.

Take this, all of you and eat it.
This is my body.

Thoughts spread out,
dropping rhetorical residue behind me as I depart.
Leaving a trail of sorts.

I pass over deserts, shimmering sands and snow-capped mountains, soaring over unconfined landscapes, back towards my biomechanical exoskeleton.

Drumming lights the way, the direction to the slow-moving surface, climbing, clawing for air, making my way upwards. The place from which I made my departure—the little pinpoint of a nobody. A wood and bark conveyer belt, a fantasy factory, a channel of fluctuating matter, vibrating and vomiting me skyward. I climb the tree to my awakening.

·····B R E A K·····

A slap in the face.
The shock of icy water.
A momentary loss of breath.

I sit bolt upright, drenched in sweat,
into the delirium of reality.

It is still muddled, waving with each breath of space, definitions and contact modifiers, still shaky, rules of thumb having trouble taking hold. Bleary and teary-eyed, without notion of how much time has passed, I try to grapple with the impressions of what just happened to me, and how it is I can still be alive.

Rainbows rival retrospective introspection, dancing deliciously before my beating heart, thumping against the inside of my chest, pumping and bumping to the rhythm of existence. Exploring my surroundings, I see I'm still inside the tent, the door is rolled up, allowing a cool breeze to send shivers across my naked form. Outside it's dark, and the orange glow of campfires carries with it the tones of hushed voices. The shelter is made like a quilt, patchwork, stitched together from bits of random fabrics. To my left, there's a basin filled with water and a drinking cup. I gratefully splash some over my face, fill the cup and pour it greedily down my throat—much to the relief of my dehydrated digestive track.

I suddenly remember how I got here, and the strange creatures stripping me of my clothes. I gag, as the flavor of the bitter medication I was administered comes back to me. Everything around seems different, but I can't really put my finger on it. It's somehow more animate, somehow more intertwined with my own livelihood. Slowly, I lower myself, relaxing, trying to analyze things one at a time, reclining, trying to recognize the supposed symbolism of my journey into uncharted domains. I feel as if I've had an out-of-body experience, I've traveled to a faraway land, the entrance has lain dormant, awaiting discovery, triggered by chemicals and intense waves of sound.

The trip has transformed me.

This exploratory trek into the synergy of spirit bringing with it enlightenment. The most obvious answer is that time and space are constricts through which we experience life, used as building blocks for logical reasoning. It is no longer necessary for me to question the viability of a true higher power. Everything is one, divisions of the same Universal energy, trying to experience itself through any means possible. This is the guiding intelligence behind evolutionary forces and repeated patterns, making themselves known from the molecular to the stellar, all contributing to the makeup of a growing organism. The question has been resolved, an answer accomplished. Humans are important. We are a part of everything, just as everything is a part of us, and all contribute to the direction the mind of the cosmos is taking at any given moment. A tapestry woven of many threads. We may not be more significant than a speck of dust or a grain of sand, but we do have a place in the greater scheme, a home inside the symphony of creation. The solution is equality. Nothing is more or less momentous than any other object. Everything has a say in how the chips fall, and power over the environments surrounding us. There can be no excuse for dissatisfaction, life is a reflection of inner-workings. Death is just another path, a step in the flow of developing ideas, a progression into knowledge.

There are two sides to every coin—everything has its shadow. Forces exerted by parts struggling for control add to the richness of life. We should never be cemented into a point of view. We must be open to the nature of this darker half, without giving in totally to its temptations. It should be used as a springboard for advancement, expansion, and growth. Just as the danger of falling into darkness can lead to stagnation, so can feelings of self-denial and restriction associated with living totally in the light. A middle ground must be found, a compromise reached, the happy medium pursued. The immense beauty surrounding us stems directly from balance.

The plague God is building, the disease He is working for, is a kind of addiction. One dangled before us so that we might be able to overcome it—use it as fertilizer to further our development.

The danger of collapse is always imminent; if we waver for a moment in our battle with these forces, we will be destroyed, becoming fertilizer ourselves. However, the battle must be fought through ideas, the hearts and minds of God's followers must be won with words and examples found in nature. The spiritual plane must be addressed. If Satan continues to ignore it, he will never fulfill his goals.

Violence will never convey with it victory.

The Devil's crusade of pain and suffering as a tactic to bring about change can only be stretched so far. He is too cemented in materialism, and the infliction of disasters upon God's followers only works to invalidate his philosophies. He may succeed in shocking people into a state of heightened awareness, but by doing it without their consent he will forever be a recipient of their reproach.

I am a prime example of this.

If I were to kill God, it would only be used against the cause of freedom. Our cause would be written off as a work of evil. In fact, it has occurred to me, this is more than likely what God wants us to do. Lucifer is being played for a fool. He believes he's about to accomplish everything, when in actuality his tirade of force is only going to discredit the truth he so desperately wishes to share with the test subjects God is manipulating.

After all, God did create Satan—more than likely He was totally aware the rebellion would occur. He let a lion loose among the lambs to help unify them behind His leadership. Fear is the primary tool of fascism. The followers of God have been taught to fear Hell and the deception of Lucifer so much, that they will obey anything the Jesus Program asks of them in return for salvation. They line up like cattle for His divine protection. The Devil is merely adding to this fear, playing into God's plan for the Last Battle, where evil will be defeated, leaving the people indebted to the Lord, cementing them to His control permanently.

Lucifer is no more than a pretentious puppet.

I am startled out of these thoughts, as the creature that ceremoniously provided the catalyst for these latest transitions of theory enters to examine me. The light from the fires outside dance his dark form across the walls of the shelter. It comes unmasked; the deformities no longer intimidate or frighten, although I grow ashamed of my nudity as it draws near my side. I flinch, and try to jerk away when it lays a gloved hand on my shoulder.

"No fearanoia, youara bettanow, Unafiedwon youara now. Here, eatadis."

I am offered a tray laden with small morsels appearing like dried meat of some kind. I pick up a piece, and after examining it closely, put it between my jaws and start to chew. Warmth and satisfaction flow through my malnourished body as I clear away the food, shoving piece after piece into my awaiting mouth. When the tray is empty, a feeling of fullness such as I've never known overwhelms me.

"Youara cleansepured now, nolongara ever dah same. Seeya dah worldmother witdah spiriteye."

It holds out a bundle comprised of a new robe, similar to its own, along with boots made of mismatched pieces of leather. I accept it, and thankfully pull the cloth over my head and put on the boots. Surprisingly, both items fit perfectly. Something about this entity is tickling the back of my mind; the answer to its awkward appearance is on the tip of my tongue.

"What...er...I mean...Who are you?"

The distorted mouth twists into what could be interpreted as a smile.

"Dah onesdat are leftafta dah Purge. Dah embodyforce of dah Croe. Youara safe witus, dis is dah timefer sleep now, youara be resting now. Relaxdah mind, lie down der."

Finally I realize what these people are. They are not death dwellers, but survivors of the Collapse—a nomadic tribe of what's left of humanity. The odd assortment of junk they clothe themselves in made up of trinkets they've discovered in ruined cities of the past, the deformities due to prolonged radiation exposure. It all adds up. They must have seen I was sick out in the woods and brought me here to help.

The space I inhabit still seems to sway slightly, and my body still tingles with a strange sense of euphoria. I don't have time to dwell any longer on my current situation or what types of chemicals I was given to provoke such a response.

A gunshot rings into the night.
Exploding outward from a hidden point of origin.
It is close—too close.

The survivor in my tent, looks around, terrified, and runs out into the dark, leaving me to my own devices. Outside, I hear frantic shouts, panicked cries, screams and shrieks. Footsteps running back and forth, scrambling for safety.

Before I see her, I know she has come for me.
To retrieve me.
To take me home.

Her voice sends shudders through my body.

"Here you are. Come on, we have to hurry."

Shiva enters the tent, gives me a look that melts all my resolve, and holds out her hand.

PHANTOMS

MY INHIBITIONS are lacking.
Beauty has burrowed into my logical reasoning.
My eyes flash, sparkling with epiphanies.

There's a war going on for my loyalty. In an unfamiliar world,
the postulate is that anyone can pose as my friend, or lover,
in order to invoke a sense of duty within me. But what choice
do I have? My feelings for this woman are the only things that
make sense lately, and after being close to death for so long,
she could be the path back towards an actual life. One not
fraught with so much turmoil and deception. A way to truly
learn who I am as a person. To find if I am more than just a
meat popsicle, a genetic creation being used to further the

goals of the maniacal and morose. After my recent journey into the infinite, the night seems an entity, flying by as I'm led away from the camp of nomadic scavengers, back to the hub of irrationality.

"I was worried about you. I do not trust those *things*, they are not sane."

Her voice sounds so comforting. In her eyes, I must seem infantile, naïve and nostalgic, always needing rescue, as she draws upon thousands of years of life experience. I am a mere trickle, a minor fluctuation in the flow of her growth. How can I ever expect her to see me as an equal?

"You didn't kill any of them, did you?"

My question is met with bemused laughter, and a tug at my scavenged outfit. "You are too concerned with the wellbeing of fools, but no, I did not kill anyone. I just fired a warning shot after they refused to let me near you."

I am one with the forest, interconnected with something greater than myself, a gift bestowed upon me by complete strangers. Just being around Shiva pushes aside further recollections of my out-of-body informational bombardment. Out of sight, out of mind. I follow the gun-toting diva as she demonstrates her ability at navigating terrain in the dark. The moon is gone, leaving only thick space, drenched in colorless substance, cloaking, clouding, choking away the vibrancy of the day.

"I know Lucifer told you to stay away from me, I know you think it's wrong of him to spy on your thoughts. But I have to tell you, he has reason to be wary. The only way to totally destroy God is to destroy the Jesus Program. Satan has spent thousands of years constructing the perfect virus. It's called *Dragon*, and it has the power to disable the Program. If God were to somehow gain access to the coding, He could immunize His network against it."

We are crossing the jagged deconstructed cityscape, circling around the edge, where the trees start to grow again. I refuse to let her words justify Lucifer's actions.

"All of the Devil's creations are monitored in order to ensure security. It's just a safety precaution. If he were to link himself up with *Dragon* and God was ready for it, everything would be over. Lucifer would lose control over his own network, God would look into his mind, and expose him—destroy him. He would die."

The killing of one faction's leader or another's, a point of view comes with its reasons.

"Besides, it's not as if he's listening all the time, your thoughts are recorded in the archives and are checked over every so often."

Nothing can touch me, my mind has been set on the part of the Devil in all of this—an instigator, a lion among the lambs, provoker of a war designed to ensure the status quo. I cannot hide the sarcasm in my voice.

"Well, I sure hope Satan is keeping tabs on himself. Being a former servant of God, he just might betray us all."

Always, her laughter is ringing, making me feel how church bells used to. She is perplexed by my paranoia, amused by my side-note observances.

She stops up ahead, turning, putting her hands on my shoulders, staring straight into my eyes, her irises glowing, feline, the color of Prometheus crimson. My stomach churns, and goose bumps cover my body, I struggle not to give into my longing and forcibly embrace her. Her lips pull back, forming a smile, warming my bones.

How I feel is that fire ants are crawling all over my insides.

How I feel is sex-starved, deprived of instinctual necessities.

"Your grievances are understandable, but let's place them aside for now. In a matter of hours, it will be dawn, and time to make our journey to New Jerusalem. We need you, at the very least to unify the resistance behind the concept of providence. With you at their side, they will feel destined to win. They have been awaiting your coming for too long for you to simply desert them."

I release a long sigh, and can't stop myself from placing my hands on top of Shiva's. To my surprise she doesn't pull them away. As the stars shine overhead, telling the same stories now as they have for all the ages, I begin to see them as real objects, more than a fabrication inside an effervescent projection chamber.

"You're right, I have to go back," I tell her. "But in any case, how could I say no to someone as beautiful as you."

I expect her to think I'm being a creep, I expect her to pull away, but instead she takes my hand in hers, gives me a look that makes my heart stop, and begins to walk slowly right beside me.

Just the smell of her is more than I can handle.
She is slowly driving me mad.

We stroll peacefully for the moment, alone with each other. Her hair, coils of silk, obsidian vessels, cascading down her back, brushing up against my cheek. Her head leans on my shoulder, her body presses close to mine.

Since my fall from grace, such joy has not been felt.
Layers of clothing are all that separates me from completion.

As I ask a question, her arms are sliding around me, clutching me closer.

"When all of this is over, what will you do? This has been your life for so long, where will you go?"

What I'm really asking is, will you stay with me? Will you stay wherever I am? Always?

Her voice pours into my ears, spilling forth from her perfectly shaped mouth.

"I will help set up a new world, a world of freedom for those who were once oppressed. I will be like a mother to all. Those seeking comfort will be my children. And I will go wherever I am needed."

"I need you."

"And now, I am here."

Our arms are wrapped, entangling us,
entwining our selves together.
My heart beats wildly, breathing is struggled.
So nervous I can barely keep my balance.
My fantasies being fulfilled.

I am lost in her company, my heartbeat in time with the galaxy, grafting itself into the spirits of love and wellbeing, keeping track of celestial rhythms, sonic vibrations, ultra-density emotion, sounds of nightlife, frogs—those not dosed by radiation—croaking, sounding their alarm at our presence, in the presence of everything and obscured by nothing, invisible to the world except in the eyes of the beholder, beautiful and surrounded with body-heat, unrelenting, sweet sweat glistening on my brow, her brow graciously flowing into and down, her cheekbones, housing radiant retinas, pupils dilated in order to increase light intake, we make contact, she is smiling, I am smiling, we are happy.

I whisper, almost inaudibly. "Now that I've found you, I'll never let you go."

A curious glance cast in my direction.

"What do you mean?"

I didn't mean for her to hear, I was talking to myself—or so I thought.

"I feel like you actually care about me, like you want to help me understand my place in things. You rescued me from the bowels of God's machine, and you brought me back from the abyss of reason. Your being here makes me feel whole. But why do you bother with me? I don't deserve it, I have no real past, and I have no future. I don't even know who I am, I don't even have a name. I'm just some favored specimen."

"Are you complaining?"

"No, I just want to know how you feel."

Her smiles ravaging my composure.
Threatening to knock me off my feet.
Her response offers much needed repose.

"You are different from the others. You are in tune with something beyond any of us, and the way you look at me, it makes me wanted. You are a decent person trying to find the truth in all this, and that's what's important. Besides, no one has told me I am beautiful before, they are too intimidated. You make me smile, and forget about what lies ahead. So be at ease, and as for a name, if it means so much to you I will give you one. It's what God's people will know you as. You will be called Abaddon, the Destroyer."

That might be a bit much to live up to.
More like Abaddon, the Fuckup.
Nonetheless, I am honored to finally have something to call my placeholder of a body.

The one time I should feel like I'm trapped in a dream.
I feel more aware, together, at ease, than I've ever felt.

I feel totally cleansed, purified, all negativity is no more.
At this moment in time.
We are the only things that matter.
The Succubus, and the Angel of the Bottomless Pit.
Lost but heading home.

My brain is bursting with new ideas, theories, concepts, regarding life, my identity, death, my decomposition. The propaganda funneled in through both sides, requiring further analysis. The conclusion is that if I never existed, if my ego is an illusion, then I can never really die.

The conclusion is that there are no divisions. The only fractures are the ones we convince ourselves are real.

We are all one.
Even the Devil and God.
Matter and antimatter, what's the fucking difference?

"...hey, are you listening?"

"What? Oh, sorry."

She shakes her head at me.
I am sure her eyes are rolled.

"I said, there's something I want to show you. Come on."

She grabs my hand in hers with incredible strength and darts off, yanking on my arm, tugging me after her. Before long, we come to a halt. She's always grinning, I can almost feel her eyes twinkling, as she pulls aside camouflage revealing another entrance into the network of tunnels. She goes first;

I replace the covering as I quickly climb after. Her head is practically inside my strange new quilted robes as we descend the ladder. We hit the dirt at the bottom, and we are off again, me being pulled along through the dark, red lights flying by, leading off into discreet distances, motion lines remaining burned into my eyelids. We twist one way, then the other.

"Almost there, it's right ahead, listen."

We slow down, and I can hear the sounds of people—voices and muted shouts, the occasional moaning. I start to wonder where Shiva is taking me.

Faint light pushes back shadows from around the next bend, she looks back and motions for me to be silent. Still holding my hand tightly, we stumble upon a scene that makes my stomach jump into my chest.

Projected onto a large screen is an image very similar to something I've seen once before. A man is inserting himself into a woman, waiting wide open, for his phallic force, groaning for him, wanting him. I feel myself begin to tremble. I start to look around us. There are followers throughout the room, pleasuring themselves and each other, a bedlam bordello, in various states of arousal, members of each sex, all laid out ahead, with the movie playing in the background. The blending of sounds, vast pitches, fluctuations, beating in time with the heart thumping in my ribs. I am sweating, my hands hot and sticky. I give Shiva a squeeze, and we walk to the side of the room and down another hallway, this one lined with what seems like dressing areas, individual rooms with curtains pulled closed, from behind each cries of ecstasy issue forth.

She whispers.

"You're used to sex being demonized; here, it's just the opposite."

There's no way, there's just no way.

Before I can resist, I am yanked into one of these side rooms, the curtain pulled shut behind us, the sound of fucking all around us, Shiva pulls me in, a spider caressing the carcass of its victim. Her lips connect with mine, and her tongue finds its way into my mouth, instinctively. I respond by putting my arms around her, finding her waist, waves of euphoria and nervousness echo out from my insides, as we kiss fiercely, enacting all my wildest imaginings.

The entire chamber is padded, and soon we find ourselves in the backmost corner. I'm pushed up against a wall and forced to the ground, she's on top of me, caressing me, soothing me with her touch, skin-lotion, lip-balm, an aloe vera embrace with a poison ivy aftertaste, her lips on my ears, nibbling at my neck. My hands useless at my sides. She puts them on her breasts, through her robes I can feel her nipples, hard, and soon my hands are inside, cupping them. We flop around, rolling over and over again, everywhere, experiencing each other, glee dripping from posturing pores, tapping into our animalistic sides.

Even if we were both grown in a lab.

At the moment, the thought is erased, tossed away, all clothes are discarded, as she feels my chest, her hands making their way down, touching my thighs while I rub hers, I lose count of how many times she tells me that she wants me.

That she needs me.

"You like it when I play with your dick, don't you."

The statement vanishes in a whirlwind of similar sentiments; I can only try to swallow, my mouth dry, as I begin to play with her. Her body is amazing, the curves threatening to overtake my will, my eyes travel over miles of silky skin, distracted, she utilizes the moment to pull me inside her. The warmth burns away my inhibition, here in the wet darkness, we have merged—our spirits meld.

Riding in and out of each other, I am reversed, channeled in multiple directions, forced to be six different people at once, all camera angles, reflecting the soft flare, lenses projecting, grinding to the beats, buried in flesh, quivering with delight, dissolving into our surroundings, mingling with minstrels of love, togetherness, lively awakening. I have found my place.

And she is screaming, yelling for more in my ears, telling me not to stop, shifting positions. I am just trying to concentrate. I never imagined forbidden fruits could taste so good. This is a new kind of high. Emotions are heightened, endorphins are released, my brain already racked with chemicals, trigger-happy technicalities sliding backwards and forwards.

I hear someone talking about us nearby, they like listening to us, peeping in on our dirty secrets, a perfect form taking shape to the touch, they are getting off now, all around us, a cascade of seamlessness, everyone so happy to be alive, all dripping, oozing with gratitude. And now harder, thrusting over and over, attempting to meet her demands, she's calling for me, calling out to me by name.

Abaddon.

It's so real that it's become fiction, digital details omitted for the sake of efficiency, the nameless have become something, more than a cause, more than a flag to carry, a feeling, an honest feeling, so deep, bubbling up from the centrifugal force, pinioning at the edge of my heartstrings, waiting to be plucked, clipped from my exposure, my vulnerability, as I make the plunge, over and over, faster and harder, the sound of skin slapping, my eyes close, waiting to fly, waiting to be taken to the edge and back, the feeling of inertia welling from within, vertigo conquered, speed increases to the point of no return.

Muscles clenched.
Tensed on the edge of climatic results.
Staring down into the empty leagues of possibilities.

Floored, a cataclysm of shrieking, limbs entangled in life retrieval, stirrings inside my abdomen, entrenched, nails claw at my back, tearing, seeking hold, a new kind of pain, pulling me in deep. I let go, all of it, my shattered life, transmitted into seeds for new growth, the darkness leaving, flowing into warm caverns, lands of sweet treats, sighs of contentment reaching my ears from all around, I explode, a firecracker burst of excitement, arriving in all of its splendid intensity— then it's over.

I wilt into a heap with her, reflecting upon the wonders of our human forms.

As we lie there with one another, in a room more than likely covered in dried bodily fluids, the moments pass without ever really passing. Ceased is the Chronos-flow. Until finally she speaks.

"...mmm, it's hard to believe you've never done that before."

I guess that's a good thing. I can barely move.

"So, are you staying here this time?" she asks.

I smile. "If that's what you want."

"Yes, that's what I want." Her fingers are running through my hair, along my cheeks, brushing me gently. "And, are you going to fulfill your destiny?" The question, posed too sweet to resist.

"I'll go to New Jerusalem in the morning, as Satan intends."

Her arms hug me violently, she smothers me in wet kisses. "I knew you would... I am so happy, this—"

"Now wait a minute, let me finish..." I try to push her away. "I...I think..."

Fingers press together my lips. "Hush...none of this now. Let's savor this moment, and remember it whatever may happen tomorrow. Get dressed, and then head to your room. You need rest before we leave."

It's hard to have a serious conversation when half the people in your general vicinity are still reaching orgasm. I make no objections and pull on my foreign attire.

She's already standing, pulling me up after her. One last kiss and she's disappearing, leaving me behind. The absence of her touch is painful, a piece of me is tearing away.

"Wait... I don't know the way."

She's calling back to me as she pulls aside the curtains.

"Just follow the lights. All you ever need to do is know where you want to go, and follow the lights. You should know that by now."

I start to shout after her, but she's already gone.
And I am alone.

Unsure of what really happened, I make my way back to the tunnels. Back to my responsibilities.

· · · · · B R E A K · · · · ·

I wake up.
So completely at rest, refreshed, prepared for this day.

I wake up, because the lights have all turned back on automatically just before dawn.

Whenever I think about last night, I question the validity of my experiences, but with the trace of a smile on my face.

I almost feel that I could kill God for her.

But I won't, I won't play into His hands.
I can't be anyone's puppet.
I have better plans.

And now, as robotically as ever, the door to my chamber slides open.

Out in the hall, soldiers dressed in black, flying by, preparing for battle. Arming themselves accordingly. Followers. I wonder what thoughts race through their heads on self-confirming conduits—justifications for anger and rage, the same emotions that hover in my heart, choking out verdicts. Pain: the aftertaste of the Messiah's mindfuck. I know what drives them, and so does God, the One who indirectly made them. All of their actions anticipated. The futility of their free will never comes into question. Arranging their deaths at the hands of a great schemer, leading them into the jaws of a vortex, heading past the boundaries of space.

Clean robes and black boots lie by my bedside. I pull them on, putting aside last night's patchwork gifts, preferring not to discuss my spiritual experience with anybody. Heading into the bathroom, I splash water on my face, refreshing myself. Staring back at myself from behind a wall of glass, convincing myself I can get through the day. No reconciliations, no firm associations between inner voices and outer shell. Haggard, unkempt, my own run-down temple. Neglected, discarded then rediscovered. The man who I've become searching for the child he never was. Phantoms of the past, disconnected from the flesh, lurking in the corners of awareness, pockets of pragmatic practices, refusing to add up, trying to lure me into an alcove of angst, convincing me my body isn't real.

Vapor trails unveil volumes.
My heart longs for her touch.

Shrugging out of the mirror's hypnotic embrace, coming to grips, I pull on my boots and head out into the hall. Waiting just outside my room is Azazel, a smirk on his face, casually making eye contact. I quickly look away. I wonder how much he knows about what happened yesterday.

"I see you decided to return," he says. "Maybe some of your questions were answered."

His pointed look full of a tingling, projected down my spine.

I hesitate before responding. "Some, yes. But others..."

"Lucifer has sent me. He's quite anxious to speak with you about what your involvement will be in today's...events."

We walk against the flow of traffic, weaving our way towards a desired exit, my mouth goes dry with the prospect of facing the Devil once more. I'm sure he already knows everything I'm planning on telling him. I'm sure he's listened while I've thought things over. I'm sure he spied on me last night.

I wonder if he's jealous.

Azazel makes his voice soothing. "Don't worry, you don't have to tell me anything if you don't want. But I will tell you this: I have worked beside Lucifer for all these long years, I've seen his character, I've seen what he's made of, and I trust him. He is, in many ways, wise beyond any of us."

"You forgot stubborn."

My remark catches him off guard. "I will not try to say you are wrong in how you feel, or why you left. But you have to remember, everyone here is depending on you. We have waited for this day a very long time."

I feel a real sense of sympathy, and almost longing, for this misguided sliver of hope everyone here seems to possess. Expecting a triumphant victory. Maybe I'm wrong, but I know in my gut, something about all this just doesn't sit right. I respond as best I can.

"I understand. Don't worry, I'll do anything I can to help you all. I'm just concerned God has already anticipated our actions. We could be walking into a trap."

Azazel shrugs before answering. "It's a possibility, but the danger must be risked. We won't have an opportunity like this once they begin colonizing the planet. That's not something I care to witness. The jungles plowed over, furrows covering the lands. His so-called perfection imposed upon everything I see. No, we must fight, and we must do it today."

I remember the charred remains of the city.
I recall the consequences of control.

"We are here," he says, "now I must prepare for our departure. Good luck. I will see you soon."

A pat on my shoulder turns into a momentarily menacing clench, holding me in place.

"Oh, and another thing. Before you consider breaking any promises you've made to Shiva, know that if you disappoint her, you'll have me to answer to."

With that he's gone, his warning hanging thick in the air. I'm once again alone, faced with my fate.

I reaffirm my resolve.

The chamber opens, and I'm strolling inside, indifferently, my calm greeted by the glowing flashes, cities on the screens all empty now, vacant and deserted.

This is what's called *judgment day*.

He's waiting, his back turned, hooked to the machines. He speaks quietly.

"So glad you could finally make it."

"No problem."

There is silence as he concentrates intently, off in another world, putting in place the gears, getting ready to infest the Jesus Network with his all-important virus—ignoring me.

I seize the moment with sarcasm. "I guess we don't really have much to talk about, being you've probably already seen my thoughts, calculated my actions. Is everything going according to plan? Should I put aside my objections and just have faith? Place my trust in you? Oh, I'm sorry, should I be addressing you as the Most High?"

Scorn creeps at the edges of my voice.
It is unavoidable.

Finally he turns to face me.

"You are entitled to your point of view, but let it be known, now and from this point forward: My actions are *not* comparable to those of God. It is true I monitor the thoughts of my followers, yours included. This, unfortunately, is a necessary safety precaution. All of my subjects are allowed to decide their own paths. Unlike God, I never will use deception in order to gain your allegiance. More importantly, I never try to erase your memories, implant you with false information, or otherwise manipulate your actions. And I will never take you to a blue room for reprogramming like some lab rat."

I can't help but give him an incredulous look.
It's the skeptic in me.

He's getting frustrated.

"And where was my choice?" I ask acidly.

"What is it you want? Would you rather I had left you in God's world of carefully constructed falsehoods!"

I feel he made his point. I reply accordingly. "Sometimes that option has its appeal, but in the end, if you had given me a choice, I would have picked this path."

"So, then you have decided to go through with your part in all of this."

"You could say that I have redefined what my role will be."

"What do you mean?"

I wonder how much of what I'm about to tell him he already knows. When was the last time he checked up on me—has he seen the unraveling of my sanity? Will any of this be a surprise to him? If he knows about Shiva, he is apparently keeping it to himself. Maybe finally realizing not to overstep boundaries this time.

He waits in anticipation, trying to hide the obvious anxiousness.

I decide to make it blunt. "I want you to call off your plan to attack God's city, and promise not to use *Dragon*."

"That is completely out of the question, and you know it." His response is not surprising.

"Then I won't go to New Jerusalem, I will leave, and you'll never see me again."

I hope he can't see I'm bluffing.

"And if I called off my war, then you would go? What is the point of this? I don't think you see what is at stake here," he says, "we are talking about the future of this planet—"

"Exactly. That's why I am asking you to do this. Refuse to meet God with violence. For the sake of the planet."

"You would have me do nothing, just stand by while God

284

spreads His tentacles through all that is beautiful? Until God restores monotony, imposes His dominance?"

"No, I only ask for you to resist in a way He's not expecting."

Red eyes search mine, as if trying to determine the seriousness of my words.

Finally, Lucifer speaks. "And what makes you think He is expecting this? He has no idea I've found a way to disable Jesus."

I struggle with myself, trying to keep from laughing. I posit a question.

"God made you, right?"

"And His programming failed."

"But He is your creator, and partially mine."

How much of who we are is embedded in our genetics? How much of who we are can be explained by DNA?

"Has it occurred to you," I continue, "that maybe, just maybe, you were created for a reason? That maybe God meant for you to rebel?"

"This is ridiculous—are you questioning my free will? I haven't been that control-freak's pawn for thousands of years. God would have no reason to want to bring about His own destruction."

"If you are allowed to succeed."

"I am *allowed* nothing! He will follow my rules today! Mine! This is the end, and when it's over, you will owe me your gratitude. God *will* die, with or without your cooperation."

"Wait, I have a better idea."

"There is no other way, this is our only option— "

I interrupt, growing tired of this hypocritical resistance to the questioning of his beliefs.

"A small force can escort me to the City, and I will sneak inside as planned. I will confront God and convince Him to stop the experiment. By taking Him into my inner world, He may finally understand our position."

Satan's eyes close tightly as a cackling begins to rise in his chest, projected around the room, bouncing off of monitors, coming at me from all sides, trying to discredit my position. Shrugging off my suggestion as if bursting a bubble in the mind of a child. His mirth causes a smile so large the anger all but disappears, his teeth gleaming with dismay. Finally he stops chuckling long enough to speak.

"You can't be serious. Don't you think I've tried convincing God to stop this madness? That's how this all started, that's what I attempted in the beginning. And I failed miserably. To God there are no positions, there are no shades of gray. There's only right or wrong, and God is never wrong."

"Anything else we do will only further God's plan, I feel that

He will listen to me, I feel He will—"

"God does not listen." He shakes his head, frustrated at explaining the obvious. "To you, me, or anybody else. There's only one way to rid the world of His tyranny forever, and there's not enough time for you to persuade me otherwise. My mind is set. Without *Dragon* you'll never make it in alive."

I draw in breath, attempting to respond, but am cut off.

"Besides, *Abaddon*, I know you've already decided to go, whatever I do. Even if I disagree with your reasons, it is a welcomed choice." The words are undercut with disgust.

So he has been inspecting me after all. My fists clench, fingernails digging into my palms. This is not going as well as I'd hoped.

At least I know he's jealous.

Lucifer dismisses me matter-of-factly. "The time for departure is growing near, and I suggest you arm yourself, whatever you may feel to the contrary. It is best to be prepared. Your idealism, I fear, will turn on you."

"And yours as well."

But my remark falls upon deaf ears. Turning his back on me, The Prince of Darkness has returned to preparing for his release back into God's world.

His prearranged reign of terror.

His appointed hour.
His call to duty.

Leaving him to his own devices, trying not to submerge myself in a candy-striped symphony playing for a lost cause, I make my escape.

Another step closer to the unforeseeable outcome of decisions based upon desire.

I tread out into the traffic of pedestrians—another colony, another hive.

I have made my choice.

ARMAGEDDON

FOLLOWING the flow.
Following the designated course.

The streaming tide, the satanic army, grows in numbers all around. Soon I find myself in some kind of armory. It's body armor first, everyone suits up, myself included. Kevlar vests bulk out underneath ritualistic garments. Weapons of all kinds, on stands, on shelves, cool black and destructive, waiting for their masters to unleash their fury. Magazines and ammo adorn the walls. The tides rush to choose their favorite designs of death and then carry on into the adjoining room. I hesitate, and the servile servants behind me begin to grow impatient. I am about to just move on without a firearm, when suddenly she's beside me. Full of grace.

"I have yours right here, Abaddon."

It's the first time I've seen her since last night, and my legs almost give out from under me. My heart beating much too fast, my stomach churning, I smile, drenched in a stupor of love. "Oh...um...well..."

"This is a weapon that suits the bringer of God's downfall." Her words are honey.

"I really don't think..."

"Here, let me show you how to use it."

Shiva gives me a long silver handgun with an ornate grip. It is cold to the touch and seems out of place in my grasp. Before I can protest further, she puts her arms around me from behind and wraps my hands around it, guiding them into the proper position.

"Here is the safety; you turn it off like this. Never put your finger on the trigger unless you intend to use it. You place the magazine in the bottom like this..."

The lesson blurs by, but I am too busy enjoying the feel of her arms to tell her to stop. She is now reaching inside my robes, placing it inside a built-in holster. Those around us are giving wide-eyed stares. Whispers spread, emanating from the point our body masses inhabit. It all happens so fast, and then with a smile and a slight shove she's sending me on my way.

The next room is some kind of dimly-lit garage, filled with small ATVs, and a few armored jeeps. Machine guns adorn all of them. Already, they are being filled with occupants. When they are all claimed, more followers walk through side doors into other garages to find their own. I wait, trying to determine where I belong, trying to find my place among the ravagers—sowers of seed, bringers of discord. As everyone begins to settle into place, I see Shiva and Azazel in a jeep across the way. I walk towards it and sit in the back, between two soldiers. A personal escort service.

I am greeted with smiles all around.
The treasured trump card is little old me.

Lucifer's voice is thick, magnified; it takes hold upon the collective, preparing us for battle as it blares from hidden loudspeakers. Everyone is at full attention.

"The time has come for your departure. You have all prepared rigorously for this day, and it will not be in vain. Do not forget what you are fighting for. Go now and liberate the Earth forever."

And the air rumbles above us, gears cranking into motion, jostling into position. The ceilings pull apart, revealing an atmosphere partially illuminated with the first hints of dawn. The floor rumbles, as the platform we are on begins rising to meet the fresh air. Everyone is prepared, everyone is on the tips of their toes.

Except me.

The vehicles are all starting. I expect their motors to be loud enough to impede my hearing, but they run remarkably quiet. All around me they hum, like nocturnal insects greeting the coming of morning. I notice the solar panels, and realize the obvious. Gasoline is probably pretty hard to come by these days.

We have arisen into crisp air beside the rumbling birthplace of that which we will attempt to destroy. A sense of apprehension rises in the back of my throat, making me wish I could prevent this massacre. It is never too late—when we arrive, I will have my chance. My one chance to convince God He is wrong.

If I fail, I will probably be killed.

But death no longer frightens me, last night's strange occurrences helped me overcome my fear. I have been reborn multiple times already, and I will be reborn again, thought streams rushing out to meet the horizons of synergy, energy flowing, chemicals reacting, the blip that is my spirit sliding into other entities, conceptual frameworks broadcast across ultrasonic frequencies. Death is not the end of anything except my ego, the mental construct convincing me that I really exist. Convincing me that my actions matter.

With a jolt we are off, Azazel driving, moving us into action, making our way into the thick of things. Part of the fencing is pulled away, and we leave the demonic compound for what could be the last time. Scouts are sent up ahead as we make our way down a small trail, the woods thick on all sides, shading us from prying eyes. No one leads, and yet everyone seems to know the way.

In the front seat, Shiva won't stop smiling at me, and Azazel is trying hard not to laugh. And the guards I sit between don't know what to think.

We seem to be navigating some kind of winding dirt road, with enough room to allow the solar-powered spectacle to steer freely, avoiding occasional debris. Steep banks of dried clay rise on both sides, and I begin to see that this isn't a road at all, but the cracked dehydrated bed of what was once a great river.

"Climate change accelerated greatly in the last years of civilization," Azazel says.

Deserted, deprived of water, leaving us to traverse the bowels of an age-old channel, a fanciful furrow, marring its way through the landscape. Another reminder of human error, another message from our ancestors. Another reason I can't turn back, why I have to accomplish what I was made for.

I will be the one to destroy God's system.
But I'll do it with words.

The prophet.
The pariah.

I've come full circle, ready and willing, playing my part. And now, here I am, surrounded by strangers, lapdogs, journeying into the mercy of mythology, unaware of our futures, unable to glimpse our pasts. Here I am, a stranger to myself, unable to communicate my feelings to the woman I love.

More chemical reactions.

You know, triggering all those warm fuzzy feelings.

The only woman I've ever experienced, confusion intercedes for experience, a raven of ravaged emotion, sitting so close, but so far away, unable to touch without drawing unwanted attention. Maybe everyone knows by now, anyway. Maybe if they don't know, they've guessed.

All around, layered sound—first the wind, rushing air, then the hum of electricity, topped off with worried whispers. All bathed in growing daylight, the revealer of life flying higher into the sky, pulled by chariots, an eye of fire, an orb of light. Those who do not speak sit silently, absorbed internally, contemplating our task with contentment caulking out the vacant spaces, easing out the kinks in their commitment to this strategy. Hopefully awaiting their final say, their day of triumph, gaining ground, grasping the upper hand, wielding the tool of selective self-appointed preemptive liberation.

As we turn down a new tributary, I can't help but voice my views, attempt to explain myself.

"I still don't think *Dragon* should be initiated until after I've had a chance to confront God. Satan should just distract them enough to allow me to sneak in unnoticed. A direct attack against Jesus, I fear, will be expected."

Shiva turns in her seat, sharply eyeing the men sitting beside me, trying to indicate that I should be quiet. Wouldn't want to deplete the morale of the engineered fodder.

"If the Jesus Network is still functional, you will never make it inside," she explains, "it will match your body signature to records of your previous lack of faith and immediately trigger the security system. The thing is, God can't focus on everything at once without the aid of Jesus. Disabling it is akin to taking away His sight."

The nameless passengers are noncommittal.

Azazel looks at me in the mirror, nodding. "She's right, there's no other way. It's up to you what to do with Him once you get inside, but we'll have to wait for the virus to take effect before you are able to enter."

Shiva winks at me, nudging Azazel. "I'm sure he'll do the right thing."

The gun's foreign shape digs into my side, unfamiliar and uncomforting. I smile at Shiva, hoping it's convincing enough. Hoping she'll still fuck me when all this is over.

By now the sun is bright overhead; water is passed wordlessly to me, followed by small baked goods, scones of some kind. I eat them meticulously, trying to fight off the growing nausea in the pit of my stomach, the accumulating discomfort of nervousness. No matter what happens, I know when the day is done the next chapter in the human story will be written, ready to be carried out, to be completed. Will the supremacy of a concentrated power structure once again envelop Earth in its stranglehold of domination, or will diversity win out? I nod off as distance blurs away with the passing scenery. Miles meld into the space we leave behind.

·····**BREAK**·····

Scouts return, full tilt, manning ATVs, pulling up alongside us to give their report.

I snap back to reality.

"We are quickly approaching the City."

Their eyes are wide, sweat drips down their faces. One of the soldiers sitting beside me swallows audibly.

"I've never seen anything like it, there are so many of them."

"Good work," Azazel responds. "How long until we arrive?"

"Ten minutes."

And they are gone, disappearing up ahead, finding a location for camp.

Rummaging through a compartment in the front, Shiva pulls out two strange looking lenses, attached to circular bands. The glass tinted green, having the appearance of an eyepiece on a telescope. Both fallen angels pull them over their heads, letting them come to rest over their left eyes.

Azazel projects his voice above the buzzing demonic horde.

"All right, this is it. Get ready, we will soon reach New Jerusalem. We will find a place to watch in secret until the moment to strike arrives. Pay close attention, we don't want anyone to die needlessly. Always remember, today we will emerge victorious."

Let's hope so.

Excited chatter rises all around us; underneath its shelter I venture a question.

"What are those eye things for?"

Shiva turns and smiles, staring at me with one red eye and one green eye.

"Azazel and I aren't equipped with perception generators like everyone else, we will need a way to see what's going on when *Dragon* begins. These allow us to view the world as it appears to God's followers."

Everything we are approaching is ominous.
My apprehension must be obvious.
Her voice soothes me.

"Don't worry, Abaddon, everything will turn out just fine. You'll see."

Once again I will place my trust in the hands of another, put aside my objections. Once again faith will be my operational function.

Everyone is slowing and turning their vehicles to climb up the bank to our left. Engines are extinguished under the cover of a dense line of foliage. In the silence that remains, I hear a background hum, a layer of droning coming from beyond the trees ahead, the sound of a stadium crowd. This is the opposite of an angry mob. Around me everyone is emptying out, crouching down, and easing forward. Ever so slowly. Creeping mold on the edge of everything, worming along, inching its way into new territories, engulfing existence. I am flanked by angels of shadow, flanked by lullaby lackeys. We are all one organism, poised, hearts ready to explode in our chests, sending blood squirting through unintended passages, making our way to this assured asinine attempt at an alteration of human history.

We're water droplets trying to change the direction of a river as it sweeps us towards arid deserts—we will surely evaporate and die. Burn up into a vapor, to be inhaled, forever after sticking to inner tissues. The synopsis of this story is surmised in our passing.

Light breaks through the trees ahead indicating empty space beyond, the leaves are ready to be brushed away and grant the gift of sight.

We approach, all of us denizens of darkness lining up for a better view. I am completely astounded, utterly amazed, taken aback.

Spread out before me on the other side of the branches is a drop off down into an immense valley—lush—filled with rampant growth and hoards of people—millions—all assembled around New Jerusalem. Its main spire, the center of my strange journey, towering toward the clear blue cloudless sky, dwarfing the delusional. Guns are trained in all directions, protecting the keep, advanced arsenals guarding this Holy Empire.

This is the land of milk and honey.

Everyone is looking their best—the appropriate attire for the atoned, Sunday clothes for the saved. Everyone is looking like an exuberant ant hill, dug up and left exposed, doused in happiness like kerosene, ready to be ignited by love, itching with anticipation. Knowing that they've all made it to this day, this perfect moment, here with their fellow Christians, their souls erupting in rapture. This is their glory. Apparently they can't see the smokestacks pumping out pollution, or the observation towers, or the industrial waste. To them it's all just pristine, just hunky-dory. They only notice the stained-glass, filtering the light, and they feel right at home.

Christ has come again.
The alpha and the omega.
What is and what is to come.
The beginning and the end.

Angels, like shepherds, carrying weapons instead of canes, wearing uniforms, patrol the tops of the white walls encircling the compound. Keeping things in check, admitting no one. The flocks of hypnotic subjects have arrived from all over the world, transported instantaneously across vast distances, to congregate, to purse and pose, like skin-pinups, like livestock, following commandments, ready to eradicate all who oppose them in the name of God. I am envious of their fervor, their certainty—but only to a point. My discarded dogma comes rushing back, reminding me of my humble beginnings. A pawn, putty in the hands of a master sculptor of deceit. Has anything really changed?

I know more, but am I any less controlled?
Are my actions any less contrived?

Shiva, standing next to me, finally close, easy to touch, to fondle, to love. She looks at me, makes contact, and smiles, penetrating my will, prodding at my insides with her cold compassion, rendering me incapable of further recollections of the past. In the present, I am to be a hero. In the present, I am Abaddon, and I will prevail. I will show God the error of his ways and convince Him to put things right. No more ceremonies, no more rituals for the sake of ego. It will all stop today. I will see to it, one way or another.

There is a quiet cackling of radio hiss and sputter, transmitting information on location back to our point of origin. This is what we've been waiting for—the end of an age, the time when Satan will be let loose from his prison to ravage the world, to convert the conscripts to his cause.

My head begins to throb, my vision wavers, dizziness abounds, and I know it has begun. The City transforms, from a monotonous center of fascist fictions to a temple of spirit, a testimony to everything that is beautiful. The guns all disappear, and the angels grow wings, they are no longer walking, but soaring through the sky, the people are raising their hands up to them. Laughing in their jubilation. The walls sparkle like gold and are now inlaid with stones of all kinds—precious minerals, trite things to which men have ascribed too much meaning. Things over which wars have been fought.

The sun beams down on us all, washing away sins.

Behold, the tabernacle of God is with men, and he will dwell with them, and they shall be his people, and God himself shall be with them. And God shall wipe away all tears from their eyes; and there shall be no more death, neither sorrow, nor crying, neither shall there be any more pain: for the former things are passed away.

Unless of course you disagree with the all those pesky underlying assumptions that go with the whole human superiority on Earth concept. Then, you're just damned.

The fearful, and unbelieving, and the abominable, and murderers, and whoremongers, and sorcerers, and idolaters, and all liars, shall have their part with fire. The heathens, the ones who were trained differently than you, seek them out and destroy them, build God's empire, the planet is yours for the taking. It's us or them.

Before me, in the constructs of man, I see paradise, as it was described to me, as it was implanted and ingrained into me. Around me, in the vegetation and green things, I see the paradise that has always existed, the face of the true supreme being, waiting there, connected, yearning for us to take notice. The serenity of simplicity, the aesthetics of just enough.

White light pours forth from the many gates of God's Temple, beckoning, hinting at the grandeur waiting within. His followers are holding hands, running in circles, jumping for joy, singing praises to the Most High. It's an orgy of servitude, a celebration of shackles.

Sheltered behind verdant photosynthesizing fibers, I feel Shiva's smooth fingers wriggling, entwining with my own and squeezing my hand reassuringly. I turn to look at her and smile, only to find that she appears incredibly pale, her eyes sunken in, her lips blue, teeth grown into fangs, lips curled mischievously, on her back I see scars, remnants of ripped off wings. My field of view expands, and I notice our army has all grown horns, hooves, and scaled flesh, reptilian and repulsive with glowing eyes. Azazel is a monster, twice his normal size, fear pulsing thick in the air surrounding him. My stomach grows queasy, as everyone else grows claws. I don't know where to look, so I stare at my hands, at the ground, searching for earthworms and insects, ladybugs, anything that's still around. Anything that actually exists outside my own synthesized spectrum, my own limited experience. It does no good, Shiva senses my dismay, and her hilarity has to be happenstance.

Her voice comes in the form of a grotesque growl, rumbling and unfamiliar.

"Just watch the City, Abaddon, ignore how we appear, it's only an illusion."

That's easy for her to say, she can choose to see through it, as we sit, surrounded with stereotypical imps, crouching in noontide shadows, awaiting their duped opportunities.

Trying to heed her advice, my attention drifts back towards the panorama of pests, emulating evaporating emotions, dancing disastrously in religious delirium, revering a magnificent master of massive monstrosities.

Those silly children of God—my old acquaintances included, real and imaginary—their hopes are all remotely dashed through the power of an invading satanic super-computer. The beautiful skies cloud over completely, smothered with smoke and mirrors, reverberating with rancid cumulonimbus clouds. Panic-stricken, piling in heaps, they're running towards the City gates in a stupor, stampeding, only to discover admittance is still denied. Judgments have yet to be made, the lingering lackluster wicked wombats need to be weeded out.

You know, all those misbehaving goats.

Unable to seek safety behind the monotonous menace of sparkling white walls, they turn to meet their tormentor; they turn to face the darkest of unknowns, suspecting the worse.

The land beneath us begins to tremble, a great earthquake, the sun turns dark as sackcloth, like blood, the sky is divided, a torn scroll, curling up. Anyone destined for captivity goes into captivity. Anyone destined to be slain by the sword shall be slain by the sword.

In the darkened atmosphere overhead, the signs point the way, a great red dragon materializes out of empty space, planned programming taking place, one head, jaws open wide, becomes seven more, brandishing ten horns, teeth shining and singing for blood.

And on its heads are seven diadems. Its tail sweeps away a third of the stars in the sky and hurls them down to earth.

Some of the once-joyful chosen are now burning alive, flesh being eaten away to fuel combustion, meeting pain, writhing like flopping fish. The rest back away from the flames, terrified, in their moment of fear, suddenly unwilling to help their fellow man. Waiting for someone to be the first to show leadership. Not wanting to step out on a limb.

Unable to fathom that Satan's virus is on the verge of rendering God impotent.

Circling around the City walls, the Dragon is devouring angels and men alike, feasting on their uselessness, fire is licking at the bodies lying motionless in the field below, massacred, their decomposition sets in quickly, like time-lapse photography, the carrion-feeders do their dirty deeds, stripping bones dry, leaving bleached skeletons haphazardly behind. It's all quite lovely—the screams, the cries for help, bleak bleating, the forces of God overwhelmed.

A new omen.
A woman, projected high above, in pain.
The labor of childbirth.

The Dragon—poised—ready to devour the essence, the innocence, the heart. Ready to destroy the Jesus Network once and for all.

Next to me, a pale flower, wearing a death shroud, grips my hand tighter, needing reassurance, preparing for the long-awaited moment. We make eye contact, she winks, and I so hope all my fears are misplaced. The visions before us are taken in, processed.

Jaws open wide, all of them, prepared, glinting in the only light not overshadowed, razorblades ready to tear apart the Son of Man. My heart throbs against my chest, blood pounds in my ears, my belly heaves, as the woman begins to give birth.

Everything spreads out.
A flash of white radiance, blinding sight.

Muting sound, an array of absence.
For a second, nothing exists.

I blink.
Silence.
I blink.

Slowly coming into focus, the scene is restored, and I am elated, as I find the woman has vanished along with her newborn child. The Dragon remains, Satan has prevailed. It's almost time for me to play my part. I await my cue.

Initial impressions are slowly shattered. I see that nothing changes, the Dragon is still in the sky, searching, confused, panicked. Something isn't right, something doesn't add up.

Except for the occasional whimper emitted from the scabbed lips of a burn victim, all is quiet. There isn't even a breeze. Miscalculations may have been made after all.

I see a break in the clouds, a shaft of pure gold, shines down, lighting up red scales, the Dragon dances in pain, a hiss builds in the back of its many throats, like a drumming rain, it falls to the ground, a squirming snake, crawling at the dust, gripping grime, trying to hide itself against the City walls. None of it works. Shiva releases my hand, and covers her eyes, unable to watch anymore. Our small, private army is overthrown with confusion, hushed questions. Fearing the worst as we look on.

Out of nowhere, hundreds of angels beset upon the red serpent, shouting cries of glory to God. A crowd of stinging insects, their swords find its soft underbelly, many times over, taking advantage of its weakness. This embodiment of evil, this boogeyman, this terror, this creature of the shadows, this thing of nightmares, now incapacitated, out on display, for all to see, discredited, humiliated, tortured. Stabbed repeatedly, some slender serpentine necks are decapitated, otherworldly wails course through my ears, filling me with an undesirable aching.

The monster—bleeding and torn—crawls away, blazing a path through the believers, trying to escape, swatting away the winged defenders like flies, but always unsuccessful. Responses grow more sluggish, opposition grows weaker, our hopes are dashed, our shoulders slump forward in disappointment. The secret weapon has been subdued.

Motionless, the Dragon offers no resistance as a chasm cracks through the land, swallowing it whole. The angels hover back to safety, unharmed. The ground mends itself, the virus has been dealt with. The intruder, the instigator left locked away.

To be released when it's once again necessary.
When fear will be used to fuel the fight against lapsing faith.
Eventually, new opposition will be manufactured.

Around me everyone is crushed, leaderless, indecisive. Shiva is close to sobbing, and Azazel is muttering to himself, bemused, disbelieving. No one knows what to do or how to react.

Down in the valley, the joy comes back better than ever. A triumphant roar rises up, praising God, the faithful falling to their knees, firm, even more engrained in the trickery of religion. It worked—I was right all along, God has been in control of this situation from the start.

Shiva's voice, projecting pain.

"This was supposed to be foolproof... What happened? He's dead, that bastard killed him. Lucifer is dead..."

Her lamenting triggers trepidation, shouting starts around us, trouble handling entangled emotions, accusations fly.

Down below, New Jerusalem glows gold, intensely for one last moment, and then blinks out. Everything has returned to normal, I am no longer the recipient of hallucinations, no one is at the master controls. I can't see into God's world of fantasy; those around me appear human once more. Further evidence of the Devil's downfall.

I am taken aback as an armored arm juts out to my left, forcibly operating a fist, clenching a gun in a white-knuckled grip. Others take notice, and breath is held collectively.

I turn my head, following the musculature to its foundation.
The appendage is anchored to Azazel.
The gun is pointed squarely at Shiva.

OBLIVION

"IT WAS YOU, you stupid bitch, I know you gave Him the code to *Dragon*."

Shiva raises her head from her hands, cheeks wet with tears, as she turns her face upward towards Azazel. I feel my hand developing a life of its own, reaching underneath my robe, fondling the metallic weapon beneath. Her words portray utter indignation.

"How could you think that's even possible, after all we've been through together—"

"Save it for someone who cares, you fucking traitor. You've

been with Him this entire time haven't you?"

Unable to take anymore, I pull the gun out into the open, and shove it towards Azazel, disabling the safety, and placing my finger alongside the trigger in one smooth motion. My voice is all makeshift confidence. "Leave her alone Azazel. Just calm down."

He doesn't respond, or lower his weapon, just continues on with his unprovoked hostility.

"If you didn't give God the code, then how did this happen, how did He fight off the virus? He had to know about it some-how, and there were only a limited number of people with ac-cess. You are one of those people, and you and I are the only ones whose thoughts have not been monitored by Lucifer."

Shiva is livid now, her face full of rage and hate. "And what about you! It was probably you, and now you just want to blame me."

"Azazel, put the gun down," I growl. "I will shoot you, I will fucking kill you if you hurt her."

Still, I am casually ignored.

"I have seen you, always utilizing your appearance to gain the upper hand, watching over the shoulders of the program-mers, sneaking out at night, alone, unaccounted for."

"You have seen nothing!" Shiva spits through clenched teeth. "You lie!"

I am screaming now, trying to get Azazel's attention. "I'm warning you, put the gun down!"

He turns to look at me.

"You can kill me if you want to, if you really love her that much, or you can learn the truth. There is a way to find out whether or not I am right."

A brief flash of foreboding filters through Shiva.

"Abaddon, don't listen to him, he's insane." She's frantic now. "Shoot him. Shoot him, Abaddon."

She's begging, she's unarmed, weapons stashed away. She's helpless. My hand begins to tremble, to sweat, I begin to grow unsure. All around us, the soldiers have backed away, silent, observing this power struggle as it unfolds, its outcome to determine whose leadership they will follow.

"If you are not God's spy, then prove it. Show us your eye."

His gun is now pressed up against her temple; he has a hand-ful of her shining hair, tugging it backward and her head along with it, forcing her to look towards the treetops.

"You're fucking crazy!" She's hysterical now. "Goddamn it, Abaddon, pull the trigger, hurry up, just kill him."

My finger resists the urge to defend her, for the moment I am frozen in curiosity.

In a flash of steel, Azazel lets go of her hair, and a long slender blade appears from nowhere, jumping into his empty hand. I intake air in fright, as he slams it into Shiva's one unprotected red eye with all his strength. Before I can compose myself, before I can respond, he wrenches the blade out, and with it her eye, pierced, skewered, shooting sparks.

"FUCK, FUCK, FUCK, YOU SHITHEAD, YOU, YOU CRAZY FUCKING SHITHEAD…"

Her hands cover the gaping hole, the empty socket, and her screams make it hard to focus. I want to comfort her, I want to beat Azazel into a pulp, but at the same time, I want to find out what's happening.

I notice the eyeball on the end of the knife is not organic, but mechanical. The others move forward, gathering around closely as he raises the contraption up for all to see—his gun is still focused, unrelenting upon Shiva's crippled form. Azazel explains over the sounds of shrieking.

"All of the angels were originally created so God could tap into their sight at anytime; transmitters were embedded near the optical nerve. After the rebellion, we removed our eyes and replaced them with cybernetics to prevent God from having power over us."

The knife is put right in my face, the eye I had loved so much, still emitting electricity.

"Look closely, and tell me what you see."

I examine the robotics, and find attached, a small chip, identical to the one Satan removed from my skull. Emblazoned with a tiny cross. A transmitter to God. I tell myself it cannot be true.

"No, this is impossible."

The others see it too and erupt in rage, discussing ways to punish Shiva for her betrayal. Cries of condemnation crackle in my ears. She looks up at me, no longer crying out in pain. She looks up at me with one empty socket and one green lens. She looks up at me and pleads.

"I am so sorry, you have to understand, I didn't have a choice."

My entire body hurts, I am in shock. The only thing I have ever loved—not because I was told to, but because I wanted to—has stabbed me in the back. Oh, I understand. What I understand is all this time, she has loved God more than me. She seduced me in His name, toyed with my emotions, played with my feelings.

"Abaddon, please, forgive me."

Never again.

I put my finger on the trigger of the gun she picked out for me, aim right at her precious, tear-stained face, and before I can think otherwise, pull it back with a resounding bang. It echoes away from us and through the valley beyond. No one is expecting this; their discussions of retribution are halted as blood rains down upon their faces. Even Azazel looks sur-prised as the pink clumps of brain stick to his cheeks.

I am crying, like a wounded animal,
a deserted delinquent, unable to be comforted.
I am numb, and the pain is pushed aside,
bitter with vindictiveness.
I am uproarious, cackling,
while I come to grips with hopelessness.

It's time to sever the strings, it's time to finish what I've started. It's time for liberation, emancipation, to cut loose, to break free. The tears trail salty towards my lips, inhaled, my nose running, my head pounding, ears ringing, eyes watching the mouths around me move, noticing the sound is not registered, not computed. Centered on the depth of my discomfort, in the dark place that is my rejection, a corpse comes into focus, sprawled lifeless, faceless, on the forest floor, disseminating experience into the collective, thoughts rotting and pouring out of an ugly, gaping wound.

Pouring out of a neglected nobody.

I pull her body towards my chest, I'm rocking, paying no mind to the leaking fluids. The leftovers of a head are gathered inward, held to me, for the last time. The treachery torments me almost as much as her lack of response.

All eyes are on me—my act of violence, my vengeance has gained me new standing. I took the initiative, declared myself de facto propagator of plans. In this moment of emergency response, in this moment of dire need, what I say goes.

There will be no more holding back.

Still gripping my pistol in one hand, I stand up and sling

Shiva's limp form over my shoulder, arms dangling behind me, I address my audience.

"Down in that City resides the one who is responsible for all of this. God must be stopped, the day of His death has arrived, and I am its bringer."

Azazel cuts me off. Always bringing up points, rubbing all his facts in my face.

"You won't even make it to the gate, the program is still functional."

My response is cold and matter-of-fact.

"You'll just have to create some kind of distraction, I don't care, but I'm going."

I turn, leaving them bustling in bewilderment, bearing my burden, striding towards the open, towards the holy assembly, towards the alabaster apparatus. Behind me the voices blend away, erased by my convictions, held at bay by my hate. I break through the tree branches, into the bright light of a summer afternoon, the one indiscriminately passing us by, paying no attention to our simian theatrics.

At the edge of the precipice I look down the steep descent, speckled with stones and shrubbery. My skin is sticky, slick with sweat and blood. My vision blurs while the target comes into focus.

I notice a winding path, a small trail of mysterious origin, a way forward. Completely sure of myself, I take the first steps toward conflict resolution; walking down, I enter into the Promised Land weighed with grief.

The incline begins to lessen and I pause to straighten my morbid cargo, preventing it from slipping, saturated, my robes are utterly soaked in her insides.

Closer now, the City calls out to me like a long-lost friend, a menstruating mirage, culling the sorrowful sores from my outstretched cinders. My approach is appropriate, as I reach flat ground, a ghoul gallivanting toward the target of temperament, my delegated demeanor demanding I keep hatred harnessed and ready for disposal.

As I near God's children, ready to stroll nonchalantly through their idle and ignorant worship of imminent extinction, they are interrupted by gunfire ripping out from the forest on both sides. Dismantled by hails of metal, two angels fall from the wall tops, landing in the thick crowds below, spreading further panic, the peons in pandemonium, pushing against each other, still searching for some kind of sanctuary. Still praying in vain for pampered protection—the kind that's reserved for only the most delusional of species.

And the land shall be a waste because of its citizens.
As a result of their deeds.

Before they know it I am among them, diligently driven towards the end I have in store. Most pay no attention, but those who glimpse me tremor in terror, looking almost beyond my exterior, sensing my intent, they back away, giving me a reasonable breadth in which to pass. I am surrounded on all sides by multitudes of cattle, looking good enough to die, ready to be reaped, situated for slaughter. I can no longer see anything but their post-apocalyptic perfection, their eyes glazed, lost in a permanent quest for redemption.

I was one of them.
They are my brothers.
I've come to set them free.

The screams still crash around me in a crescendo, as the livestock are sacrificed for the cause of their own freedom. I simmer, and it melts away, leaving only the emptiness of lost desires. Leaving only two pieces of meat—one automated, the other disabled indefinitely—trudging together, the former overly attached to the latter.

The mob ahead dissolves, dissipating to reveal solid walls and a gate. It opens, allowing an arriving group of armed angels to dive eagerly into the fray. Staying my course, I step through the doorway just before it comes to a close behind them. Up close I see layers and layers of wire threads, knitted together to create a mesh of mechanical mastery molded into structures, overtaking and overlapping the stained-glass and souvenir baubles that pass for windows—color entrenched in copper coils. Transubstantiating from grotesque to guilt-free.

My emotions in limbo, I feel no comfort for having made it this far undetected. I feel only the dampness invading every aspect of awareness. I feel only the warmth fading as it exits the mess that I've brought with me.

The trash that needs to be put where it belongs.
Here in this conformity capital of the world.

Captivating, the central spire beckons me with its wired coating, enabling me to ignore all the other facilities. The auxiliary control chambers, the genetic testing labs, the residences of researchers, the churning incinerators, are all second-string to this one phallic fable. This sparkling house of cards.

Waiting for someone to send it tumbling down.

I am finally face to face with the base of operations for the religious bombardment I've been subjected to, the sentinel of the supposed Savior, the idolized implement for ensuring total domination through sanctified scare-tactics. A blood-sucking ballet of barbiturates.

It's a ghost town, there's no one watching, I'm left to my own devices, left to such splendid havoc. So much for being under surveillance. Taking my cue, grips tightening on the firearm and dead flesh, my gait quickens, as I shorten the remaining distance to the tower efficiently and without incident.

Standing at the base of this transient temple, this perpetrator of hoaxes and myths, the sheer gargantuan scope dwarfing my disgust, I prepare myself for what I must do next. I will kill anyone it takes to get to Him, I don't care anymore whether He is expecting me or not. I'm here just the same; ready to strip away His superimposed immortality.

There appears to be no visible entrance, but when I take a step closer a door opens out of the intricate patterns of circuitry to reveal a hallway lit with blinding intensity. I squint, becoming accustomed to the increased illumination, and make my way to the stairs at the end of the passage. Wiring covers every surface, I feel like I'm inside a massive reactor, my footsteps mix with the sound of pulsing electricity and the rush of invisible fans. Climbing the stairs, I find myself in a round room unable to proceed further. As I search the alloy walls for clues, the floor shakes and bursts into motion, rocketing me upwards at tremendous speed. I struggle not to drop Shiva's carcass, widening my stance to maintain balance, as I ride to the top of a carnivorous cathedral. I brace myself as the lift slows to a stop, revealing the receiving end of my animosity.

The direction of my bitter rage.

In the center of this circular space the size of the tower's diameter, is a hub, a throne positioned on a pedestal, occupied by a gnarled old man, perched gaunt, motionless and nude, withered and shriveled mottled casing covering organized organs, long beard unkempt spilling into a lap, eyes set back behind layers of wrinkles, blank, absorbed inwardly, breath escaping in ragged gasps with the rising and falling of a narrow, sunken chest. Advanced technology takes shape in the form of a nefarious nervous system, from all over the aged form wires are arranged of various shapes and sizes, protruding from the corners of eyes, from the ends of fingers, from ear canals, coating the balding skull, surrounded by liver spots, emerging from the abdomen, from the tips of toes, slithering down the sides of the chair, the raised platform, and rushing away in all directions towards the room's perimeter, where they angle upwards, flowing to meet the ceiling far above, rejoining and exiting view through a large, centered hole.

This sorry excuse of a man is God?
This helpless fool?

I shake with mirth, chewing on the irony of it all, laughing to the point of tears. It makes no difference, it doesn't change what I've come to do.

Regaining my sense of purpose, I drop Shiva violently on the floor, spreading people-pulp across pristine metal surfaces, raising my voice and weapon simultaneously.

"I give you back your pathetic doll, and I've come with a message: Your time is over."

Equipped with adrenaline and endorphins, I take aim at the unprotected scalp and squeeze. It is vaporized like a melon; wires broken free from their moorings now dangle random bits of flesh, their circuits broken. Before I can feel adulation, before I can feel the fulfillment followed by relief, I am taken over with trepidation.

The gun falls from my hands, sliding away, as I witness their transformation into spotted paws, adorned with sharp, slicing claws, the floor shrinks below me as I spout upwards to larger than life proportions, muscles rip away my robes displaying the new growth of fur beneath, many twisting horns work their way out of my head, my screams come out in earthshaking roars, tossed to the winds with a forked tongue clicking against rows of sharp teeth, jaws spread wide in rage and shock at this sudden departure from reality. I snivel and hiss in pain as burning crawls its way across my skin, burrowing deeper in the breadth of each passing second, bringing me to my hands and knees, cringing before His seat.

Shiva's unoccupied body is now more beautiful than ever before, giving off a faint glow, the brutality and gore all gone, her hair is golden, clothed in white, feathered wings pinioned out in unnatural positions, resting beneath the apparition of a young man standing in sandals, wearing robes, crowned in thorns, long hair trailing to shoulder level, eyes—pools of knowledge—bathed in excruciating luminosity, a faint smile playing on thin lips surrounded by a brown beard, hands held outwards, palms up so I can see the holes.

My error is obvious.
I behaved precisely as anticipated.
God's neurology has already been completely scanned.
Uploaded onto the Jesus Network.
I only killed what He had already left behind.
With the Devil's destruction,
the Holy One now has complete command.
My perception generator is being sent new information
I am being controlled via Satan's imitation implant.

Jesus makes eye contact, and his face portrays absolute exuberance. I try to escape, but I'm too weak to get up on my overgrown talons—strength has been weaned away. I've failed to find freedom, unable to control my emotions, my struggle for selfish justice has caused me to serve God's intended purpose as an unwitting pawn in His hand, a thread used to sew His schemes. No better than the Devil.

I have taken on the form of the Antichrist.
I have become the Beast.

The Messiah winks, and chains materialize, wrapping themselves around my engorged limbs, holding me at bay, disgruntled and damned, as glimmering beings of piety enter and surround me. Where I am touched, I bubble and blister, the angels' delicate hands reacting vehemently, seizing me into submission. I struggle to cast aside fury and finally deal with the consequences of my actions. This is no one's fault but my own.

Lifted into the air, I offer no resistance as I am carried away from the Lord, brought back down to ground level. Once again all the contiguous wickedness is masqueraded as immaculate beauty, but I ignore the infused versions of deceit as I am paraded up onto the ramparts of the now majestic City walls. There is no sound of further fighting, leading me to believe our meager resistance has been subdued.

The monstrosity that is me is unveiled, put forward for the scrutiny of all. The crowds of chosen ones chastise me, celebrating my capture and subsequent imprisonment. Without warning, a break in the sky grows, peeling back the last dregs of dark, replenishing the day, a new glowing dawn, a stream of figures pour in from beyond the horizon, led by a fearsome king, with eyes of fire, all clad in billowing silk, glimmering with holy light, riding a white horse, he wears a cloak dipped in blood, the armies of Heaven trail behind.

What picturesque real-time theatre.
How deliciously macabre.
The fearsome ruler approaches,
plunging a flaming sword straight into my gut.

Wounded, I am thrown into the mob, fed to a pack of hungry dogs, freefalling through empty air, only to impact abruptly with the sweet, brown earth. The epiphanies enter, rushing to the forefront of understanding.

Our every living moment is spent at the mercy of the Universe, every day is a gift.

We see our sustainer, our mother, our umbilical cord, as something to dominate.

Never happy with the fact that we are provided for at all. Never seeing that we don't have to wait for an afterlife, we are already immersed in a world of spirit, more profound than anything we could imagine.

To be saved, you must first be convinced you are damned.

A decree comes from angels on high: "You must put the blasphemer to death!"

God will be redefined, from a single being manipulating perceptions to an all-encompassing force so far beyond our capacity for understanding that we can never hope to quantify it. A vibration we are all a part of. A wavelength attempting to realize itself.

"Kill him in the name of the Father."

Consciousness is divinity.

"Kill him in the name of the Son, and the Holy Spirit."

There is no deity whose will I must subjugate myself to, there is only the unsurpassable beauty encompassing existence in its entirety, and to take notice of that is to fulfill my role as a sensory organ.

So I might die in peace, spreading out and blending with the oneness of all things.

Self-restriction only inhibits this process.
But so does anger and unnecessary indulgence.

I must admit, pulling the trigger, killing Shiva and God was a mistake.

Everything's a learning experience.

This is why I can lie here, bound, face down in the churned dirt, as hundreds of happy little fists pummel my vulnerable vessel, my fragile form. This is why I can bite my tongue, while hundreds of happy little feet kick my skull and rattle my brains. This is why I can smile as I watch the blood flow and listen to the breaking of bones, smile as I feel the pain.

Here I am.
Destroyed.
By the very people.
I was meant to save.

End transmission

One thing happened God did not intend. This record began circulating among His subjects after being salvaged from the Devil's archives. Narratives have the power to open minds, but in order for this to be achieved, the message must be dispersed to all who are ready to reach a new level of understanding.

Only you can know who is prepared for transformation.

There is still hope to end mental slavery:
Become a prophet – visit perceptionexperiment.com/aware